THE PRAYER RUG

THE PRAYER RUG

MALEEHA JAFFERY

First published 2025

Copyright © Maleeha Jaffery 2025

The right of Maleeha Jaffery to be identified as the author of this work has been asserted in accordance with the Copyright, Designs & Patents Act 1988.

All rights reserved. No part of this book may be reproduced, stored in a retrieval system, or transmitted in any form or by any means, digital, electronic, electrostatic, magnetic tape, mechanical, photocopying, recording or otherwise, without the written permission of the copyright holder.

Published under licence by Brown Dog Books and
The Self-Publishing Partnership Ltd, 10b Greenway Farm, Bath Rd,
Wick, nr. Bath BS30 5RL, UK

www.selfpublishingpartnership.co.uk

ISBN printed book: 978-1-83952-895-8
ISBN e-book: 978-1-83952-896-5

Original cover art jessicapalmerart.com
Internal design by Mac Style

Printed and bound in the UK

This book is printed on FSC® certified paper

'...and so becomes a companion to the heavenly host of angels, for they are on the carpet of proximity [to God].'
Al-Ghazali

1

It had been a mistake to mention her in the lecture.

It was always hard to know how to play these things. A lay audience but still with a sprinkling of academics and experts; meeting their varied expectations would always be difficult. The working title he'd been given was 'Woven Tales from the Lower Indus Delta'. It was all going so well. He knew his subject – loved it in fact – that much was undeniable. His slideshow had been immaculately prepared with photos of his dazzling collections from around the Indus valley and surrounding areas. He had mentioned the gender division of labour with craft items – generally embroidered – being produced by women, whereas any tie-dying or block printing was almost exclusively carried out by men. The embroidery was also part of the social fabric of the women's day, while the men were outside and working the fields. He hated admitting this, but he knew things were changing and this was to do with the spread of technology in these previously untouched lands. The biggest threat to traditional textiles was television.

He had also told them about an anecdote regarding how in one tribal area any guests into the Sindh region – otherwise known as 'the land of quilts' would be treated with the upmost hospitality: welcomed, fed and watered while seated on appliqué patched quilts as a barrier from the intrusive desert sands. If, however, they didn't pick up on the delicately nuanced

2 The Prayer Rug

cultural cues and overstayed their welcome, their hosts would very subtly fold over one corner of the duvet as a clear but polite sign that it was time for them to leave. It was normally Europeans who would fall foul of this, but that was always the case with any cross-cultural dialogue, he guessed, no matter in which direction you were doing the travelling.

He knew as he worked his way through his talk it was getting nearer. He had now arrived at the slide immediately before it. This was of an Afghan hand-knotted rug – so a slight geographical diversion from the Indus, it had to be said – but it was one that had a story to tell. Its large blue and turquoise floral medallions radiated outwards to the familiar paisley motif across a peach background. At first glance it just looked like an ordinary garden carpet from the region, and depending on the quality of your eyes, that was just what it might remain. Nope, no one from the audience could see what was there. He wasn't surprised. Right, he was here now. He had thought about leaving it out entirely ... but the shawl was so very beautiful. It had no particular lineage he could trace, no mirror work that was reputed to offer veiled protection from the 'evil eye' of folklore, no subversive hidden designs showing the ethnic and religious affiliations of the minority embroiderers in a controlled area. So why was it even in his collection? Why had he photographed it and added it as a slide to his presentation? He wasn't even sure himself.

'In the late '70s I was a student right here at SOAS. I first saw the woman who was to later become my wife walking down the stairs following a seminar. One look at her long raven hair and bee-stung lips and I was smitten. She was wearing this shawl that afternoon – and when she left me years later, she didn't take it with her. So I kept it.'

He could sense the momentary bafflement in his audience. At least a third of the women there were wearing scarfs or shawls of some sort – though none over their heads he noted. Perversely, that had made him feel better when he had first walked into the auditorium. There was nothing that distinguished any of theirs from the one they were now scrutinising on the screen. Before they could dwell on this any further, he quickly clicked on to the next picture.

'What the hell was that about?' whispered the curator of the accompanying exhibition to a colleague.

'I think he's having some kind of breakdown,' came the reply. 'He's quite near the end now, so let's hope that he holds it together.'

They needn't have worried as he finished with a perfectly composed flourish.

'Finally, does anyone know what this may be? Any guesses?' The audience looked at a piece of scarlet material covered in the finest delicate embroidered thread: swirling designs resembling one of Vincent's skyscapes. 'The fabric is actually an old red coat – the British Army uniform of the day. The skills of these embroiderers could turn anything into a silk purse – even an object that was the very symbol of their oppression. Thank you very much.'

There was polite and prolonged applause afterwards and he was thanked by the organisers. The final part was what he always dreaded the most – questions from the audience. There was always one – and several if you were particularly unlucky – who had managed to hear a completely different lecture to anybody else. They would ask a question – usually a pointlessly long and incoherent one – that was unrelated to anything in the preceding talk. To be fair, it hadn't happened to him very often, but the fear was always at the back of his mind.

He had come up to London and to SOAS the week before – the first time he had been back here for over three decades – and wanted to reorient himself before his own lecture the following week. The talk that evening had been from a prominent religious leader who had given the most soulless interpretation of the lecture title possible – all research and dogma – and not without a healthy sprinkling of prejudice. He evidently wasn't the only one who felt like this. At the end of the lecture the first question from the audience was from a woman who Giles had seen again this evening. She was asking about the mystical elements of religion, and even before she finished he could see the speaker bristling.

'This isn't well documented but there are accounts of meetings between Christian and Muslim mystics – for example St Francis of Assisi was rumoured to have met with Shams of Tabriz and there have been other meetings between St Cuthbert and Sufi saints. Is there anything you can tell us about this?'

4 The Prayer Rug

Good on her, thought Giles. If forced to take sides he would have come down firmly as an agnostic if that made any sense, but he just hadn't liked the speaker's approach – even if he had an MBE. Especially as he had an MBE. Why had no one ever considered *him* for one? What was the point of awards if they never went to the right and most deserving people?

'It's important to note that Shams of Tabriz was quite a shadowy figure. We cannot even say with any historical accuracy if he even existed.' Giles caught the change of tone in his voice from that of the lecture and wondered if he would try to deny that St Francis had existed too. 'I am not aware of any meetings between St Cuthbert.' As if he had been around at the time anyway to know. He then indicated that he was ready for the next question. Giles had actually felt tempted to ask his own question but decided this would be bad form – especially given that he would be speaking himself the next week and as his question would definitely have been considered off topic: 'Mr Archimam, as neither a believer nor a non-believer, I'd be very interested to hear what your own experience of God is. What do you actually know?'

The woman was evidently not impressed either, as a few moments later when he glanced back at the rows near the front she had disappeared. He needn't have worried on his own account though, as there was only one question – about the black block that many of the appliqué quilts had as their centrepiece – that he was unable to answer fully. All he really knew was that these distinctive cut-up designs had actually travelled into the region through the influence of Christian missionaries, and thankfully the remainder of the questions were largely relevant. There was a modest drinks reception in the foyer afterwards, but he had no desire to hang around too long. He bade a cursory farewell to his academic contacts at SOAS, double checked he had removed his memory stick, then gathering his coat and hat, he left the building.

It was now dark, and he wondered if the portable street kitchen that had fed what seemed like generations of students was still in operation. The queues used to snake all around the campus he recalled, but he remembered reading more recently that the university wanted to evict the kitchen from their premises as it was no longer in keeping with their image

– whatever that meant. The familiar blue statue was still there though, and looked as if he was wearing freshly cut garlands today, not just those material replicas. The statue was also covered with a light sprinkling of what looked like glitter or dew, but he realised that it had just been raining earlier, that was all.

2

Howra had felt sorry for him when he let that slip about his wife.

She'd had a busy day. Earlier she had been to an exhibition curated by an arts charity who worked with inmates of prisons. All her attempts to physically get into the institution where he was being detained had failed, so she knew she needed a different approach. As luck would have it his work was on display, and although this detail wasn't strictly relevant to her brief, it was an added bonus that his work was of such good quality. And so interesting. She had stared at his picture for a long time before taking a postcard from one of the guides and writing her message to him. She thought long and hard about this. In her delicate position she would have to be discreet. He was evidently serving a long sentence as his picture showed him in his cell with all his belongings and the prison bars clearly discernible above him. Every detail in the picture was made up of words: phrases and sentences that had formed the feedback on the anonymous postcards he had received from the fortunate and free members of the public who had viewed his exhibition entry last year. She spent a while reading the comments. They were overwhelmingly positive and she briefly wondered if he would have included any that weren't – or would anyone even have sent him any that weren't? It was doubtful. Though not impossible.

Up until that moment she had her question for the speaker carefully formulated in her mind. The slide was one of the early ones and she had been so engrossed in the richness of the visuals, and his descriptions of the unique tribal techniques and formations that she had almost not seen what she had been sent to. It was a double bind for her. She loved the look and feel of the fabrics and seeing them on the screen as photos allowed her the distance to appreciate their beauty. She was one of the women who Giles had noted was wearing a scarf herself when he had scanned the audience. (Well, it was the scarf he had noticed first and then the woman after – but he was that kind of man). Hers was Kashmiri – she knew that much – and definitely not to be worn over her head – she knew that much too. She had been attracted to the amber and maroon patterns on the predominantly black background and how the right scarf could immediately dress up an otherwise ordinary outfit – even jeans. Yes, she liked that hybrid style. It was a chilly evening as otherwise she would have worn something silk rather than woollen. It was vaguely extravagant, she knew – but it was silk that was her fabric of choice. The exhibition in the gallery was off limits as far as she was concerned though. It was housed in several rooms and over a couple of floors, and when she had peered into the first room before the lecture started, she knew she couldn't go any further.

'You've got plenty of time.' It was the student who had been handing out flyers for all the talks. She must have thought Howra was backing away because she thought she would be late.

'Oh no – I was thinking I'd just go and get a cuppa first. Is there a cafe on this floor?'

Back in the amphitheatre she had looked hard at the slide and then faded out the speaker's for once wholly inaccurate descriptions of its provenance. She knew immediately it was the one. She had been sitting quite near the back today, row 'k' and in the centre too – unlike last week when she had stupidly sat near the front. What a dickhead *that* speaker had been. She had had to leave at that point, as if she had said what she thought of his answer, she would probably have been escorted off the premises. She did briefly consider waiting until the reception afterwards and discreetly cornering him, but she still didn't quite trust herself to not lose her rag in these situations,

8 The Prayer Rug

and as she was still on probation, she didn't want to blow it. Once she had made up her mind she had just quietly left her seat and walked home.

She wasn't initially sure what to do this evening though. She couldn't ask him something so challenging in a public forum – and when she could feel his discomfort too – so thought she would gently extract the information afterwards. But he had left immediately, and it took her a few seconds to realise he was no longer either in the crowded auditorium or the foyer outside. She sprinted up the stairs and outside into the evening air, hoping he wasn't still in the building, just in the gents or chatting to a colleague somewhere. She did feel though that he had left. With relief she spotted him standing in front of the statue and thought she should just follow him for now and not confront him at all. Not yet. It was possible that he actually knew nothing, and it had been an entirely innocent acquisition. Anyway, there was one thing she had noticed. Those paisley designs in that Afghan rug. It had taken her a few seconds but, once she had spotted them, they just seemed to overtake the central motifs completely. The professor had actually given more clues than that dozy audience had deserved. The patterns very gradually but perceptibly transformed across the rug – into helicopters. The female weavers had – initially covertly – begun to weave the very imagery of the Soviet invasion into their traditional designs.

He was walking through the outdoor passageways between the various academic buildings, in a way that clearly indicated he knew where he was going. A slim leather bag was over his shoulder and – pushing all thoughts of war from her mind – she briefly wondered what it would have been like to have followed an academic route herself; she had always known she was smart enough – but at the time when she should have been making those types of decisions, it was other things that were consuming her energies. Well, she knew from Mick, her probation officer, that no avenues were completely closed to her – just because she hadn't followed a prescribed path at the time. When she had last seen him for her fortnightly reporting session (soon to be monthly) they had spoken at length about what she felt the future now held for her. He told her he wasn't discouraging her from following a conventional education route – that was the path he himself had followed through studying various evening courses. But he had always known he wanted to support those on community sentences, rather than custodial ones, and there just happened to be a designated route for this.

'What is it yer want, bab – I mean Howra. Excuse me that, just a Coventry colloquialism.'

'That's okay. I've been called much worse ... Don't laugh at me. I know where I am – I'm not denying that – but I don't intend to be on probation forever. I've only got six months left. You're gonna think I've got ideas above my station, but to be honest, one day I'd love to be doing what you are – or something similar – it doesn't have to be as formal as your role is.' Mick put down his pen as he liked to take copious notes to add to the growing case files of all his clients. The paperwork would need its own home soon. When he was involved in serious thought, however, he had realised he couldn't write cogently at the same time and remain attentive. Okay, he had told her, she hadn't gone down a traditional learning route, but it was evident she was smart – he had realised as much from her initial interview when he had gathered the relevant information for her pre-sentence report. He had liked her immediately – he did a mental scan of his current case load and realised there were currently precious few clients that he did actually like. He then immediately retracted this thought. It wasn't for him to like them. It was for him to get them through to the end of their sentences so any possible future harm to the general public would be minimised, and any welfare needs of the clients themselves could be identified and addressed. And actually, he thought, feeling slightly more charitable, there were many who he did like, it was the usual systemic failings that did nothing to support their needs. Or his. How could he possibly be expected to support almost fifty disparate souls at any one time without – just occasionally – feeling slightly put out?

Anyway, now was not the time to be ruminating about the faults in the system. He would take that to his own supervision with a senior next week. It was the young woman currently in front of him who was in immediate need of his energies. There was no possibility of her being given a custodial sentence. When she had turned up for her interview she had spoken openly about her offence. It was a relatively minor one by all accounts but there was no accounting for the impact these things had on people. Some would

10   The Prayer Rug

deny all knowledge of any wrongdoing – even if the evidence had been staring them in the face. Even if the evidence had been able to speak and the witness statements themselves had come to life and spoken up in the very voices and vernaculars of the wronged, as the best voice recognition software currently could not do. It was the amount of bloody paperwork that would be his undoing you see. When he had first started out almost thirty years back – dear God – it had been nothing like as overwhelming as this. And did it actually assist him in any way to support those people? Well, that was a resounding 'no'. He was finding it hard to keep up with the report writing now, so one of the recommendations from his last supervision was a trial of some new 'assistive technology'. He was doing it again – allowing his interior monologue to take over. Back to the client. She was not one of the ones who had initially denied all wrongdoing or tried to excuse her part in what had happened. She had been composed and measured when she spoke, detailing the events leading up to 'The Incident' as she persisted in calling it and he could feel her remorse from her very opening words:

'This is the thing – I did something that may have been nothing to anyone else. But for me and where I was – or where I liked to *think* I was – it was a massive transgression. I don't give a shit about what punishment the system wants to hand out to me – that's irrelevant. It won't impact on me either way whether I get custody or not—'

'Oh goodness, there's no possibility of that,' he interrupted, but she was paying no attention and continued speaking and he realised then that she just needed to talk and – what the hell – he had all the time in the world, didn't he? For a client in need. Bugger the set questions – it all came out in the wash anyway, if you were patient and created the right conditions for this. He seemed to have multiple service washes on the go at any one time – maybe he should have set up a counselling service in a laundrette? Just let them talk, he would say – or would think whenever he was forced to go on any refresher training on interview skills and new tools for extracting information. Just let them talk and take note – and everything relevant that was needed would just emerge by itself if you created the right conditions. He knew now to keep his mouth shut though. Such an underrated skill. All the latest techniques were nothing more than just common sense and using the ability to listen – which no one knew how to fucking do these days. Including him at the moment. He had zoned back in quickly to what she was saying.

'It's what it showed me about myself, you see. That I couldn't recognise myself from my actions. Just who the fuck was I ... He was such a good-looking man though – a proper specimen.' Though all for being one for allowing the space to talk, Mick didn't think he wanted to know *too* much about this so-called specimen. His was not to judge though. They – or we – all fell for the same reasons. They just manifested slightly differently in the world that was all. Some were more socially acceptable than others, but all were essentially symptoms of the same things. He knew immediately that she had what it would take. If he thought about some of his colleagues – and he was observing without judgement here – yes, they had all the relevant qualifications, had read all the related theories and knew about the appropriate assessment tools to use – but did that in itself mean they were up to doing the job? Did they know how to reflect? Whenever he peer-read some of his colleague's reports he would frequently find himself observing how flat-packed and one-dimensional they seemed, rather than giving full-scale holographic account of The Incident in question. He was starting to think that his new-fangled technology could do the report writing job better than those solely human hands could – certainly some of the suggested words it came up with when he had been speaking in frustration into the microphone had provided him with some much-needed light relief – courgette syndrome anyone?

The young woman opposite him could probably do a better job of a compassionate assessment of others – in time. Once she had recovered from her own situation that was. Anyhow, that was what she was on probation for, and he intended to support her all he could.

* * *

Howra knew this part of London reasonably well. She wasn't sure where the professor was going though, as he had headed away from where she knew the nearest Tube station to be. Maybe he just needed a longer walk

12 The Prayer Rug

to clear his head, she thought. It was a fine evening with just a light chill in the air due to the approaching autumnal season. She wondered if he was regretting what he had let slip about his ex-wife – he had certainly left in a hurry and from her (limited) experience these public figures tended to do the opposite and loved hanging around till the very death throes, hoping to milk any possible acclaim. Free booze always helped and there always seemed to be some kind of intelligentsia-groupies who would hang around with them. Probably hoping something would rub off on them – like you could grow intellect through close proximity. Not that she rated intellect anyway. Just look at that twat from last week, she thought again. Although she had made the wise decision to walk out, she had no doubts that Mr MBE – who couldn't even answer a straightforward question without giving off the unmistakable stench of hypocrisy – had hung around until the last train home. Actually, he had probably got a taxi and put it on expenses. After getting pissed.

There were several garden squares in this part of London, and she watched from a shortening distance as the professor turned into one and walked along a path towards some benches around a fountain. It was already lit up due to the fading light, and she was surprised the park was still open. There was a brief written history of the horticulture of the plants, along with some information on the people whose statues were dotted around. Yes, they all looked worthy – unlike anyone from this era. Just who would be making statues of this lot? She was surprised but irritated that there was one figure she had *never* heard of before now – and that she really felt she should have done. Never mind – she would just have to blame her ignorance on her disrupted education and the failings of the system itself. Maybe she should set her own targets now she was on probation, around trying to educate herself in a wider sense too? Like reading. You could never tell what might be on the syllabus of some of these courses, so she was in two minds about what to do. Maybe she should just join a local library? Yes, that would be a good start. That would make Mick happy too, if she was to show initiative from the outset. She wanted to find this particular statue now, but she was aware that if she took the direct route to it she would be walking right in front of the professor – and she didn't wish him to notice her again, any more than he may have done already – well she had been a member of the audience so that was unavoidable. She would have to take a circuitous route – or maybe she should walk straight out and follow the road round the park railings before re-entering through another gate? Yes, that seemed a better idea and he didn't look like he was going anywhere in a hurry.

Giles sat on a bench and wondered what had possessed him to speak of her. It was too late to unravel that particular tapestry and augment its designs in an alternative way. Those stitches had been set in time no doubt, and even if he could find a loose end somewhere and just pull and watch the whole thing disintegrate, he knew he would never do that. The finished textiles had been imprinted in his mind now, been displayed in his home. He had spoken in public repeatedly over the years – not just of his knowledge of their mythological significance and regional peculiarities – but of his very love for them. He had not spoken in public of how he had lain on them, loved on them, run his hands all over their stitching and used his knowledge to try and unearth all their hidden secrets. How then could it ever be possible that he would wish this one away? That it had never been produced and come his way, even fleetingly as it now seemed? He couldn't.

It was he himself who was torn you see. It was as if someone had taken shears and cut the very heart out of his own woven dream. It was the first thing that any visitors to their home had remarked upon over the years. For he didn't believe in treating these objects as museum pieces, despite some of their evident rarities. No, not for him the vacuum-packed prisons and trunks that were the homes of choice for some of his colleagues. He needed them around him at all times. He always had done. Even before her. Now though he was often tempted to clear the whole lot away. Give it away even. Yes, that seemed more acceptable than just bagging them up somewhere, or loaning them to exhibitions even.

He looked through the bars that bordered the square, out onto the street. He knew the surrounding area had been some kind of artistic enclave over the centuries, with writers, painters and musicians gravitating to an undefined but known of centre for creativity. He wondered where these spaces existed now – online communities probably. He could see some of the benefits of this but also many of the drawbacks. If only someone could bring back the coffee houses of the seventeenth century, he thought. Where there was open debate, recitation of poetry and plenty of punch-ups. All you got these days was rows of people plugged into headphones, eyes glued to laptops and souls shrouded in the false raptures of Twitter feeds, fake news updates and the resulting dopamine hits that eventually left you feeling like you'd just wanked all your energy away on things that didn't even matter. Under the alleged auspices of keeping up to date with what was going on. Like the news was what was really going on ... Right, that was it. He had a book he was in the final stages of editing, plus a few more lectures he had to honour his commitments to, but after that he had a new mission:

He was going to bring back the coffee house as a space for engaging with the genuine artistic and creative issues of the era ... but – through the tempering lens of the past and those who had *genuinely* once made a difference. Some of these statues would have been a great place to start, he thought. A square that wasn't just dedicated to dead white men and their sometimes dubious histories either. That, he had to admit, was one of the huge limitations of the original coffee houses, in that there hadn't been a woman in sight – unless she was either pouring the drinks or having them poured into her. That would need to be rectified immediately.

Giles knew from the world of academia how many of his male colleagues he had wanted to headbutt over the years, and had somehow managed to restrain himself. Professors generally had other ways to express their hatred of each other, and in his time he had seen the slow burn of damning peer reviews in literary journals, the subtlety of research grants suddenly drying up, book proposals being rejected then seeing almost identical treatments being published just a few months later ... After all this who wouldn't long for a straightforward fight in a carpark after dark? At least you would know where you stood – or fell. In his world you could land in the piss-ridden gutter of a pointless course at an unrecognised institution with half-witted students and quart-witted colleagues and have no clear idea of whose kick you had even landed there. At least he had managed to avoid that ignominy over the years. It was just his personal life that wasn't even very personal these days that had imploded on him. Just why the fuck had he mentioned her again? Anyway, despite all that, the one thing he had always admired in her – with no reservation – had been her passion and inclination for ideas; she could leave him for dust with her nought to sixty acceleration, but such was their relationship she would then make an emergency stop (when he couldn't see a thing in the road) and send him hurtling through the windscreen when he couldn't come up with a satisfactory explanation for the views on that particular shared road trip.

Once they had been traversing the plains and meadows of theology (never a good idea, not even with your beloved – especially with your beloved) and she had as usual been at the helm, her long fingers gripping the steering wheel as she spoke.

'I need to face facts, Giles. If someone did a gender analysis of all the characters that appeared in all the bibles of all the world religions, what would the ratio of male to female be? And the women who do put in an appearance, how many of them are mothers, wives or just plain old sinners who drag the great and good men down?'

'I don't disagree. When have I ever believed those stories? On my good days I'm an agnostic at best. And if anything –' and he paused here as he gently placed his hand on one of hers as she continued driving – 'it's you who insist on believing that there is some equalising higher power at work here.' He watched as she momentarily slowed as a fledging and possibly still flightless bird decided to start hopping around on the stretch of road before them, not yet aware of the dangers just on the very edges of its wooded sanctuary. She then removed her left hand from the steering wheel – shaking off Giles's in the process – while she ran her fingers through her hair. They had the top down as they always did on these road trips, both of them loving the added exhilaration of the wind through their hair and the sun on their faces – and even if it was cold and dark, still wanting the wind.

'Someone very well-meaning told me once that as far as they were concerned there were lots of female saints and there was essentially no difference between saints and prophets, so why was I bothered about all the prophets being men …'

16 The Prayer Rug

He was interrupted in his not altogether painless reminiscing by a squirrel that had bounded right up to his feet, and now sat expectantly in front of his bench. He rued that he had nothing to feed him and briefly lost the thread of his memory. Where had he been …? Oh yes, the coffee houses – they would have to positively welcome women in some way, as he couldn't imagine anything worse than a load of egotistic male bores dominating proceedings like they did on bad comedy panel shows. The squirrel was now standing upright and bizarrely holding out a paw, as if he knew Giles had a secret hoard of nuts or fruit upon his person to give to him.

'I'm sorry fella, the only thing I have is this stupid memory stick and that won't be of any use to you.' If the squirrel had heard him (and understood) he gave no sign of this as his pose remained unwavering. He was looking Giles square in the eyes too, so he gestured – ridiculously he thought – with his two palms splayed in front of him, hoping to demonstrate his complete lack of provisions. The squirrel continued to stare at him a while, before looking slowly from one palm to the other and withdrawing his own pleading paw. 'Tight bastard,' Giles imagined he might be saying. Though it was true he had nothing on him. Maybe he could have fed the squirrel with some of his old memories of happier times?

Thinking about it now though, Giles wasn't even sure they were happier – maybe he had just become used to the ennui of his marriage? Could he honestly say that it had been a complete shock when she had left him? No, he couldn't. His friends had been kind – supportive even – but he could tell they weren't shocked either. What was it he *really* missed anyway – was it her wit (before their years of shared domesticity had turned it caustic), her beauty or her extensive trousseau of embroidered gems? Given the choice of taking her back (though he knew that unlikely; the last he heard she was married again and living abroad) or having just one or two of her textile treasures back in his possession, he knew what he would prefer. He even knew which ones. He closed his eyes while he imagined them and recalled first the embroidered shawl/throw; it was a pale green silk and had been embellished with a broad, diagonal criss-crossing pattern in an earthy amber hue, like a wooden trellis just catching the early evening sun, and contained within each section had been a uniquely realised flower. All were differing designs, but somehow when viewed all together they blended and complemented one another perfectly.

If the truth be known, the shawl itself had had a slightly disconcerting use over time and just how she had managed to procure it for her own private ownership, he was never entirely sure. The other unusual factor was that it was of entirely English provenance, whereas most of what they both collectively owned and coveted between them came from the diverse regions of Asia. It had been produced by the daughter of a minor arts and crafts aficionado of the nineteenth century, who had subsequently been brought back into the public sphere. It was used as a mortcloth both at his own funeral, then his daughter's – and finally at that of her 'companion'. He recalled his wife's slightly salacious speculation that this companion/housekeeper was actually her lover, but social mores being what they were back then, they had to disguise the true nature of their relationship in some way.

'Just look how beautiful they both were,' she had said to him once after coming across some old sepia-tinged photos of the two of them online. 'Yes, the lady was slightly older but she was still stunning. I wonder if that shawl was actually created as a gift to her future lover, before they had even met?' That had made no sense to him at the time. Surely gifts (and especially ones that were genuinely labours of love as this one was) were always produced with their known beloved recipient in mind – for how could it be otherwise? He recalled how he had tried to tell her that it was much more likely she was just enamoured with the act of embroidery as creation for its own sake. It was immaterial what happened to the object afterwards. Thinking back now though, he didn't feel on such secure ground with his former thread of reasoning. In fact it was starting to catch and unwind before his very eyes. He then opened his eyes with a start and shook his head rapidly. Bringing her to mind like this always did that to him, took him off on a magic carpet ride of who had said what, and when, and what he now believed they might actually have been saying. Anyway, he knew that simply as an artefact of stunning beauty he would have liked to see and feel this shawl for one last time – and just supposing it *had* been a gift from

18   The Prayer Rug

one lover to another – well that was now fine by him too. He knew he would never see it again now though, so that was that.

Howra knew she was inconspicuous now, as she walked in the darkening shadows in the quietest end of the square. There were a few old Victorian street lamps illuminating the trees and the surrounding shrubs, but people would only be visible in silhouette now, which was perfect for her purpose. She could see that Giles hadn't moved, so she took this opportunity to take a look at the statue she had wanted to see. It was raised high on a plinth – and was of head and shoulders only – but much larger than life. There had either been a recent anniversary, or someone was still very connected to the life of this spirit; there were various bouquets of freshly cut flowers and a couple of potted plants too, lying just at the base. She read the carved inscriptions on the plinth with details of the woman's name, role in the war and the awards she had been given by both the French and the English (posthumously of course). She had only been thirty when executed. Howra stared up at the woman's eyes and her short, rolled hair, such a feature of that era, noting the beauty and strength in her profile that the sculptor had so skilfully captured. She made the short circle round the base of the statue, looking skywards, and saw the stars just becoming visible in the darkening blue of the sky. She wondered if this woman had made it onto the history national curriculum. Somehow that seemed doubtful and even if she had, Howra had missed too much of school through her enforced moves to other countries in her childhood, so it was possible this could have entirely passed her by.

   She then looked towards the bench that Giles had been sat at. He was no longer there. This was not good. She quickly scanned the nearby pathways and other benches and began moving swiftly towards the centre of the square. Shit. It was just like her to become distracted by something in the environment and lose sight of what she should have been observing. When was she going to learn? This was not the time to be berating herself, however, she knew. There would be plenty of time for that afterwards, once it became abundantly clear that she had screwed up. Again.

He was nowhere to be seen in the square now. She thought quickly. He was hopefully just heading to a station, so maybe she should just take her chances and leave by the exit onto the street at the wooded end and head towards the Tube? It sounded like a half-realised plan as she actually had no real idea of where he might be going, but as it felt a reasonable assumption and in the absence of anything else in the moment, she decided she would just have to go with it. He wasn't going to suddenly materialise in front of her and say, 'Hello, Howra, I understand you have a particular interest in one of the objects from my talk? Would you like to join me for a coffee in one of the many establishments in the area, and I'd be happy to explain everything to you about how I came across it?' Howra didn't actually ever drink coffee. Tea was much more her thing, but people always seemed to use the phrase 'over a coffee' these days. What the fuck am I thinking about all this for, she thought as she hurried her steps out of the park. This section was much darker, but it housed the closest exit that led directly to the Tube. She would just have to take a chance.

As she turned left onto the pavement outside, she felt the light crunch of something hard but still fragile below her right foot. This was going from bad to worse. This was always a hazard after a downpour. The snails all seemed to make their way out and deliberately submit themselves to the fates of general human blindness straight after it had rained. Maybe those antennae were not so great at sensing what was really all around them – either that or they were just too slow to get out of the way of her size eights in time. She sighed as she wanted to avoid looking down at the inevitable sight of crushed fragments of shell, sticking to a trail of slime on the pavement. She couldn't do it though. She removed her foot, all thoughts of finding the professor temporarily gone from her mind, and glanced at the floor.

Well, for a start there was no slime. She felt instantaneous relief. Yes, she had destroyed a home, but the inhabitant had already left the premises so her conscience was at least clear on that account. The ultimate backpackers snails were. Humans were nothing but dilettantes with their 'gap years' that ultimately only ever led them back to their safe base. Do it like the snails if you dare, she thought. Running the risk of death after any rain shower, though she had never been sure why they did always choose to come out then. It was an investigation for another day. Maybe the esteemed Mr Attenborough should make a programme about this? Maybe he already had? Then again, snails were not especially rare or exotic insects. She bent closer to the ground now. It looked like it had been quite a large shell as well. Good luck on the next leg of your journey, fellow traveller, she thought. Hope your new home is much sturdier.

Giles searched for his travelcard before entering the Tube station. The image of her shawl flashed through his mind again, and it was this slide of his presentation and his accompanying commentary that he knew would be caught in the audience's memory. He was a bit worried that one of his venomous ex-colleagues, who he had spotted in the back rows of the audience during the Q&A, might have asked him publicly why she had left him. That was Max who currently headed up an archaeology department – although Lord alone knew why as he had none of the patience nor discernment that this subject area required. He was only concerned with digging up the personal past of anyone vulnerable in the vicinity, in order to prolong the already substantial harm and create evermore destruction. Excavating some beautiful remains with the purpose of keeping them intact was beyond Max – beyond most of us even, he thought.

He took an empty seat at the far end of the carriage and closed his eyes.

After resigning herself to the fact that she wouldn't be able to track Giles any further that evening, Howra decided she would get herself some dinner instead. The station had multiple Tube lines, entrances and terminals and she knew it was an unrealistic hope. She had garnered what she had needed from his talk, even if she hadn't ventured into the exhibition. It wouldn't be too hard to find when his next public appearance might be, so she knew there would always be further opportunities. She decided to walk through the international terminal. It was very busy with fellow travellers, and when she heard the growing strains of a piano concerto, she felt a sudden inexplicable desire to pretend she was there for another purpose, rather than the one she was all too familiar with. There were two pianos in the terminal, and she stopped as there was a small crowd gathered around one of them where a young woman was sitting and playing. Howra knew nothing about the technical aspects of her performance – and while the melody was unmistakably known to her – she could never have named either the composer or the piece itself. To her ears, though, it sounded transcendentally beautiful. And she wasn't the only one. A smartly dressed young man who couldn't have been older than thirty was holding a lady who could have been his grandmother in a dance hold and leading her across a small section of the concourse. They almost certainly were not English. She didn't know why that was so obvious, but it was.

She only had a small bag slung over her shoulder, but looking around her, she suddenly yearned for a glamorous set of luggage. Not just one of those wheelie cases – though that too would be an improvement on her current lone item – but to be one of those travellers who had a complete set of matching box trunks, sturdy but highly decorated with gold hinges and locking mechanisms, in graduated size, full of the accumulated treasures of her many journeys – rather than the traumas that she currently held. And of course, she couldn't be expected to lug all of that around on her own. She would need a personal porter, with his own immaculate uniform to push her trolley around for her as she waited to board her carriage (first class of course) to take her on the next leg of her journey. She sighed as the pianist came to the end of her current recital. As the casually gathered audience applauded and dispersed, and the young man bowed to his dance partner, she wondered why her mind was taking her on this reverie. She knew she was right where she had to be, and what her purpose was in being here too. That was what she needed to focus on. And right now she was hungry. She took a lift to the upper level of the station, where the Victorian construction could be seen in all of its magnificent splendour, and traversed the alley of restaurants there. She chose one that was neither one of her regular choices (on the rare occasions that she ate out) nor too fancy to be comfortable where she might feel conspicuous. This was still a learning journey for her. She sat outside under a lit and heated canopy, and once she had ordered, she looked out onto the huge clock face she could see at the other end of the terminal. She pulled out the book she had in her bag and settled down to read.

٣

3

It had started early.

  To say as early as childhood would have been wrong. To say within her infancy even would have been wrong too, for the expectations were already there before she actually came into being. They preceded her birth, as actually, her birth itself was no more than an irrelevancy, a mere footnote in the already written cannon of lives that not a single volume to date had managed to overwrite to any great effect. Granted, it could have been said that some of those ancestors hadn't strictly followed the designated path of the emperor, but there was a level of freedom still that meant the bloodlust, savagery and conquests of all sorts could still be tolerated, excused and even celebrated as the rightful prerogative of the Sultan. Of course, when we look back in the annals we wish to see the compassionate and benevolent reformer, extending social, artistic and religious freedoms that encompassed all minorities of the kingdom. But one of the (unfortunate) quirks of leadership is that it is actually the opposite that somehow provides a guarantor of power.

It could have been any soul that was born into that milieu.

Though it wasn't any soul. It was hers.

She wasn't born to be a ruler, however. Not in the traditional sense. Her role was that of a consort and from childhood she was schooled in a bewildering array of arts, customs and traditions to ensure that she would be the perfect princess. The beauty was hers already, but even from childhood there was something missing. No, perhaps that isn't quite right, not so much something missing but something surplus that would have been befitting of a different role, but within hers needed to be whittled away. It was fortunate no one was really too aware of this, however. To begin with, that is.

But by the standards of royalty her upbringing was unconventional.

First of all there was her mother.

She became aware of the Sultana's idiosyncrasies in her childhood.

'Do not disturb the *sahiba*[1] this morning,' her *ayah*[2] would inform her. Every morning without fail. She often wished that her mother wouldn't disturb *her* as regular as clockwork (preceding the era of clocks) or as regular as the call to prayer then, as she herself would be awoken by her mother's singing and dancing in the fragrant courtyard outside her apartments. It wasn't just the singing (which actually mellifluous enough, beautiful even), it

---

1. a respectful form of address for a woman, madam
2. maidservant

was the accompanying jangle of the bell-laden ankle bracelets that she would insist on wearing as she whirled barefoot, with increasing mania, until she would collapse with exhaustion, and Roshni, despite her natural inclination towards sleep, would be wide awake. The Sultana would rarely ever remove these, which had the effect of serving as an early warning system to whoever happened to be in the vicinity, of her rapidly approaching presence. Occasionally Roshni's lady-in-waiting would manage to commandeer a couple of these bracelets and mischievously attach them to the legs of an unsuspecting member of the royal menagerie - most commonly one of the monkeys - and then let him into the inner sanctum of the *mahal*[3] to run amok, and convince those around that it was the Sultana herself who was on the approach. The creature himself would be much enamoured by the unfamiliar jangling emanating through his own movements, and once he'd been rumbled, would protest most vociferously when the servants were ordered to catch, detain and deprive him of his newly realised sonic powers.

'Little shit, see how you like it once you are banished to the tiger's enclosure,' cried the head *mali*[4], who much to his chagrin had been temporarily relieved of his beloved gardening duties and ordered to assist in the capture and de-braceleting ceremony, as they tussled on the floor and the monkey tugged at his generous moustache, taking his howls as a cue to tug even harder. Even worse, when it came to maintaining royal dignity and decorum was when the Sultana managed to mistake a monkey for one of her

---

3. palace
4. gardener

younger children, and would then berate her entourage of maids for the 'child's' nakedness, poor hygiene and the fact that he or she had been left to wander the grounds unaccompanied and despondent - and had even managed to make it into the animal enclosures. The staff, though long-suffering, were hugely loyal and protective towards their mistress and her changeable moods - as changeable as her bewildering array of outfits - and would do whatever it took to placate her distress at what she perceived. The fortunate monkey of the day (they seemed to have themselves a rota) was then lured with remarkable ease into the inner chambers with promises of succulent food, then forcibly dressed in the finest silks, organzas and brocade from one of the younger prince's or princess's wardrobes and then duly paraded in front of their 'mother'.

This usually had the desired effect, and she would respond by hugging, kissing and sometimes dancing with her new offspring of the moment. She would often then run off to her dressing rooms and bestow some of the finest pieces of her jewellery on the creature, who usually had to be prevented by a vigilant maid from attempting to eat these - or worse still, stick them up an orifice. Roshni as an elder child would watch these shenanigans and wonder for the umpteenth time what had made her mother this way. These particular moods were the harmless ones though. There was only ever a minor conflict if one of her younger siblings would wander in and see the monkey bedecked in their favourite clothing, mother's jewels (and mother's affections) and would predictably throw a brief tantrum and attempt to chase the animal outside - or sometimes even attack it. This was never wise, as the monkey, having had its fill of food and fuss, would then unceremoniously remove its clothing, hurl it at the child, along with the jewels – which could cause serious damage – and pandemonium would ensue for a few brief moments. But no real harm was ever done.

The more serious moods, which she (along with the staff) did her best to protect her siblings from, were completely different. As a younger child herself she had known on one level that something was amiss, but was neither able to articulate this nor speak to anyone. She would have liked to have spoken to her father, but a conversation of this sort with the Sultan – even if she was his daughter – was never going to be possible. She saw him at court every week for several hours, stifling her yawns but sitting dutifully through the dull and, to her mind, entirely meaningless ceremonial rituals, but as for a private audience, this was generally out of the question. Even if she had had the presence of mind to ask. And she never had.

It had been a calligraphy lesson.

Although there was much that she did share with her mother, her looks and her deportment being the most obvious, the most valued and the least – to her mind – relevant, there was much on which she diverged. She had never had her mother's love and talent for dance for one – it was this that was commonly believed to have entranced her father all those years ago. And of course, a Sultana, once a Sultana, would never perform in public. It was partly the showy, seductive elements of this that would induce Roshni to run away when any of the women of the household tried to teach her and she would abscond with the ringing of their laughter in her ears, but beyond this she had no real talent for anything involving fine and delicate movements. So calligraphy was a torture. Especially when she would rather have been outdoors and talking to the animals, or eavesdropping on the dirty conversations of her maids and their latest hidden exploits.

It was a requirement, however, and part of the extensive training needed to turn her from an uncut diamond into a rival to the Koh-I-Noor herself. So the calligraphy itself was of no interest to her, but the writing now - this was where she found herself. She remembered her first time. The first time it had happened. We never forget that do we? Her teacher was astounded, as he was well aware of her complete absence of both passion and aptitude in this area. She had come to him diffidently at the end of the lesson, and asked in her quiet but firm way for as large a piece of parchment that he could spare - or failing that, several smaller sheets. Well, he was more than happy to oblige but did not honestly hold out much hope of her producing anything of beauty, in either structure or formation. But that wasn't her intention.

She had worked late into the afternoon and evening and had sat herself in a far courtyard of the grounds, away from any prying eyes - the birds and other animals didn't count and were welcome companions in this, her new quest. She had begun with only a vague idea of what she was going to write - perhaps something suitably juvenile and rebellious about her unwanted life as an imprisoned princess of the Mughal empire. What emerged didn't even seem as if it was from her. She sat and listened to the birdsong, even more rousing than her mother's dulcet tones, and just let the words pour forth. The sun was almost setting once she was done, and the parchment was almost filled with her immature hand. She remembered running: no delicate and graceful swanning into parlours for her. That was the first thing that provoked her mother's ire. Then it was downhill all the way.

'And who might this be, causing this unholy disturbance in both the earth and the heavens? Even God himself would not dare to be so bold, not when I am in need of sleep such as now! And look who it is. Are *you* God? I think not! What dost thou want, infernal monkey who belongs in a cage? What brings you here in the guise of a princess – my daughter no less. Do you think I know not my own child? Your hair, clothes and jewels do nothing – nothing you hear – to persuade me that you are anything but an imposter!'

She looked open-mouthed at her ayah who had tried unsuccessfully to bar her entry to her mother's chambers. She just stared back as if she knew what might be coming, as sure as the monsoon follows the dry and suffocating heat. All too late now, but she tried to back slowly away from the tented veranda where her mother sat on a silk-lined swing as if a child, but stared at her as if she were actually seated on her imperial throne and Roshni were just a mere mosquito needing to be fanned away.

'And does the monkey have a tongue? Oh look, may Allah bless him! The monkey has been trying his hand at the regal, refined and rarefied art of calligraphy no less. Come hither animal – now that thou hast disturbed my precious solitude – and show me the fruits of thy labour.'

'Mama,' she began but her ayah gestured to her to just play along. And what, pretend to be a *monkey*?

She tried to ignore the tremble in her hands as she handed over the sheets of parchment to her mother, who snatched them from her and stared hard at the top sheet. The hardness of her expression then changed.

'By the fates of the worlds, this I was not expecting. And from a monkey, no less.' She then took Roshni in her arms and lifted her onto her lap while the child smiled and held on to the twisted golden cords with both hands and waited for her mother to swing them and their cares away. Sometimes, when her mother was in the right mood, she would swing as high as she could, and they would be able to catch glimpses of the city beyond the palace walls in the distance. Roshni had never ventured out into the city. She was told by her ayah that the palace itself contained more delights and wonders than the city – and indeed the whole land beyond ever could. And besides. It was *dangerous*. Her mother began swinging them high into the air, and she felt it couldn't have been a more joyous end to the day. She closed her eyes and inhaled the fragrant musk from her mother's skin and heard the strains of a familiar old *ghazal*[5] that her mother usually sang in the mornings to wake her up, now intermingled with the breeze and applause of her ayah as well as the growing crescendo now of the birdsong, as they too briefly soared high into the air, invading the space of their feathered friends for a mere while. She could almost imagine that she was feeling the touch of their wings brush past her face and arms, and briefly opened her eyes. She saw the city first. Far in the distance – but this evening she felt that as she reached out with

---

5. a genre of poetry, containing spiritual themes and often set to music

one hand she could touch it. And if she could touch it she could one day venture there. Her mother then bent down mid-swing and kissed her lightly on the cheek: her lips soft and full to the touch. Then she saw the birds. Circling in the air around them as they slowly descended and the city disappeared from view, they were a sight to behold. She realised now that her mother had finally recognised her for who she was.

Her next thought was that they were maybe giant moths rather than birds, as they continued to circle around her and her mother as they reached the ground, and her mother tenderly lifted her off her lap and began to dance her familiar swirling dance around the now stationary swing, her bare feet moving with extraordinary speed as she tossed what looked like petals from the jasmine tree around her. But where had so many petals come from? Roshni had no idea, but for the first time in her life she danced too. Danced with abandon like her mother, and forgot she had no real skill or talent for this. For once she didn't care. To her even greater delight her mother then picked her up – and she was by no means a small child by then – and twirled her around with her.

Through her joy she could finally see. The birds and the moths were the ripped-up shreds of the parchment on which she had written her precious story. Her mother had been tearing this up as she had swung, throwing the debris into the air. Roshni started crying. Silent tears of course; they were always silent tears and she knew her mother would never realise. After a lifetime, her mother stopped her dancing and Roshni felt ill with both the whirling and the distress of her lost story. Her mother had not even read it.

'Well, if any more proof were needed, monkey, no child of *mine* could ever write in such an unforgivable scrawl. Though for a monkey, it was probably passable.'

She ran crying from the courtyard before even her ayah had realised something was wrong.

A few days later her calligraphy teacher asked her what she had written on the parchment he had given her. She didn't wish to even think about what had happened, let alone have to formulate a swift answer in response. She said she had just used it for additional practice, but it hadn't been worth keeping so she had handed it to one of her maids to be used as additional lining for the many bird cages in her apartments. She hoped he didn't mind. He looked searchingly at her as he wasn't completely convinced by this answer, but he thought better of questioning the princess, who was but a child, and even younger than any of his own daughters, any further.

She had always hated seeing the birds caged like this and kept as mere decoration, when they were actually alive and needed to spread their wings through the uppermost leaves of the surrounding jungle of the city, as well as spread their badinage through their early morning salutations. One of the (very many) bizarre behaviours that her mother would exhibit would be to occasionally carry these birds in their cages out into the extensive grounds of the palace estate when she was disposed to. They would dutifully sing along to the jangling of the dancing bells on her ankles and – Roshni supposed – look out from between the gold-and-jewel encrusted bars (lined with gold and jewel encrusted excrement, rather than parchment). She wondered if this was not an additional cruelty, letting them physically see and feel the freedom of the wider grounds while they were still indisposed by the confines of the cage. But she then recalled how one day she had spotted her mother opening the cage door of a pair of stunning looking pheasants – who at least were not being hunted as game while they were ornaments of the palace. The birds were bewildered. Roshni had been observing from behind a small jasmine tree and one of them had not even moved. The other had appeared more interested in the Sultana's gentle words of encouragement and had moved right up to the open door; if he had flown then, no one would have been able to stop him. But he did no more than simply extend his neck outside of the cage and look around him. His feet stayed right where they were before he stepped straight back, to her mother's evident disappointment.

'Fly ye damned creatures! Dost thou not know that these opportunities are but rare and fleeting? How wilt thou explain this to thy charges, when they too wish to fulfil their God-given natures and take their leave of all the empty delights that the palace has to offer, and trade this willingly for the dangers but ultimate freedoms of the jungle? O fearful ones! How much better to be savaged by the soaring clutches of a descending eagle, once having tasted the free air, than live a lifetime in the gilded security of the bejewelled prison! Thou art not deserving of thy wings and I shall arrange to have these clipped, forthwith, as they do nothing but betray the real degraded states of thy true and shameful natures! Now, who goes there?'

Roshni with her customary lack of guile and decorum had – being intrigued by what she was witnessing –

stepped forward out of her hiding place and right onto a surrounding bed of immaculately laid stone and chalk pebbles. The resulting sound had broken her mother's delicate reverie – and this was never advisable. It could go either way. She decided that ignorance would be the best policy here.

'Mama, I had just been observing the beautiful hues of the *shafaq*[6] in the darkening skies.' The Sultana immediately turned skyward and Roshni could see the appreciation on her face. 'They reminded me of the bleeding of the colours when Mustafa hangs the block-printed saris out to dry, and they float in the wind like the changing meadows with the seasons.'

Roshni, even at a young age had been partial to a rather poetic turn of phrase – and this was one of the few things her mother did appreciate, and her father even did admire. It was enough of a distraction as the Sultana momentarily forgot her vocal chastisements of the reluctance of the birds and stood up straight – she was a tall and imposing lady – gazing upwards, and then she reached out as if to allow the strains of pink and fuchsia to trickle through her fingers. Roshni walked up closer and surreptitiously closed the cage doors so her mother would hopefully not recall what she had been doing there, and that she may have been spotted. It was all in these tiny details. The Sultana's fragile equilibrium could usually be restored – if you knew what to do and were quick enough. Roshni definitely was. She then went to pick up the cage – though it was slightly too large and heavy for her to carry with ease, and when her mother

---

6. twilight

realised this, she smiled affectionately and took it from her with a smile and a kiss.

'My darling princess. What is this destiny that thou hast been burdened with? Forgive us all for what we have left you with, for we knew not what we were doing.' Roshni trailed behind her mother and watched the two pheasants staring at her as they made the trek back to the palace apartments. They seemed happy enough. Didn't they?

So, while calligraphy was definitely not her forte (though poetry may have been her destiny) and it was fair to say she hated dance with a passion, there were other elements of her education which – while not exactly part of her specific calling – were still pleasurable and, more importantly, tolerable enough. Firstly there was embroidery. A princess needed to be able to stitch with style and panache. Although Roshni never veered towards the very traditional designs that were most beloved by her mother, she did have a certain unique and creative flair that the Sultana – despite finding unconventional – couldn't really find it in her to object to. This was one of the few disciplines that she had taken it upon herself to teach Roshni personally, rather than engaging an artisan teacher. If she couldn't teach the girl to dance, she'd be damned if she wasn't going to be able to bob and weave with the best of them. Roshni was not at all resistant to this arrangement and would apply herself as best she could to her mother's tutelage.

Her mother had a particular penchant for mirror work:

'To ward off the eye of the evil one,' she would whisper theatrically to her. But she was also partial to more traditional embroidery. Initially her mother would tell her that it was of *upmost importance* that she knew what she was making before she actually started; seeing where you went with things was just a luxury when it came to embroidery, but as Roshni still happened to be a child she was allowed some leeway with this. Well, quite a lot if the truth be told. Despite telling her that she needed to plan in her mind the colours, patterns and overall design that she was aiming for, she would never really enforce this in her daughter's own work until Roshni began to suspect that she didn't really believe it herself. She was telling her what she felt she ought to, having taken on the – in her mind – auspicious role of A Teacher, though when it came to it, Roshni and her mother both worked mainly from their intuition and allowed the design to develop as it chose.

'Remember, my Roshni, textiles are not meant simply to be worn and appreciated aesthetically by the eye, for how dismal a fate that would be. No, they are to be *felt*. It is the direction of the stitches that will affect how the light – my light – plays off them, how they will feel to the touch and, most importantly of all, the quality and weight of the background material itself. Is this to be draped in the air as a tent for an opulent shelter, spread across the floor as a covering for a veranda, nailed to a palace wall in a private chamber, or' – and at this point she partially unrolled a huge roll of linen – that must have taken a maid the best part of an afternoon to wind – and hung it across her body – 'to be draped across that most worthy of all destinations, more so than the air, earth and walls of the most sumptuous palace, that of the human body.' She then, ignoring Roshni's looks

36 The Prayer Rug

of bemusement, began to dance seductively around the chamber, holding the fabrics up against her shapely body while the child sat waiting patiently for her instruction of a new stitch to begin. Finally, her mother sat down, and with the ringing of the bells still in her ears, Roshni would listen to and take in the finer points of her learning for the day.

The Sultana was distracted you see. There had been notice of some new arrivals at court who had requested a meeting with the Sultan. They were foreigners no less, from exotic climes in a far-off region known as *Europe*. Roshni had heard of this place. Some of the maids had been speaking of it earlier: a place that according to legend was so cold that the sun was never seen and the men – and women too – in order to survive in that most uncompromising of climates had been forced by necessity and the need for survival to grow thick hair all over their bodies so they now resembled bears more so than actual human beings. This thick hair even covered the men's swords – though Roshni wasn't entirely sure why their weapons needed to be covered in fur too, as surely they weren't going to be feeling the cold. A sword was supposed to look threatening was it not? Anyhow, Roshni was looking forward to seeing these bear-like humans when they arrived. And their bear-like swords too. She had only encountered bears in woven tapestries and fables previously. When she asked her mother about the appearance of these Europeans, however, it was a full ten minutes of precious embroidery time later when the Sultana could halt her laughter enough to continue with the lesson. And even then she was semi-distracted up until lunchtime by odd bouts of smiles and comments to herself about the European swords. Roshni was not best pleased. Surely it was the foundation of all righteous learning and genuine knowledge to ask questions – her ayah was forever telling her this – but whenever she did, she was either met with derision, laughter or told that knowledge of this type was not for the likes of a princess. She had decided right then that *all* knowledge was going to be at her disposal from thereon in; she would just have to be careful from whom and how she sourced this.

Anyhow, towards the end of the lesson things took an unfortunate turn. The Sultana had been teaching Roshni a range of stitches and techniques; she had been practising these and perfecting her use on various scraps of old material. The ultimate creation that was being worked towards was a large wall hanging that Roshni was adding to incrementally, each time she had mastered a new style or use of embellishment. She had been making good progress on this and, to her delight, her mother had been consistently praising the development of this larger piece of work. It was a scene of the jungle surrounding the city, and part of this was made up of the caves, where bats dwelt underground that sucked the blood of the maybe outwardly pious but ultimately irredeemable unbelievers. So she had been told. How bats knew who to attack she wasn't quite sure, but they had made their way into her scene and there they had stayed.

Roshni had become quite enamoured with working on this scene; she had used fragments of mirrors and also small pieces of shells to represent the bats. Strictly speaking this was starting to resemble more of a mosaic than a purely textile work, but this was permissible as it was the overall design that mattered. And the overall design was starting to look rather enchanting. She had even been working on it in her own free time, sometimes by candlelight in the solitude of her chambers when she was unable to sleep, and it had therefore progressed at a much swifter pace than could have been anticipated. Bizarrely she found that the more she worked on it – imagined the scene with its animal allegiances, as well as dangers, concocted mini narratives around it which she would occasionally tell one of her younger siblings and then brought fully to life within the confines of her growing tapestry – the less she found she was attached to the actual object that began to grow before her eyes. Yes, her mother's praise had been heart-warming as it was so very rare, as was her father's as he rarely took real note of anything she did, but then an idea began to form in her mind. She realised she didn't want to keep the scene. Her original plan had been to have it prominently displayed on one of the walls of her spacious octagonal bedroom chamber, so it would be one of the first things she would see upon awaking each morning (and would hopefully offset the disturbance of the all too early hour of this, at the behest of her mother's whims). Additionally, it would also therefore serve as the last thing she would see at night, to override any of the unsettling events of the day. But the more it took a tangible form, the more clearly its purpose unfolded before her. She would have to give it away. Yes. She would give it away – and not just to one of her maids or another designated princess friend (who was really no such thing). She would give it to one of the Europeans. Maybe there would be a visiting princess her age among the delegation, or one back at home that she could gift this to? Or even a prince – it really didn't matter to her. That way when they were suffering in the lands of no sun and shivering despite their thick layers of fur, maybe they could gain some solace through gazing at a scene of the heat of the jungle, with its particular wildlife as well as nocturnal inhabitants.

There was but one thought that made her sad though. She herself was within touching distance of the jungle. She could even see it from her swing, or when she climbed up the narrow spiral staircase of one of the turrets in the palace. But she had never physically set foot there - had never felt the leaves underfoot or brushing her face, seen the animals that existed in the palace menagerie in their natural habitat, or hidden herself in the caves to see what the bats' judgements would be of her. Had she been living a worthy and virtuous life or a wanton one? Would they attack her with virulence or circle her but not dare to touch her skin? It pained her that there was no way she would ever know. Still, she was resolute. The tapestry may have been her creation, but it was not hers to keep.

'Oh, my Roshni, my light - how hast thou conceived of such a scene, that thine own mother has not, even in her own advancing imagination, begun to see!' It was the following day and Roshni had decided to unveil the full splendour of her tapestry under her mother's discerning eye. She was relieved. It had been the right decision. Her mother's pride was palpable, and when she haltingly mentioned her idea of gifting it to the visiting European delegation, her mother was positively in the throes of ecstasy.

'My radiant one! How thy light dost hide the passions of thy young heart, for you are but your mother's daughter indeed. What a splendid plan is this! It is through this that my Roshni shall escape this prison and live the life of a *European* princess!'

This unexpected turn of events was not at all to Roshni's liking. Or understanding. She wasn't too happy being a Mughal princess so how would being a European one, living in the bitter cold and having to grow into a bear with a man with a hairy sword, be any more desirable? She decided not to speak of her immediate objections to her mother, however, as a mood of happiness combined with lucidity, such as this, was one to be savoured and not curtailed. There was still a considerable amount of work to do until she felt it would be finished and suitable to be presented as a gift; Roshni had high standards and if her final envisioning didn't quite match the scene that had evolved in her mind's eye over the past few months, she would not be prepared to relinquish it and would allow some other suitable gift to be chosen.

She watched as her mother ran her long fingers over the length of the jungle scene. Almost every finger was adorned with a precious gem in a gold setting. The joy in her face was a rare sight, and for a brief moment Roshni wondered if she shouldn't perhaps keep hold of the tapestry – if only to gift it to her mother. She was sure she hadn't ever travelled into the jungle either, nor communed with the bats. (The Sultana frequently claimed to have travelled around the world – and into other worlds too, but since the Sultan had kindly but firmly barred her from any talk of this kind – and the servants from humouring her – she had never spoken of her alleged sojourns again.) Certainly Roshni could never remember her mother even having left Delhi, let alone setting off on any extended adventures such as she had claimed to. Though she of course had been alive a lot longer than Roshni had. And some of the tales her mother used to tell her at bedtime (sadly very infrequently now that her place as the youngest child had been usurped by several others) certainly sounded as if her mother were speaking from experience. Fantastical though they sounded. Roshni now disregarded these musings. She was convinced her mother hadn't ever traversed through the jungle, but as this particular creation had already in her mind been given to the pending visiting party, she resolved at that moment that, once this hanging had been completed, she would start a new one – and this one she would keep completely secret from everyone until it was perfect. For this one she *would* gift to her mother.

The day of the visit grew ever nearer.
 The tapestry grew in detail and texture: colour and composition.
 The palace had been a hive of activity with the workers – maids, manservants, chefs, gardeners, musicians, artists and performers – from all corners of the kingdom it seemed – all vying for supremacy in their supposed importance in the proceedings. Having the unenviable job of keeping this motley crew in some semblance of order was the head courtier, who took responsibility for overseeing all major functions. To Roshni's growing alarm – and none too insignificant irritation – her mother had become almost possessed by the idea of this being an opportunity of presenting her eldest daughter – now fast approaching adolescence – as a possible future marriage prospect for one of these foreign bear-princes. That the Sultan himself

would never have given his blessing to such a match (and that Roshni herself had no desire to marry *any* prince from any region, let alone a frozen one with no daylight) was of no significance to her. She would often be completely consumed by these fleeting fantasies and Roshni had begun to learn now with her own maturation that the best strategy was just to allow her these to play along and immerse herself in her mother's world of the moment. It would abate soon enough and be replaced by another, initially alarming but ultimately soon to be forgotten initiative. Like the magpies congregating in the palace grounds, whose attention flitted from the shiny bands of brocade to the gleaming fake baubles that they managed to pilfer under the distracted eyes of the maids to line their nests (but then discarded amongst the lawns and flower beds before they even made it there, to the eternal annoyance of the uncovering gardener).

So she allowed her mother her wild imaginings, and kept herself focused on the completion of the tapestry – it was the edging and framing she was working on now – with brief interludes for wardrobe fittings for the array of outfits she would need to wear for the various receptions of the visiting ladies at court, followed by the obligatory banquets. The male visitors would of course be visible to the ladies behind their *purdah*[7], but this only worked one way; the men themselves would have no idea whose gaze was appraising them. Which was of course how it should be.

---

7. the practice in some Muslim societies of screening women from men or strangers, especially by means of curtains or barriers

A stunning silk tented enclosure – replete with awning for looking at the stars – was swiftly being assembled on one of the largest lawns. This was where one of the many banquets would be held, and Roshni loved the fact that a garden pavilion such as this could be assembled with such ease and completely transform the outdoor space – and with one of the many fountains forming the centrepiece. But then this would be completely disassembled the next day, or whenever its temporary function had been fulfilled. She had been making her way back to her chambers while an idea began to form in her mind: how the interior of a banqueting tent could look by lamp and starlight with the embroidered tales and woven dreams of her imaginings forming the decor. It was her favourite time of day now, the early evening, but she could see a glow in one of the smaller courtyards in the distance. Her ayah would often have gated fires burning there which sent out a warning glow from a distance. This was their secret method of communication that all was not well with the Sultana and that she should be vigilant. As she approached, her unease growing with every step, it seemed to hit a crescendo as she saw it was her mother herself who was tending the fire; this wasn't customary at all, but Roshni was learning to take these things – with the ringing of the bells – in her stride.

She decided normality and an absence of the obvious line of questioning might be the best initial tactic.

'Mama, hast thou seen the banqueting tent? It is resplendent with the stars visible above!' The Sultana paid her no attention. Her face was hard-set and her eyes were shut. Roshni could just about make out the murmurings of a prayer being recited at great speed from her lips.

'Begone, O evil one. Thou didst try with thy familiar mischief to fool us with thy false covenant of protection. But thou didst underestimate the powers of the wise Sultana in thy midst. How clever did thou think thyself with the mirrors for supposed protection, when all the while it was the hidden, the background, that my poor innocent one was covering with her beloved design.' Roshni could approach the fire no further, for upon hearing these words she knew what it was she would find in the charred remains of the embers.

Her resignation and composure deserted her.

'Mama, what wast thou thinking? It was a scene of the jungle on an ordinary backing that I was to gift to the Europeans! Nothing more! Why hast thou done this?'

'Do not be intemperate with me, child! Hast thou forgotten the depths of gratitude that thy owest to one's mother? Snivelling wreck of a child! Shameless creature, allowing Satan to trick her when her lineage itself should have been ample protection. O Allah, can you assure me that this is even my child and not another devious means of subterfuge employed by the dark lord himself?' She grabbed Roshni's arms so hard that the girl cried out in pain, and she then pushed her face close to the fire itself. Her tears were now turning to screams and this only had the effect of further enraging the Sultana. 'Can thou not see child, it mattered not what you might have embroidered on this cloth – even the verses of the Holy Quran itself would not have served as any amulet. It was the cloth itself that had been damned! Burning was the only remedy, for the cloth itself had been worn and woven by the impure!'

Roshni could now clearly see the flames eating away at her hours of labour. Her eyes first alighted upon the roughly stitched outline of a lion that had all but disappeared; this in itself was not too upsetting, for the lion was not yet fully formed with any amber hues and woollen textures to give him any substance. The other animals that were completed though, with beads and pieces of glass that she had meticulously stuck with a vegetable paste to give some texture to her stitching – in her mind, these were real. The burning was akin to a murder and through the crackling of the flames she could hear the wails of the mynahs, the cries of a baby elephant and the growing hysteria of a pack of small monkeys. Roshni was quiet now, but silent tears continued to roll down her face and a few began to drop into the flames themselves. The Sultana did not see what happened next, for if she had done, her reaction would have been unpredictable – even for her. Roshni was not aware of it herself for a good few seconds.

The fire was continuing to burn – but it was the cave.

For some reason this section of the fabric had not caught the flames like the remainder had. The bats were still intact. Just. But the cave seemed to be growing. Roshni knew that didn't make sense, but the shrinking canvas was subsumed by the cave itself and the collective spirits of the now dead or dying animals were all congregating there. And accusing her.

For she was the one who had brought them to life – they themselves had had no choice in the matter. She was the one who had envisaged them and chosen their composition, and she was the one who had chosen the contaminated world they had been born into. The diseased cloth. The world that should have been a blank slate for them was already – as her mother was repetitively chanting now – *haram*[8]. And so haram that she had taken it upon herself to completely destroy that world – and all of its inhabitants. With no dialogue with its originator either. They could be granted no pardons nor clemency from her now. They were all but gone. Roshni blinked a few times, as the smoke was heavy now, and with the combination of this and her own weeping, she couldn't be entirely sure of what it was she was seeing. But as her tears began to fall on the fire, the images that had now mostly been burnt into oblivion suddenly started to reform in front of Roshni's eyes. They floated up from the flames themselves and then into the air. First she saw the lion, and perhaps he was the most startling of all, as while she had not been afforded the opportunity to complete him on the tapestry, he was now fully formed and resplendent as he leapt into the air and took his place in the hanging tapestry that was now suspended in the growing cave directly above the fire.

She knew she was both distressed and in shock but neither of these two emotions could quite explain that away. She looked again as a couple more droplets of tears fell and – this time – there was no doubt. This time she clearly saw the birds flap their wings and fly upwards to join him. Unlike the lion who was silent, they were animated – even boisterous as they flew with abandon. She was slightly worried now. She knew the bats would be up there and what – according

---

8. believed to be sinful

to folklore – their purpose was. But if the animals were all ephemeral now, what was it that the bats could really do? Well, the answer presented itself soon enough. They did indeed circle the animals, but they didn't (or couldn't) land and appeared to be unable to do them any harm. Looking back many years later, these unexpected sights unfolding in front of her were the first time she could remember an extraordinary happening such as this. Even at that age she knew enough about how her mother was treated – with reverence as she was, after all, the Sultana – but that was a role. If she had been almost any other woman (or even man) in the kingdom, it would have been a different story. As the solace that the sight of the newly animated creatures imbued her spirit, her tears stopped falling and those she had already shed dried quickly in the heat of the fire.

Slowly, her mother relinquished her grip on her.

She was still chanting various incantations, and just a few moments earlier Roshni had wanted to demand an explanation for how her mother could possibly have thought the material was impure in any way. She had already seen it and had been regularly inquiring about the progress of the tapestry, extolling its merits and virtues even – and how this in itself could perhaps lead to a most precipitous marriage proposal and a life of adventure abroad. Actually, upon swift reflection now, Roshni began to wonder if this had perhaps not been a blessing in disguise; she could maybe escape a future with a bear as a bear now (as she did actually quite like being a girl, though maybe not a princess), avoid contact with any swords – be they hairy or not – as they didn't sound much fun, and could then dedicate her time to recreating

or even reimagining her original tapestry. This was a lot for her to take in at that moment, but she no longer felt any shock or profound distress.
It was then that she heard the laughter.
It was Noura: her cousin who was closest to her in order of birth, though not in knowledge, intelligence or sensitivity. She wondered if Noura had ever applied herself to creating anything in the way she had. She doubted it. Although unspoken there was one thing she and her mother always concurred on. Noura was best avoided. The Sultana was already hurrying away from the gardens, and Roshni knew that, for her mother, all these episodes (that unbeknownst to her then would colour her own life well into her adulthood) would be forgotten by her at least, the very next day. Noura was standing at an open balcony and looking down at the scene.
'Roshni, what hast thou done now to upset the Sultana? Will thy bearing and countenance ever be those of a true princess? Somehow, I findest that doubtful.' Roshni was glad that Noura was at a distance from her and that the light was now fading, along with the flames of the fire. Her tears would at least be hidden for it didn't sound as if Noura had witnessed the entire scene. Thanks be to God.
'*Salaam*[9], Noura.' Then both on impulse and to change the subject: 'Hast thou ever heard of a sword, Noura?' Noura liked to be in the know, Roshni knew. About some things at least, if not others.
'What is this nonsense thou speaks, Roshni. Thy brain truly does belong in a furnace. Along with thy outfit. Maybe the wise Sultana should have thrown that onto

---

9. Islamic greeting

the fire along with the other rubbish she was burning.' Roshni felt that vague pang of hurt she customarily did when either her mother or Noura spoke in that effortlessly heartless way of theirs. That was their way. By now she knew better than to ever reveal how painful Noura's put-downs were. Tears were just more ammunition in her eternal arsenal to use against her. Roshni was the pre-eminent princess due to her father being the Sultan and for this accident of birth she could never, in Noura's eyes, be forgiven. Had it been at all possible, Roshni would have gladly traded places with her cousin and lived the more obscure life that would then have been afforded her, if she chose. As it was, Noura would do everything she could to usurp her cousin and Roshni did the same in order to reject any limelight. Unfortunately for both girls, this truest of reflections of both their constitutions only cemented the relative hierarchy of their positions within the household and wider kingdom. For nothing seems to work out as it should. Or is it that everything does?

Roshni was unsure how or why she thought this, but she *was* sure that swords – whatever they were – would be something Noura would probably like when she was a grown-up princess. And probably lots of them. Mughal, European – Noura wouldn't be too bothered. Anyhow, in the absence of any real understanding of what these common-for-her intuitions actually meant, she reluctantly went up to join her cousin on the balcony. As long as she had her specific purpose in front of her, she would cope with the Sultanas and Nouras of the kingdom. Somehow.

It was the next day that she was summoned to speak to her father.

50 The Prayer Rug

She was not concerned. Even though he had never explicitly admitted it, the Sultan was only too aware of the Sultana's idiosyncrasies. There had been rumours at the time of their marriage that the extent of these was kept carefully hidden – and to be honest, even if it had not, the Sultan had been so taken with his young bride's extraordinary beauty that he had vowed to never take another wife (rendering the harem redundant) as how could any other ever compare with the radiant beauty of his true love? Unfortunately, since that time he had reneged on this level of faithfulness, taking various concubines, but had been careful to keep this from his daughter and had threatened all in the know with a swift and certain death if she should ever discover the truth. He knew that she would take this as a heinous betrayal of her mother. And deep down he too knew this for what it was.

She entered his extensive library – she was well on her way to being its most ardent visitor – and found him seated at a desk with a large manual in front of him. She stepped forward to kiss his hands.

'Roshni, our brightest and most enduring light! Please take a seat with thy poor and undeserving father.' She did as she was bid before he continued. 'Thy mother tells me thou hast decided to discontinue the tapestry that thou had begun with the purpose of gifting it to the visiting European royalty. I am sorry to hear this, my light. But I am sure we can find a more fitting present for them. Thy humble father wondered if there was anything else thou had in mind?' Roshni could not believe her ears. It wasn't her mother's rewriting of the truth – she was used to this – but the fact that her father was offering her an opportunity to possibly do the one thing she knew her true calling to be – though it be considered an unlikely one for a princess. She paused, almost afraid of what she was being afforded.

'I am most unworthy, my dearest father, of any opportunity that thou hast blessed me with from the goodness of thy heart. But if thou couldst possibly consider this – I almost do not dare to utter it – there has been another creative endeavour that is much closer to my heart that would give me the utmost delight in sharing. I have been working on a modest collection of poetry – I would n'er dare to have recited this in public – but if this could maybe be presented as a bound volume for the visitors, that should greatly please me!' Once the words were out of her mouth she could barely contain her joy. The library was her greatest sanctuary, and to be able to contribute to an equivalent in another nation – she knew it nothing more than a token gesture – she was not unmindful of her modest age and talents – but it would give her a real purpose behind the heavy golden chains and bejewelled shackles of her unfortunate regality.

Her father stared at his precious daughter.

And then finally he spoke.

'Roshni, my child – I am astounded. Hast thy mother and I not bestowed the very highest levels of freedom and privilege upon thee? We can tolerate one of the arts such as tapestry being relinquished – though it be abundantly clear that neither singing nor dance be thy forte either – but the rigours and exactitude – the creative heights and endeavours needed to *write*. Roshni my beautiful but sadly deluded child, these are the preserve of *men*. Of *sons* and not daughters. By all means transcribe an already written poem in your calligraphic hand – but how canst thou readily believe – as thy apparently dost – that thou art capable of *independent creation*? The female disposition is to study the arts to the highest level verily, but composure is beyond even the considerable – for a female – talents of thee. For I shall illustrate this simply and clearly:

'Thy bhai[10] hast imagination; thou hast *no* imagination.'

With that he kissed her perfunctorily and immediately returned his attention to the volume in front of him.

Roshni took her leave without a word of protestation, let alone any flare of righteous anger. That was not in her natural disposition, and she had no clear idea of what it was she would be protesting about, for she had no real proof of her creativity. Her poems were just childish ramblings. But why Shiraz had been imbued with a quality – virtue even – when he had exercised no real proof of this either, she wasn't too sure. Had he ever written a poem? Or a story? If he had, he had never shared them with her, but her naturally charitable inclination veered towards him maybe having presented his work to her parents without her knowledge.

Her brother was certainly talented and skilled in numerous areas: an accomplished hunter, shooter and horse rider, his habitat of choice was most definitely outside of the confines of the palace. A few years older than Roshni, he was already a charismatic presence at court, though still a very young man. The Sultan had high hopes for the future of the kingdom

---

10. brother, especially an elder brother or relative

in his hands, though a few of the senior members of the palace had reservations. But still, he was in his very early adulthood and no great ruler ever came to power fully formed. There was considerable growing to be done on the job, even for those who managed to leave a great legacy.

As Roshni walked through the long aisles of the great palace library, she gazed up at the domed roof above, which looked befitting of a grand mausoleum or mosque. It was here she paused and wondered if the view of the stars from the banqueting tent would ever match this one. For here you could see the same moonlit sights, particularly if you climbed up to the mezzanine and were then in touching distance of the glass roof itself, but you were also shielded from both the elements and the unwelcome company of other people. There would be no possibility of that at the banquet. Roshni was starting to dread this. Unlike Noura, who she knew would love the limelight. And Shiraz.

On a whim she decided to walk straight to this upper level. On the gallery hung a number of miniatures that had been produced by a succession of royal artists over the years. None of these were formal portraiture, as these belonged in the more ornate grand reception and state rooms of the palace and court. These were all more relaxed and naturalistic scenes of various predecessors of her mother and father, intermingled with flowers, gazelles, peacocks and other animals (though Roshni did note that there were no monkeys). None of them – the men nor the women – were painted looking directly at the viewer; they were all in profile and seemingly unconcerned or unaware of being observed while either contemplating a book of verse, or smelling the sweet aromas of a flower from a nearby tree. Roshni and Shiraz too were represented, but only as very young children in the one picture. She had no desire to be immortalised in this way either now or at any point in the future – maybe that unwelcome honour could be passed on to Noura too?

Turning away from the artwork and surveying the scope of the library from her vantage point here, she marvelled at the lifetimes of work that had been assembled due to her father's generous patronage. The thought of these scholars, poets and theologians feeling that overwhelming compulsion to seat themselves down, with their self-imposed veils from any ephemeral distractions, and letting the word pour through them was extraordinary to her, as she thought of the sheer effort and craft it took her to produce a tiny gnat-sized verse in response to their majestic panthers. How could it be possible? Yet it was possible – the evidence was in front of her and she was seeing it with her own eyes. Her father's careless dismissal of her sex then came back to mind, and she hid her unease by gazing skywards at the roof. The sun was high and strong today and it was an odd sensation being in the library at this time, for she was more accustomed to nocturnal rummagings here when the Sultana's singing and bell-ringing were too much of a disturbance.

It was right there and right then that she made her oath. She wasn't sure to who or what, perhaps it was to herself and maybe it was of no consequence anyway. She was going to write. What she was going to write she had no real clue either, or for what overarching purpose evaded her too. All she knew was that it was a need within her – not just to learn about the arts in order to converse with other bored aristocracy about their merits, or engage with their creation in worthy areas (which happened to be of no interest to her) as that was the expectation of a princess. She knew then that it was what she was here to do, and if she did nothing else of note in her entire life, it would matter not. If no one ever read her work, it would most likely be a blessing too - so she decided there and then that it would be kept a secret. From everyone.

Roshni had always known she was blessed and one thing that her father (in his own way) had instilled in both her and Shiraz was the awareness of the weight of responsibility that came with being royalty. She remembered her father saying once that his own grandfather - himself a noble emperor - had told him in his own childhood that during the course of his hopefully long reign he would never recall the legions of people he had met, but he must always be mindful that they, however, would never forget their meeting with him. Even if fleeting. Perhaps especially so. Therefore the bar was higher than the imposing minaret that both surveyed and sang for the city. Other people could build reputations over time, could be forgiven for falling and would have ample opportunities to redeem themselves in others' eyes. Not so those who had been burdened with the royal seal. Any oversight, even if minor, any perceived lack of grace or courtesy and any behaviour not considered as befitting a guardian of the seal and that would thereby inform and colour any witness's view of them for all of eternity: no chance for redemption here. It was their role to rule which, according to him, was indistinguishable from their role to serve, and to remember at all times that it must be the highest levels of service that were to be employed *with no concessions*.

'Thou shalt never be released from thy duty, dear child.'

She remembered Shiraz reacting with horror at the time. Even at that young age he seemed to be resembling one of the more distant Sultans, who the dynasty no doubt hoped would be buried as deep as Ozymandias himself in the sands of time and people's memories. With some, the cloak of royalty sat as comfortably as the tigress reclining in her substantial enclosure; while for others it was more a case of a lizard darting frantically across the palace walls, once caught by the illumination of the lamp of a servant trying to dispose of him. What was evident to both children – even at that young age – was that the Sultana herself was heavily protected by a number of existing conventions. Firstly, as a female consort she had the purdah which prevented her appearance at any mixed gatherings. While she did appear at many segregated ones, Roshni was always amazed at how she managed to consistently uphold such a different demeanour (one that was genuinely befitting of her station) on these occasions, to the extent that it was only those who were part of the inner sanctum of the palace, the trusted entourage and close family, who were even aware of the other elements in her behaviours. Her mother to her credit (though sadly to her larger distress) was a consummate performer at these functions. Roshni had always observed that in the immediate aftermath of any official duty she had to undertake, she would always be that much more, *more* in the days following this. It was hard not to conclude that it was the role of Sultana itself that was partly the cause of these fluctuations in her equilibrium, not just any underlying vulnerability.

She did recall hearing once from her ayah – though never any member of the royal household – that her great-grandmother had, in her day, fought against and eschewed the purdah and demanded that she and other women (and not just those from regal backgrounds) be able to freely attend any artistic and theological events on a similar basis to the men, rather than having their senses forcibly enclosed through what she called 'the curtain akin to the death shroud', one that was designed to kill the spirit rather than kill the passions. She had achieved a measure of success with her courtly and educational innovations, but sadly, as is often the case, inroads made by one generation can easily be undone and even regress through subsequent ones who, though close in terms of lineage and ancestry, are from a different milieu regarding their attitudes. There was no question with the current Sultana, however. It was felt that her particular disposition would only avail itself to inappropriate attentions (and temptations) though the Sultan himself would never admit this openly. When his eldest daughter was born, he had been quietly concerned lest her nature be similar to her mother's in this way. He realised in time that he had no cause for concern. Not in that respect at least. For Roshni, though having inherited her mother's beauty, had only ever displayed a steady countenance and composure that he secretly wished had settled more on Shiraz than on her. There was something in this child though that kept him at a distance. He couldn't quite love her as he did his other children. It wasn't just that she was a daughter. It was that she was Roshni. He never felt he knew her as he did the others. Shiraz, however, was an open book in terms of his virtues (a few) and his ever-expanding dancing peacock of vices.

She was still up on the domed mezzanine when the Sultan walked directly beneath her and left the library with a weighty tome in hand. She knew her father was well read but, as he walked back out through the doors, he had no idea that she had remained in the library and had seen him. What was that book?

* * *

The years went past in a steady and heady haze of ceremonial functions, courtly machinations and rumours of uprisings and manoeuvrings in far-off and upturned corners of the patchwork quilt of the kingdom. Roshni had grown into a young woman, but had still retained the reserve and steadfastness of her childhood self. Some of the unkinder comments made by the ladies of the court were that it was Noura who was actually more constitutionally suited to the station of princess, but this of course was coloured by their own expectations for the role. Noura was no doubt a more extrovert personality, more inclined to opulence, more drawn to intrigue, but if there was ever a need for a scholarly mind in that younger generation, it was only ever going to be Roshni. Shiraz had grown more accustomed to pursuing decadence and pleasure in all its forms, and the Sultan's growing despair was these days no longer contained. In fact, not just scholarly – there were days when he felt that if he could, he would hand over the running of the kingdom to this daughter of his. Though if he was honest with himself, he could see that she wasn't quite right for all the publicly required tasks of a figurehead – and of course she was a woman. He was finding himself spending more and more time ruminating on the possible creation of a specific behind-the-court role for her. Of course, her soon-to-be expected designated role would be that of wife, but Roshni herself had shown a distinct lack of interest in any of the potential suitors who had asked for her hand in marriage. So far.

In recent years she had become almost reclusive, though behind the confines of the purdah this was acceptable – nay even desirable. Yet, even within the private chambers where she would have been most able to receive and entertain friends and guests of her own age, she often struck a solitary figure with her books and her growing attachments to the animals of the palace. Her younger siblings were all very sociable though and, in their own way, so too were the animals. She had not displayed any of the disordered thinking that the Sultana unfortunately had at her age, and she remained resolutely loyal to her. The Sultana herself had stayed as she was. Her singing voice as resplendent as ever, though these days she no longer wore the ringing anklets that for so long had become almost part of her very identity. When she was in a quiet mood, she would now walk into rooms without the previous jangles, and as a result would terrify those around her as if she were now an apparition itself. She no longer danced either, and these days Roshni would find that her nocturnal singing – which had once kept her awake at night and woke her all too early in the mornings – now had the opposite effect and would almost immediately send her off into a deep sleep.

It was one morning after one of these deep sleeps that she awoke and decided that today she would again ask for an audience with her father. For she had made her decision. And it was him that she needed to speak to first, before the most appropriate way for informing her mother could be sought, so as to minimise any unnecessary excitement.

'Roshni Sahiba, thou art consumed with agitation in thy soul today, what becomes thee, I wonder?' Her ayah as always, as if to confound her advancing years, was still as sharp as the cut-glass gems in the array of ornamental headpieces that her mother owned – but Roshni neither liked nor coveted.

'I have a supplication I wish to make to the Sultan, and it has been decreed that it must be today, for alas I have already but delayed long enough.' Roshni was sitting at the mirror of her dressing chamber and was brushing her long hair, a task that she had insisted on doing herself for many years now, rather than it being done for her. Also mounted on the wall was a reworked tapestry of a jungle scene with a cave full of flying bats to one side. Farishta looked at her shrewdly.

'Even for a humble soul such as I, it takes not the milk and honey from the blessed creatures to know what it is thou hast decided!' Then in a most unexpected turn in proceedings Farishta proceeded to weep, allowing her tears to fall straight onto the pristine marble floor without attempting to intercede in their course. Roshni felt a mild exasperation but as she was experiencing no minor attack of nerves herself, controlled her immediate urge to begin straightening the embroidered silk cushions a short walk away in her living quarters – or even pummelling them as she sometimes did when on her own. This was not advisable as, firstly, tears or no tears, this would earn her a rebuke, and secondly, she knew it was a sign that her discomfort was approaching what Noura would call 'bat out of hell' levels. Noura would customarily apply this to something of a critical nature such as her *kameez*[11] not being adorned with the right type of beading.

'My precious one,' Farishta continued to cry, 'At least permit this unworthy one the dignity of a final question? May Allah protect us, for it isn't to be that our dear princess shall be leaving us forthwith and transitioning – into a – into a *bear*?' This was not helping matters at all. Roshni decided that she would have to be as honest as she could with her loyal ayah at this stage.

'Dearest ayah, who hast cared for me since my own infancy as if I were her own blood and sinew, let thy soul rest in peace for there shall be no bears involved in my decision.'

'Thank Allah for his most beneficent of blessings! It shall be a noble Indian *raja*[12] no less who has swept away our light to illuminate the darkness of his own cave, but how can we be distraught?' She was still crying. 'We who have benefitted from the light ourselves are in the best of positions to know of its resplendence.'

Roshni could hear no more of this. Leaving her ayah veering between intense agitation and excitement, she wound up her tresses into a bun and then made the walk across the outdoor gallery towards the imperial chambers.

---

11. blouse
12. an Indian king or prince

4

Giles had opened his eyes just in time.

He then heard the familiar beeping sound signalling the impending closure of the doors, and he quickly leapt to his feet and jumped off the carriage. The evening had taken its toll on him, and he was wearier than he realised. He stepped out into the now much chillier night air and began the short walk to his home. Technically these houses were all terraces, but with their multiple storeys, high ceilings and period features, they were in fact a world away from the terraces in other parts of the city or the suburbs. Giles knew how fortunate he had been. He didn't own the whole of his house, but having the ground floor and substantial basement was more than adequate now he was on his own. He needed very little space himself – it was more a home for his precious ornamental companions than for him as a person. But once they were happy and suitably displayed, how could he be anything but overjoyed, even if he had no wife to share in this? As he walked in, he became aware of his phone vibrating in his pocket. It wasn't an incoming call though, just a signal that someone had left a message. He turned on lights, removed shoes and enough clothing to be comfortable, drew curtains and settled down to listen:

'Hi, Giles, it's me, Maurice. Was in the audience tonight and thought you did a grand job of it. Just hope you are okay though. Couldn't help wondering about that reference to the ex. Hope to chat further about the possible documentary soon too ...' Maurice was an old friend and colleague but one who was often out the country. Giles was surprised on two levels, both that Maurice had even been in the audience, but also that he had managed to completely miss his presence. The auditorium had had odd lighting though, but in a strange way it was this that had made him mention her. For when he had walked out onto the stage and was momentarily fiddling around with the IT, if it hadn't been for the kind applause, he would not have known there was anyone even there. As he couldn't actually see any of them once the lights had been lowered. For the whole of his lecture, he could have easily imagined that he was talking to an empty audience – much like most first semester undergraduates these days. It was only when he had finished and it was time for questions that he was actually reminded in a concrete way that there had been a whole (and substantial) body of people out there, listening (perhaps) to his every word.

This was something he had never experienced before. He knew he could be clearly seen, but of course hoped that most of the collective attention would be on his slides – there was no earthly reason why anyone would want to be looking at him if that was the alternative. He wondered if he might specifically request this again in future, and if this was what actors on the stage experienced during a performance. He was actually starting to see lecturing as a performance now. An act, rather than a pure exposition of knowledge. Maybe next time he could add in something else about his collection? Maybe a casual reference to a one-night stand he had had on one of them with a colleague from the manuscripts department? Yes, he was very tempted to start doing something like this. If only to keep himself entertained.

Later, with thoughts of his future lecturing engagements – and former sexual dalliances – still on his mind, he lay in bed and allowed himself to be enveloped by sleep.

* * *

Howra too was tired when she arrived home. Hers was a much more modest rented flat in a large concrete estate of maisonettes. She tried her best not to breathe in the objectionable smell of cat piss as she ran up the outside stairs, and across the walkways. The book had been just what she needed and had managed to displace the initial curiosity generated by her find. She recalled that she wouldn't be required to report to Mick next week, and her original plan had been to spend some time in reading and research – both into the professor's next movements and what her own future plans might be. As she made herself a cup of tea, her mind wandered away from all this.

Slowly settled at the large multi-purpose table where she ate, wrote and worked, Howra surveyed the object in her hands. It was possible that it wouldn't even work ... but it was worth a try. A part of her was loath to switch on a computer at this late hour though; people spent more time touching their electronic devices than the people they loved these days, and if she needed to read something she would willingly destroy the environment and print it out or read it in book form, rather than on a screen. If the truth be told, she wouldn't have minded having someone to touch just then, but in the absence of that, this was going to have to do. She was curious though and knew she wouldn't sleep as well as she might if she didn't try. What was the harm? She turned it on and when her prehistoric computer finally indicated it was ready to go, she had just about finished her drink – this was good actually as she didn't want to be spilling liquids everywhere as she was apt to do. That was her mistake – firstly in the dark and then inevitably making assumptions. It hadn't been a snail's shell at all. It was the plastic cover of an old memory stick which even she could tell was from a previous era, that she had crunched underfoot. But unlike the resulting slime that would have resulted from the unfortunate demise of a snail, the stick itself seemed largely intact inside the cracked cover. Slightly misshapen, perhaps, but that was the extent of it. Maybe it was that very fact that would make it compatible with her own antiquated device?

After a seeming frenzy of activity, the computer was indicating it was ready and waiting. The screen was blank in anticipation and she imagined she could almost hear its gentle breathing. She was definitely losing it. The sooner she made progress on her tracking of the professor, the better, as far as she was concerned. Something tangible to occupy herself and ward off these thoughts that seemed to imbue insensible objects with human emotions. She knew there was a word for that for animals and our fondness for imposing our own frameworks on them, when in all likelihood she reckoned they were way ahead of the game. We weren't crediting them an advanced view at all. Someone should come up with an equivalent for objects. Maybe she could – if she could actually get her mind under control for more than seven seconds that was. To stop this endless thought she reached down and inserted the silver end of the stick into the port of her computer. Despite the now crooked exterior, it slid in easily, and a few brief seconds later, the computer registered its presence too. It wasn't password protected so she opened the contents and scanned the list of files.

* * *

She knew her father well. He was at a loss as to what to say, but appearances being appearances, he had to adopt a hastily thrown on robe of all-knowing and all-seeing to hide the nakedness of his ignorance. He had sent his vizier and other staff from his chambers in anticipation of Roshni's visit, and this in itself was rare as there were precious few who were ever granted the courtly privilege of a solitary audience with the Sultan – family or not. He was hugely grateful he had had the foresight to do this. They were barely keeping a lid on the huge *biryani*[13] pot, desperately trying to stop the delicious aromas of regal gossip from filling the appetites of the lower orders – and that was just Shiraz. His complete lack of discretion in his conquests, coupled with a lack of political acumen that even the Sultan now acknowledged was already shaking the foundations of the kingdom was now a serious concern. It would not

---

13. a highly seasoned rice dish made with vegetables, meat or fish

have surprised him if even the jungle animals – as well as the suspected inhabitants of those caves – knew all that he'd been doing. The last thing he needed was a scandal involving a daughter, his eldest and most sensible to boot. In order to give him time to gather the folds of composure in his thoughts and words, Roshni continued speaking.

'My mind is made up my dear abaah[14]. But I shall require very little in the form of provisions henceforth.' She paused then and took her father's right hand between both of her own before speaking as gently as she could. 'I do of course recognise the slightly irregular circumstances of my decision and the fact that thou hast not yet been party to it. I am letting thou knowest before any other living soul. I have even kept it from ummi[15].' The Sultan wondered immediately if it was the ayah who had been behind this; servants could be masters and mistresses of cunning in these palaces, so much so that he often wondered who the real rulers of his fracturing kingdom were. He dismissed that thought though. That one wasn't bright enough, and he knew better than to distrust his daughter's word. He still couldn't speak and Roshni herself was reluctant to continue any further, just to fill the space between them. He finally found his voice.

'And where didst thou hear of this – this …' he finally managed but had no idea how to continue.

Roshni gave a brief but beautiful smile. This was turning out to be easier than she'd thought.

'Why of course, in a dream dear abaah! How else could we have met?'

---

14. father
15. mother

Dear God, was it possible he could have misjudged her so badly for all these years? Had she exchanged spirits with that Noura, daughter of his least favourite brother? A dream? However, he knew that in some circles decisions made on the basis of so-called divinations were perfectly acceptable, it was just that he himself was a tactician and strategist and had no time for anything of this nature. No, it couldn't have been Noura. She was more hard-hearted in her pursuits, and in her own way would have been a great ruler too. He then wondered if it was some late onset of a similar affliction that had blighted his wife. But no, Roshni's thinking did not appear to be disordered in any other sense. What was happening to him? He was losing his own clarity of judgement in the process. He would need to accept that perhaps this request – as irregular as it was – was hers and hers alone.

Eternal damnation to those confounded *djinns*[16]! How would he ever reconcile this? No matter though, he was the Sultan and if he needed to put on a fake cloak and accept Roshni's decision he would do so. But still, there were certain protocols that would need to be followed, as was the case with any royal nuptials, if only for the sake of the image of the kingdom.

'My precious jewel, your request takes thy father by surprise somewhat, but thy wish can only be my command. It be unusual yes, but there is a former precedent for this in the hallowed lineage of our family.'

* * *

---

16. a spirit in Muslim mythology able to appear in human and animal form and possess humans

68 The Prayer Rug

'It's going to be the next European City of Culture, you know.'
What, that shithole? Mick thought, but managed not to say aloud.

He had wanted to laugh in her face, but she was a well-meaning lady who was working as a volunteer in the prison's education department so that really wouldn't do. He wasn't really sure what she was doing there, but he wasn't really sure what he was doing there either. In the education department that was. Not the prison. No, he was sure why he was in the prison. A resettlement visit just prior to release for yet another inmate about to join his overstretched caseload. It was – as was frequently the case – proving difficult to track this one down. Prisons were like galaxies with their seemingly endless boundaries, but they were not generally redeemed by the presence of any celestial bodies to illuminate the way to whoever it was that one was supposed to be visiting.

The officer was apologetic but resigned and asked him to wait while he investigated what had happened, so in the meantime he had struck up a conversation with the woman who was in the small library by herself.

She had seen the lightly questioning contempt in Mick's face quickly transform into humour before he composed himself. The inmate he was there to visit was a nice young man, despite what it said on his record. She hoped – as she always hoped – that when one left at the end of his sentence he would never be returning – either here or to another institution, but she knew that it was largely out of her hands. Mick was right though. It was a shithole, although she wouldn't normally use that language herself. So much of one that no amount of long arm government intervention or regeneration policies could really transform the lives of the local people. Something else would need to happen there first. This much she knew from when she had studied sociology many years ago.

Mick scanned the books and thought about his latest project. He hadn't expected to find it so engrossing, but after years of direct case work and supervision, it was a welcome relief to be doing something slightly different. Approaching the so-called City of Culture through the scenic route of the surrounding countryside to the north, rather than the well-known, polluted ring road that most were familiar with, he inexplicably felt bad about his initial harsh judgements. For who was he to condemn an entire city that he had never once even visited for himself? He had travelled through it, yes, but actually stopped and entered the town centre, walked through the growing pedestrianised streets, eaten in a cafe or sat in a park? Never. That thought was soon overridden by the officer reappearing. His new client had been tracked down and was in an interview room at the far side of the prison. He bid the volunteer farewell and went off to meet what felt like case number seven thousand, three hundred and forty-eight.

It was a reasonable journey back down south later in the day. His work laptop safely locked away – he never opened it on journeys – and a quick check around him that no one was overlooking his reading materials, he settled himself down with the latest transcript:

5

Session One:

[A man N sits at a table in a dimly lit room in a prison. He is surrounded by huge piles of books, on the table, and on the floor. A doctor's notes appear transcribed on screen: Session 1]

I read about it earlier today.

Hold the front page, doc, yes I can read. They would love it if I was an illiterate bastard as well as everything else, 'cept I'm not. That was one problem I never had, although I had a shit load of others. You'll have read the reports on me won't you, doc? Probably files and files worth of assessments and questionnaires and statements and words, words, an endless stream of words. If you don't know what the fuck is going on, just write a report about it and convince yourself that you do, and then everyone else will believe you know something too. I feel sorry for you, doc, having to wade through all that shit and then sitting down with me. I see this as my chance though you know. The best gift anyone could get this is, even in my situation.

Especially in my situation.

The chance to tell it like it is.

I like to believe that I own my experiences you see – that they're as unique to me as my fingerprints – which have been taken enough times let's be honest – but I always seem to find that some smart arse has come up with a theory or a framework and just tried to brick me up in it, like the bloody princes in the tower. Or was it the princes in the bloody tower? Don't know and it doesn't really matter, the point I'm making is that if I've lived it, there may be *some* parallels with those that came before, but following anyone's footsteps I am not. Treading the untrodden path maybe and to the same destination no doubt, but you are not sticking a fucking framework round me. May as well call it for what it is, a straitjacket, that's what. Or a diagnosis. I know that's probably your livelihood, doc, and I don't control shit about what criteria you think I meet – in any case, I have more fucking letters to my name than most professors do. Just not any of the right ones, that's all. The ones that get you jobs and respect and all of that.

Anyway, it was called the paradoxical intention.

Basically, whatever scares the shit out of you, don't run away from it, run *towards* it. Tell it, is that all you've got, 'cause actually you wanted some more, you did. That wasn't nearly enough for a real man – a screaming girl maybe but not a man like you. Now, if you say that in some of the situations I've been in and didn't know what you was doing, you would be following in the footsteps of my mate Oscar here – *[N thrusts a book across the table, from one of the piles he has in front of him, while the cover and title is shown on screen –* Salomé *by Oscar Wilde]* – lying in the gutter but looking up at the stars. Or seeing stars at any rate, whether they were really there or not. A dozy girl I was once with managed to do the opposite. Looking up at the stars then falling over and landing in the gutter. How the fuck do you manage that? Mind you, I'm a fine one to talk, I am. So basically, the moral of the story is, don't go looking for any stars, just spend your life seeking out the gutter and telling it it isn't nearly as much of a stinking piss-ridden gulley as it likes to think it is. You want more fag ends, more broken glass and more dog shit. Please.

I caught that, by the way. You did try to be discreet but I saw the beginnings of a scrawl there on your notepad, as I must have said something important back there. Don't worry yourself as I'm not gonna bother asking. I haven't even got myself started yet, you're gonna be filling pages and pages when it comes to me, don't you worry. It's nice this though. Just being able to talk

72 The Prayer Rug

without too many questions. This is how it should be. Now make sure you keep those notebooks won't you, as one day all those pages might be worth something you know. May even be of *special historical interest* in some quarters perhaps. Think about it, you could be sitting on a future goldmine right there. I'm guessing you probably didn't even want my case, is that right? Don't worry yourself as you don't need to answer – and it's not me that's even supposed to be asking the questions, is it? You drew the short straw but you might just end up pulling the longest, hardest dick, haha. Sorry. Shouldn't speak like that to a lady.

Anyway, where was I? Oh yeah, the eternal paradox.

Let's start with solitary shall we.

Like life itself it's a game of two halves. You lot like to go back to childhood don't youse, think all the answers are there? I think you may be right on that count, so before you ask me to tell you about it, why don't I just give it to you from the off? Yes, it's a game of two halves all right, but not separated by anything as neat and tidy as a break at half-time, with pep talks and rests and time to regroup – nope, yer just have to keep on ploughing through, and all the action and goals are actually all mixed up with the fights and sendings off, all the way through, and sometimes it just feels like one long punch-up all the way through anyway. That probably explains the line of work I got into. Anyways, I'm jumping the gun a bit here. Maybe you should be keeping me on a tighter leash as I'll be on as many diversions as Walthamstow streets these days otherwise? Mini Holland – you heard that one? Bloody hell … does that mean I can smoke what the fuck I choose in them streets an' all? If I ever see them again that is. Or maybe you just want me to talk and you'll make your own sense of it afterwards? That's probably the case isn't it, doc? That's what your doctor letters mean after your name, don't they? That you know how to make sense of my nonsense?

I had it all through school to begin with. There was either too much noise or agro and shit going on – and if I couldn't cope with that I'd get put in something that resembled a cell even then, so I got acclimatised young you could say. I think they call it a 'time-out' room these days. Shame you've actually gotta hit someone to get in there like. Probably why I don't mind it at all now – it's actually how I like it. I had the same at home. One of eight I was and before I got put into care – don't get me started on that one, not today at any rate – I would just abscond from home and go and sit in my own cave in the forest behind the railway tracks where I lived. Wasn't even out nicking stuff or drinking – I mean I did some of that, of course, but that wasn't what it was about. Not really. It wasn't even a proper cave. It was just an old tree that had fallen over in a storm once and the earth around it had been disturbed, and combined with the slope it was on it naturally formed some kind of mud shelter. That's what it was in my mind anyway. This isn't some fucking Boy Scouts story so I had no friends there, no secret passwords or stash of biscuits or shit. Not even any fags or girls to take there – it wasn't exactly a love nest. It was cold and semi-exposed and I kept nothing there. The only thing I had was an unspoken contract with the animals of the forest, that I knew I was the gatecrasher but I wanted nothing from them. Just to share their space for a bit. Just to sit there. I can tell you about this now, but at the time I had no way of forming it into words. Would have just sounded mad, I would. All I knew was I needed a sanctuary from all the mayhem, so that is what I made myself.

I dunno, thinking about it again now as I'm speaking to you, maybe a love nest was exactly what it was? It was there you see. It was there that it happened for the first time. Some of the details are hazy but others are as clear as the moonlight that would stream in through the gaps in the earth at certain times of the month. So I couldn't tell you anything about how old she was or nothing. I didn't remember ever seeing her actually in school before – I guess she could have been from another one – though thinking about it now, I don't think she was ever in any uniform either. I remember the first time I saw her. She was in the high street one weekend and was on her own just like me. I walked past her and looked her dead in the eyes. Green they were. I didn't register if I fancied her or nothing back then, but all I knew was that I couldn't stop staring. I never even gave her much thought after – I think I was on one of my many suspensions from school then and was about to end up in a special unit – can't even remember what I was supposed to have done half the time. That's the thing that got me. I was never a bad kid you see – rough and gobby – but that was about the extent of it. But 'cause no one really cared or understood, I stand before you now *[he was sitting previously and now stands up]* as an officially Bad Adult. Because if that's what the paperwork says, it must be true right?

Shall I tell you how dangerous this stuff is, of not questioning what's on the official paperwork? There was one kid who was in my first home. He had a collection of files that would have rivalled the Tower of Babel – except I think he was on a personal mission for it to reach all the way down into the bowels of hell, rather than up to heaven. I wonder if Satan would have objected to that in the way that God did? Maybe burning all the files of his collected misdemeanours away so the kid couldn't actually reach him and would be stuck where he was on earth? Or would he actually have welcomed this traveller, as long as he was a genuine bad 'un? And not a pretender? I'm being waylaid here I reckon. The point I was making was that some professional muppet once mentioned in a meeting that he – in addition to a number of other things – had a diagnosis of a 'personality disorder'. I have no real clue what that even means, doc, but I'm sure you do. The thing is, once this was recorded in the minutes of that meeting it somehow completely erroneously became part of his story. Not his real story mind. But the story that the so-called professionals continued to tell about him in all the subsequent meetings they ever attended. He asked to see his files years later you see, some kind of Freedom of Information request. I actually bumped into him down the gym where I used to train. Told me that they had to be delivered in a van and he spent months going through 'em all.

Never trust what they record. That's what I say. It's all being recorded anyway. If they've thought it or said it or done it it's all been recorded. They can write what the fuck they want in the minutes – and the more attached they are to them, the more you know they're writing their own shit there – it will all come back to them, trust me.

The same as it's all coming back to me now too.

None of us escape this.

We can build the highest tower we want, with all the so-called recorded minutes of every pointless interaction we ever had, but we won't ever be able to escape the real truth.

The only saving grace is that it works both ways.

Saving Grace ... you know, that would have been a good name for her.

After that you see, I kept seeing her round the neighbourhood. Not often enough to really think about it much, just when she seemed to be on the periphery of my consciousness, she would make an appearance somewhere. She was never in a uniform though, even on school days. Maybe she was older though. Yes. Yes, I think now that's what it was. She was older. I thought she was a girl but maybe she was actually a woman ... me and a woman eh? Wasn't I the lucky one.

It was late autumn. I know because it was half term, so I wasn't in school that week. I was never in school much by then but at least on that week no one could do shit about it. Ironically I'd had a fight with the only brother I kept in touch with over the years, my eldest one, Connor. He was just bigger and stronger than I was back then, but over the years it was me that actually honed my skills and then made something of them. Back then though he had wrestled me to the ground and got me in a choke – and then laughed at me when I had called for my mum. That was what did it for me that time. She came in and saw what was happening. And then laughed at me too. Started instructing him on choking me harder and I think that was what did it for me all over again. Luckily when he finally let me go, I managed to get out of there before either of them saw I was crying. By the time I got to my shelter, though the tears had stopped, I was consumed by this *rage*. I'd always had a bit of a temper on me, but this was off the scale. Worse than anything I've felt as an adult, though maybe I had got so used to anger by then that it was a normal response. This was my first time, you see, and I guess we all remember our first time, even if there were shit-loads of other times over the years, and we'd managed to forget half of them – sometimes deliberately but sometimes 'cause they'd just merged into the whole sorry mess of life, like all the casual fucks that merged into one foul looking she-demon with scaly skin and hooded eyes. My anger was off the scale. I couldn't settle in my shelter even and this is one of the things I have never been able to forgive myself for. You see, the forest had never asked anything of me. People found it strange that there was such a sprawling estate, a whole town with a station near such an affluent area bordering the forest, but it was just what we knew – a world within another world but neither would ever help the other out. The forest wasn't like this though.

It was always there for me, like a proper mum and dad should have been. It never refused me entry just because I'd been kicked out of school that week. It didn't matter if you had no pocket money or a trust fund, what you looked like, how you spoke or how old you were, whether you lived in a tower block or a four-bedroom detached house with a bloody conservatory And the thing that really got me years later – when I could finally bring myself to think about it – it never wanted anything in return. I didn't need to commit to life as a conservationist or even know how to garden. I didn't need to know anything about nature, full stop. It was just there for me to access and appreciate whenever I needed, like the best lovers who don't actually exist in the real world should be. She was my lover all right. That evening I was a bastard though. First I started by just kicking and punching a few tree trunks. Fucking stupid the punching was as all that did was hurt my own knuckles like hell, but the kicking – now that felt proper good that did. I was swearing as I went, imagining every tree as one of the bastards who had got a kick from treating me like shit over the years *[begins slowly kicking over the chairs in the room].*

So there were the obvious suspects such as my mum and Connor, a couple of other brothers and sisters, some wankers from the neighbourhood flats and several from my many schools – teachers as well as kids. Much more teachers than kids in fact.

I was getting proper stuck in with the roundhouse kicks on the trunks. I started with an oak – why not? Its bark was thick and old so I didn't think I could do it much damage. It was fucking stupid. I knew it was just going to mash up my shins but to be honest I think that's what I wanted. Just to get it out of me. The tree wasn't going to kick me back, was it? And let's be honest, if it had it would have all been over – I would have landed in the underworld in a split second. But it wasn't going to be injured by my pathetic attempts either. Nah, just me. Again.

That was when it happened.

I was taking a breather and crying again – openly this time but the forest wasn't gonna laugh in my face and tell everyone what I stupid cunt I was ... pardon the language, doc. Momentarily forgot I was talking to a person and not just to myself, seeing as that's what it feels like I've spent most of my life doing. Who the fuck knows how to listen these days? Anyone? I was bent double with my eyes closed now and breathing hard and the tree was just standing stock-still in front of me. There was no wind at all, so even the few remaining leaves were motionless on their branches. Somehow the evening had come on suddenly. It was daytime when I had run out but it seemed like my totally pointless exertions had prematurely robbed the forest of all its natural light. Even then, in the immediate aftermath, I was feeling remorse for what I had done, so I looked up and leant forward against the tree, and wrapped my arms around its trunk. That was when I really started crying. Thank fuck no one was there at that moment to see all this. The trees didn't count though. More than anything just then I wanted that tree to hold me back – sounds fucking stupid I know. But that was when I felt it. That despite what I thought I wasn't quite alone.

I let go of the trunk and wiped my eyes on my sleeves. As I looked around I could hear this heavy rustling sound from behind a clump of bushes. I had this random thought that there might be some kind of wild cat living undiscovered in the forest and suddenly I was consumed with this urge to find out for myself. What could happen? I could get bitten or eaten alive but compared to how I was already feeling, would that have been so bad? I didn't think so. I walked towards the sounds and could hear my own footsteps cracking the twigs and disturbing the dried amber leaves underfoot. A smoker's dream that could've been. Wonder what it would have been like to inhale that stuff, instead of all the shit I always seemed to be smoking? Rather than stay still though, the animal got even more animated as if it was trying to hurry me up. Time was short. Didn't I know it.

As I got nearer, I could no longer even feel the ache in my shoulders or the pain and wounds in my legs. I was nearly there, just a few yards now, I thought, and the creature – whatever it was – had now decided to be still. I could hear nothing. But I was there now. And I could see it. Right up against the bark of a tree and looking me dead in the eyes ... was the girl.

I just stood there transfixed for a while. She didn't say anything and neither did I. For some reason she didn't need to, and me – though I was always known for talking – just didn't want to either. After a few minutes of just staring at her I realised that it wasn't half as quiet as I had thought. I could suddenly hear the birds all around me in the branches above *[birdsong can be heard]*. But it was like I had never heard them before with their chorus of songs and chatter – or maybe it was just I had never listened. And you know like I said it was getting dark? Well that all changed too. It didn't suddenly get brighter though; it was just that the light *changed [green light slowly bathes the stage]*. And it was all to do with her – that much even I knew. The light which was illuminating the entire clearing now was coming directly from her presence. It was her eyes. I couldn't even look at them any longer. It was like being baptised in a smoky phosphorus pool, as if all the collected fag smoke in our front room was suddenly made to linger indefinitely and had took on this green colour. 'Cept there was no stench with this light. It was like spring had interceded and decided that nope – sorry, winter just wasn't getting a look in this time. There'd been enough of a winter in my life, even by then.

Ahh. I can see this is the bit you're really interested in, doc – the first signs of my properly losing it. I can tell by how you're fiddling with your pen, you see. You want to make some kind of note here but you know I'll notice it and for some reason you don't want that. Do you reckon I missed my calling? Haha – I do amuse myself sometimes you know, even if no one else finds me entertaining. You're good though, doc, I'll give you that – not a flicker of a smile, not a raised eyebrow, nothing even when I suggested it was maybe you who was the client. I did catch you when you was about to write though.

Anyways, I know exactly why I'd be a shit psychiatrist.

Because I can never fucking stop talking.

[Dr's notes appearing transcribed on screen:
- *Against all professional body guidelines, no initial contracting done with client in this session. To do so would have been inappropriate and contrary to building any trust and rapport going forward.*

The Prayer Rug 79

- *Will build contracting into subsequent sessions.*
- *Will make this clear in my logs and take to supervision – presuming I'll get some at some point that is …*

Further sessions to be arranged]

There is much they can take from a man – there is much they have taken from me – yet if they only knew how much still remained, that was essential and untouchable, how their punitive and puny inclinations might be curtailed. Fourteen months it has been now. Fourteen months since my enforced withdrawal from my former life. People always try to assign blame in these situations and look for explanations. Well, I have none. No blame attaches to me and neither does any explanation that society could ever find acceptable. So, I resolved I should not even attempt to give one. They believed what they chose to at my trial and continue to do so. The guards make their feelings known. The other inmates I barely see. My one constant, however, my one companion is eternally here. During my arduous journey to this institution, I was led to believe I was to be kept in the harshest possible conditions, those of solitary confinement. They believed that the incarceration of my physical self was the greatest punishment that could be dispensed. How little do they know. Is there a purpose to any remonstrations that I do not belong here? Not that I can see.

Mick scratched his head and began shuffling through the sheaf of papers as the train pulled away from yet another nondescript station of a town he had never heard of. It was evident that the last paragraph had erroneously made its way in from a different text entirely – and whoever was responsible for the transcription process was most probably labouring under a similar workload to his. It was probably the equivalent of a more literary form of slave labour, where they would be paid a pittance for every reel of tapes they transcribed. He wondered then if his own voice recognition software could have helped out in some way, though he had no idea of the exact date or circumstances of the transformation of the spoken word into the written. They were probably full of caffeine and devoid of real sleep. He had spent much of his own life in the same state. A quick scan through indicated that the remaining pages did seem to come from the original text, so what story this interloper had made its way from, he had no idea. He considered flagging this up to his source. The tone was completely different too – from another era possibly – but the last thing he wanted to do was get anyone in trouble. After the appearance of the green sprite, he found himself speculating what this new voice had lived through too.

As the train got nearer the urban final destination of his work and home, he found his thoughts returning to more mundane matters. He replaced the papers in his file and then in his bag before pulling out his diary to check what the next day's agenda held for him. Leafing through to the correct week he was pleased to see a blessed day with no meetings but several ongoing reporting clients, which meant no assessments or report writing either. How perceptive this unknown case had been about the dangerous assumptions that formed the basis of reports or were thrown about in meetings, as if this polluted forum itself could somehow lend credibility to things that had no foundations in truth. The words would be birthed into the world of air, to initially float like helium balloons but if repeated enough times (either through thought or speech), gradually taking on the form of dead weights round the body of the subject, more difficult to free oneself from than the most extreme of physical incarcerations – the words being branded upon the souls of the unfortunates. He put his diary away now too and closed his eyes for the final twenty minutes.

6

Giles had heard about the rumours; for all the air of deception and skulduggery no one – despite their collective professorships and publications – seemed to be able to resurrect the dying art of discretion. His work had never involved people in such a direct manner – objects seemed imbued with so much more humanity to him – but even he knew that there were still such things as client confidentiality – no matter what someone had been alleged to have done. He had never once considered this as applying to rugs or tapestries. He knew there were infinite mysteries contained within their weaves and yarns – but he also felt that they actively *wanted* to share their stories, who had conceived of them and for what purpose. They would almost beg him to be unstitched of their forms, unravelled of their purposes, with their dyes and beading being bleached back into the pale hemp-like hues of their original state of purity. Only through this retrospective process could they ever, truly be known. There was no professional integrity at stake here, no complex rules of data protection or the supposed sanctity of the client–professional relationship; he operated only from love. No one knew the source of the leaks – or could even verify that any of the rumours were true but they seemed to be growing by the day.

It was a bright morning, so he was sitting outside on the decking with a cup of coffee, and pondering the day that he had ahead of him. He had a long drive to a private residence who had contacted him via the university about a mysterious find they had unearthed. This was what made the job for Giles – all these unexpected treasures that could be mined from anywhere and arrive as gifts at his door. It made all the personally unedifying aspects, like the lecturing, much more bearable – and of course, without this he couldn't financially keep himself in the manner to which he had become accustomed, like a self-kept prince of books and blankets. He didn't mind these contrasts to his life. They were mutually supportive and it was often after a particularly heavy schedule of education, talks and seminars that a dazzling new find would somehow make its way into his life, like a stranger in a late-night bar enticing him into their bed. He tried as he always did – mostly in vain – to stop his mind getting carried away with the promise of excitement and new possibilities of a liaison like this. He finished his coffee and a few minutes later was getting into his car.

He was just about to start the engine when he caught sight of Katrin. She lived in the upper floors of his building and was descending the outside stairs and leaving something in one of the numerous wheelie bins – there seemed to be a new one there each time he looked. It was the small upcycling one that was a real new one on him. And it didn't look like the others in its shape or size either. He had absently been noticing it over the last couple of weeks when he had been arriving and leaving, but never given it much thought. He opened his window as Katrin approached.

'Off to another one of your royal engagements?' Katrin seemed to think he lived a charmed life, and he had had a hard time over the years explaining that he did actually work. It was just that it gave him too much pleasure to ever complain about in any way. He laughed.

'Actually, this one is. A minor aristocrat, whose family seem to have squandered most of her inheritance, is convinced she has uncovered a gem in an attic or something.' Katrin had smiled as soon as she'd approached the car, and with her smile widening, she simultaneously rolled her eyes.

'Haven't they all?' Giles laughed. Katrin had known what it was like to have no money – then some money – until her former self-made husband had left her and her then young twin sons and gone over to the States on a business trip. Never to return. She found out later that he had a second family out there, complete with two more children. With her sons now grown and away from home she finally had time to enjoy her life – though it was a shame she had had to wait until her twilight years to do this. Better late than never though. She had occasionally attended Giles's talks over the years and would often sit in the audience and deliberately ask the most obscure and occasionally obscene questions possible – verging on unanswerable in fact – but Giles the forever-ready one with his creative slant on the enviable background knowledge he possessed did a sterling job of it. Sometimes. Combined with his obvious love it could make for an engaging sparring match. And it was largely unscripted.

'More than that – I think this one's living the life of a recluse. She's still got money though, which always makes for a better standard of solitude. Listen Kat – I've got to run now but we'll catch up soon.'

'Have fun with the posh bird and her comfort blanket then!' she said before walking back inside.

Just shy of two hours later he was driving through a dense forest on the outskirts of the city, looking out for the turning he had been directed to. He was driving progressively longer distances between each property, and also finding each one more and more obscured by thick foliage, high fences and the sheer length of their driveways. He knew he was far from living a deprived life, but across from his own front room and towards the back of his garden he would be assailed by the sheer density of housing and humanity stretching far into the horizon. All he could see here was seemingly endless nature. Could he live like this though? As long as he had his precious artefacts he felt he could easily live in a caravan – or even a cave – if they were spread out beneath and around him. People were just an optional extra. Nice enough though. Some of them. He interrupted his own reverie as he had finally arrived at the property of his potential client. He braked gently over the gravel in front of large iron gates. There was no intercom he could immediately see, but before he could get out of the car to investigate further, a tall wiry man approached him from a door in a small built-in structure in the boundary wall. Giles opened his car window and waited for the man to get nearer. He was even taller than he had first appeared.

'Good morning, sir. How may I help you?' There was a very faint perceptible Scottish lilt in the man's voice. His manner was polite, but Giles got the distinct impression he was not a man to be messed with.

'I'm Giles Lewis – I have an appointment with Mrs Luscombe. I'm slightly early though – I wasn't sure how much time to allow for the drive.' The man's expression remained even, and he raised himself back to his considerable full height.

'Not a problem, sir. She has been anticipating your arrival. Just one moment please.' With that he walked back into the outbuilding and a few seconds later the gates opened, and Giles began to slowly drive through. The house clearly wasn't one of the modern rebuilds of her neighbours; it was visible at the end of the drive and was much smaller than he had thought – though the grounds were stunning. With their mature and varied trees, he felt as if he were driving through an arboretum, and half expected to see signs with the Latin names and genus of the original inhabitants. The drive felt long, though in reality it couldn't have been, and the considerable shade from the trees felt a comfort rather than oppressive – as dark canopies sometimes did to Giles. As he left his car to a small expanse of gravel at the end of the driveway and walked up to the main entrance, he was surprised to see the same travelling turret of a man opening the door to him, just as he approached. Giles was by no means a short man himself, but this man had several inches on him.

He didn't really know what to say then, but it appeared he wasn't expected to speak as he was gestured into a spacious hallway and through to the right into a sitting room. Here he found views of a very gently tiered garden of plants in full bloom. It was a beautiful day and the French doors were wide open. As the besuited butler-cum-bouncer had departed in the same manner as his arrival, he was left on his own to take in all the impressions of both home and garden of this possible new client. Giles would always start with the house, for how could it be otherwise, what with his passion for the sensual indulgences of people's interiors? And he was on his own too – he didn't have to cast furtive glances at odd moments during breaks in conversation, while a companion was engaged in stirring their tea or momentarily gazing into space. The worst feeling for him was getting caught doing this, so being on his own right now was an unexpected bliss. There were sometimes valuable clues in the obvious and displayed interiors as to the value of the object to be discussed. Not always though. Sometimes the recipients of these gifts were most unlikely: living in bland and nondescript houses where magnolia was deemed daring and pastels positively obscene, but still having come across an incongruous gem. He knew better than to judge, but judge he still did.

He wasn't sure exactly what drew him to it. Maybe it was the open invitation of being left unchaperoned, with the wide-open doors allowing the sunlight in, coupled with the excitement of being in an unfamiliar environment with no immediately available reference points. (The woman had been very cagey about the exact nature of her find on the telephone and in his experience of these matters this was very irregular.) Whatever it was he really didn't have a choice, so with no further thought he strode purposefully across the room – and straight out into the garden.

'A pleasure to make your acquaintance, Professor.' The voice was both gentle and genteel, though with the slight jaggedness of age. He started as he couldn't immediately see where it had come from. He turned back into the room and was doubly irritated with himself; not only had he been caught unawares (where had she been seated?) but going out into a garden of all things – and not even giving his attention to the interior of the room. Well, he would just have to rely on the information she gave him now as he'd blown his opportunity to form a preview – be it right or wrong – on what he may have been presented with. As he prepared to step back inside, a figure seemed to glide in front of him from behind a small cherry tree. He gathered his composure quickly.

'Mrs Luscombe? Do excuse me but your garden looked so enticing I couldn't quite help myself.' It was absolutely the right thing to say – and true to boot – as her slightly anxious and preoccupied face relaxed into a smile. Her hair was a thick auburn that had been tempered by a peppering of grey and was pinned up away from her face, though longer than most women her age would choose to wear it. Her voice and movements were of an older woman, but her face was relatively youthful. Giles was hopeful that she had indeed uncovered something unique and he was looking forward to the rest of the morning.

'You must come and take a closer look then.' Giles was relieved to hear this. He followed the woman back round the tree and the space opened up into a small square courtyard. He had nothing to do with his own shared garden, as it was Katrin who did most of the work out there – though luckily she had no objections to him enjoying it. Consequently, he had no idea what he was really looking at – though one thing did hit him immediately as they walked across; he had only taken a few steps when he had to stop as he felt a sudden sharp pain on the side of his neck. It subsided immediately, however, so he didn't think it was a bee, but when he looked down, he saw what looked like crushed red and amber stones of various sizes lining the path through the planting beds. Every step sounded like highly crystallised gravel under his feet, but evidently he had somehow scuffed one into the air or something.

'Ahh, sometimes the path just takes exception to being stepped on, but more often than not, it is a none-too-bright bird, who has mistaken the stones for berries, but once realising his mistake has then expunged them from the air.' The other thing Giles immediately noticed were the fragrances: some form of unconventional herb garden perhaps? He wasn't too far off.

'Up until last year when he passed away, my father lived with me here. I'm afraid I couldn't see him in a home – awful misuse of the word – so I had him here with me for a number of years. It was actually due to him that I'm meeting with you today – but we shall come to that. He was in the advanced stages of dementia when he died, so I created this space as a sensory garden for him. My dear mother had died many years before, and I knew there were certain aromas that he would forever associate with her; she had lavender in their wedding bouquet and when she cooked she loved using rosemary, so whenever he came out here it was as if his tenuous links to their shared memories were fleetingly restored for a time. It took me a while to get the balance right, with the sights, smells and sounds. Once I was sure that I had though, the poor man went and died. Maybe I should have prolonged the process just to keep him with me.'

Giles took a good look around; there were silver mobiles of carved birds and flowers hanging amongst bells from nearby branches. He wondered what the real ones thought of these imposters created in their image, even if they did chime beautifully with the breath of the wind. His eyes were then taken with the thick long grasses growing in a miniature patch of meadow in a corner. He couldn't help himself. He walked over, and while Mrs Luscombe was momentarily surveying the water feature in the centre, he knelt down and ran his fingers through the dark green locks. With his eyes closed he could almost imagine he was seated at a loom in a distant past, weaving a tapestry. When he opened his eyes he saw that she was smiling at him.

'Yes. You were definitely the right one.

'Both my mother and my daughter – who is now a young woman herself – had long hair. I had always kept the lawn perfectly short and manicured, but one day I looked out and saw Dad crying, crawling around on the grass on all fours and lamenting that someone had cut off Mum's hair – where was her beautiful long hair? He was at a stage then when he still had many lucid moments, and the idea for a garden especially for him was not even partially formed in my mind. It was seeing him then that actually gave me the impetus to do it. It made such a difference to him; it was remarkable.'

Giles stood up, feeling his action had been slightly inappropriate.

'I confess I have never been a gardener – partly due to the land constraints of my London residence – but even if I had acres, I am not sure I would know what to do with it.'

'Well, I've grown to believe over the years that knowing what to do is somewhat overrated. As long as you can appreciate with an empty mind and an open heart, that is what really matters.' She said nothing further for a bit so Giles continued looking round and absorbing all the sensory delights. She appeared to be in no hurry and he himself had the whole day at his disposal. He let his gaze wander over to the water feature. It was a statue of a hybrid mythological creature that he couldn't have named – sort of half man, half bird of prey. He realised how good it felt to look round without being surreptitious about this. With the sensation of the thick dense grasses still running lightly through his fingers, he became aware of the besuited man who had now appeared again in the garden and was murmuring something just out of his earshot to Mrs Luscombe.

'Where would you like to sit, Professor Lewis, before we get started? Here or back in the house?' Giles needed to think about this. He was slightly intoxicated by the garden – and if this had been a purely social visit, he would have had no hesitation. However, he reminded himself that he was here for work and meeting a client, so it did feel right to talk tapestries back inside.

'Oh please, just call me Giles. It is very kind of you to offer – maybe indoors? So I can also see the object in question without causing you undue logistical problems? It is beautiful out here though.'

'Indoors it is. We can always return to the gardens later.' With that she led him round in a kind of semi-circle, back onto the pomegranate path, until they returned to the other side of the house. From here they entered a conservatory, and she gestured to him to take a seat before sitting down opposite. There was already a teapot on the table between them, and just as they had taken their seats, the man in black appeared – again – but this time carrying a tiered stand of cakes and biscuits. Perfect. Giles was starting to feel less and less interested in the primary purpose of the visit, and more and more intrigued by this woman – and her incongruous companion. He seemed to double as some kind of butler stroke close protection officer. An all-purpose manservant he guessed.

'Forgive me – I made the assumption that you would like some tea after your long drive down here. I'm afraid I don't have coffee in the house, but I can easily send for some if you'd prefer. It is no bother.' She smiled suddenly then. 'Nothing is.'

'Tea is perfect. I can't imagine anything nicer. There is something about sharing from the one pot, rather than an individual coffee anyway.' Immediately upon saying this Giles wondered what on earth he was talking about; if the truth be known, he had always preferred the bitterness of coffee and couldn't actually recall ever having shared a pot of tea with anyone – let alone a veritable stranger of a client.

'I knew you'd understand.' She slowly poured a cup for him before looking directly into his eyes for a moment or two and speaking further. 'It all starts and ends with my father you see. You already know the ending, with his deterioration from dementia – but it was only really the beginning of things.'

Giles was surveying the plants that were also in their company now. Many were hanging from baskets and draping low – almost to the ground, like rivulets of water – though what really caught his attention was a group of cacti standing guard in a far corner. The main one was as tall as he was, and almost looked a parody of a giant cactus that you'd find in a cartoon of the desert with a roadrunner zooming past. Its trunk was sturdy and with its two asymmetric arms studded with thick sharp pines, everything about it said *don't fuck with me*. You wouldn't want an embrace off him, thought Giles – even if you were of the female cactus variety. Especially if you were. Near its base were several others in varying paler shades of green, some with a soft-looking fuzz rather than those hard-as-nails needles. Many of these were round like globes, but some were strangely flattened and two dimensional. In amongst them there was just the one that looked slightly incongruous: at first Giles had thought it was another plant due to its proximity to the cacti, but although it too was spherical, it had not a single pine growing from it and the colour was off-palette too as it wasn't green either. He realised then that it must have made its way in from the sensory garden; it was a large, smooth, highly polished stone that he could imagine the old man running his palms over, much like a crystal ball.

He took a sip of his tea, registering with pleasant surprise how deep and fragrant the flavours were – maybe it was some kind of special blend? He would have to ask her once they had got business out the way. It was just then he saw the stone levitate. Shit – this wasn't his imagination. He somehow swallowed quickly and stifled a coughing fit. To his horror the stone then continued its trajectory in the air. He was aware that Mrs Luscombe was speaking again now: he could hear the intonation of her voice and the educated inflections of her accent, and this seemed strangely comforting to him given what he was now seeing, though as to her actual words and any associated meanings he was completely oblivious. He sat as if transfixed, and nodded here and there – though his attention was still on the whirling dervish of a stone. Suddenly – and beyond any conscious control of his own it seemed – he managed to tune back in.

'... so while I may look and seem quintessentially English I am really nothing of the sort. The Indian connection is undeniable now and it is all due to Father. That is why Prof – Giles – it was you that I contacted. I have actually been a follower of your work for many years, so imagine my joy when I realised I had a legitimate reason to contact you – rather than seeming like some kind of antiquities groupie.' She paused then and stirred her cup, and Giles bizarrely found this seemingly everyday action so oddly provocative he almost felt like running back out into the garden for some air. At least it had distracted him from the stone though. Wasn't it rock stars and artists that had groupies, not professors and academics? Maybe he had found himself one. He wondered then how old she might be. Bloody hell. Just what was wrong with him? Maybe it was the herbs in the garden ... Maybe the lady in her innocence had no idea what it was she was actually growing?

'I'm so pleased you did so Mrs Luscombe.' He was unsure what was going on with him right then, so wanted to keep things on a formal footing while he tried to gather his composure. He ignored the comment about groupies and continued, 'Maybe this might be a perfect moment to see the object in question, given the richness of the context you have been so kind to furnish me with?' He had no real idea what on earth she had just been telling him, but it turned out that this was exactly the right thing to say – again – as she smiled just then and looked truly beautiful. Nothing like an external stimulus to take the focus away from any potential awkwardness. Just when he felt that, at least conversation-wise, he was managing to behave like a semi-functioning human being, the bloody stone decided to make another appearance. Fuck. It was now several feet off the ground and nearly at the height of the giant cactus.

It was only then that he saw it clearly. Rather than having left the conservatory as he had assumed, the man-mountain had been seated just behind this gang of large cacti in the far corner. He wouldn't have noticed him at all if it hadn't been for his shining bald head that had kept making an appearance from in between them.

'I shall be right back, madam,' he said and shot Giles a not entirely friendly look, before leaving the room to retrieve the object of the visit.

* * *

Howra's head was full as she made her way to her reporting session with Mick. She pressed the buzzer beside a grand-looking set of wooden double doors, before entering and climbing the steep stairway to the reception. The office was located in a former music hall that had apparently been popular in the last century – but it was now all partitioned up and the office was currently housed over a branch of Boots. There were several men already seated in the waiting room, and as she approached the glass window she noticed one staring at her longer than necessary. She ignored him, gave her name to the receptionist and sat down where she couldn't see him – or anyone else – but could look undisturbed out the window. The bloody place was always full of men, but that was no reason to gawp at her like she was an alien species. She knew she was several minutes early, and Mick was one of those very thorough officers whose appointments would invariably run over – and his clients always seemed to show up too – not many DNAs with him – so she prepared herself for a wait.

Her mind was slowly replaying her latest accidental discovery and she was undecided whether to bring it up or not. She considered getting out her novel, but she didn't feel her mind would be able to focus, what with her other competing thoughts all vying for her attentions.

'Come on you wanker,' muttered a voice from somewhere behind her and she heard footsteps heading over to the glass windows. 'I've been waiting twenty minutes now. How come if I'm late it's a DNA but if you lot piss about I just have to take it?' She couldn't hear the response from behind the screen, but a long explanation was given, which the man interrupted several times with various expletives, until Howra wondered why he wasn't just asked to leave. It appeared then that this was exactly what happened – either that or he had just got tired of waiting and decided to leave of his own accord. He marched to the end of the waiting room and slammed the door behind him, and she could hear his heavy footsteps thumping down the stairs before some shouts from the street, directed upwards to the office, could be discerned. She thought this very stupid of him – whatever had prompted his leaving. She herself had reframed the experience (to be honest she had actively welcomed the support from the outset) and decided that probation was infinitely preferable to the infringement of liberties that an actual incarceration would involve. No, she couldn't countenance that and knew she would have struggled to cope. A slightly inconvenient journey, just every couple of weeks now, to receive such bespoke support from Mick was like a Godsend for her at this stage in her life. Though many thought she shouldn't have been there, her 'crime' was definitely worth it.

She saw an officer appear at the door and stare at her briefly before calling out a name. It was evidently someone previously unknown, who was there for an initial assessment. Smartly dressed attire amongst the jeans and tracksuits and her own knitted dress, rose up from his seat and followed the officer through the doorway. She recalled her own nerves when entering the same door for the first time, not having a clue what to expect and never having known anyone in her extensive networks who had ever been in a similar position. As soon as she had sat down in the chair opposite Mick in his tiny office though, she knew everything would be okay. He had exuded reassurance and she was thankful to whatever systems for allocation existed – or pure random chance – that meant she had ended up on his caseload and not that of anyone else. It was just then that he appeared, grinning as he saw her seated there and she followed him into the main office.

'You okay, bab?' he said as his customary greeting. She was never sure whether this was a question or a general statement on her well-being. She took it as the former and nodded while resisting a mischievous urge to call him Dad, just to see how he might respond. On her first appointment she had been startled by the labyrinthine nature of the corridors; they weren't even organised in straight lines, though she guessed there were no hard or fast rules around these things. They snaked around several corners where you had no idea who or what you were heading towards. There were odd touches of the theatrical lineage of the building that still shone through the attempts to rob it of its former glories and give the impression of a Professional Work Environment. She recalled how Mick had told her a bit of the original history of the building. He had said that sometimes – during odd quiet moments when it was actually his own mind that was quiet – he could hear the strains of piano or the odd soliloquies. He was a bit of an odd one himself to be honest, but she wouldn't have traded him for anyone else.

She took her usual chair to the side, farthest from the door. This was the chair for clients so, if one of them happened to kick off, Mick would have an unobstructed path to exit the room. There was also a red strip running around the walls and she knew this was a panic alarm that he just needed to hit if needed, and she guessed help from the other officers would arrive. It wasn't very discreet though; couldn't they have a more covert alarm system in a place like this? She didn't know why she was thinking along these lines. He was never going to be in any danger from her. No one was, but she had still ended up here.

'You're looking well, bab. How has life been treating you over the past two weeks?'

They spoke about various obligatory things like her general well-being, housing situation and how she had been occupying her time:

'I'm struggling with this one, Mick. My work – menial and crap though it was – was what gave me a structure. I have so much time to myself suddenly that it's hard to know what to do with it.'

'This is a common one, bab. People think having time is a luxury to be envied, without any consideration of how hard it is to fill once you've let go of all addictions or distractions – not that I'm saying you were a hardcore addict or anything.'

'Well not drink or drugs-wise but I had plenty of others.'

Mick paused before he said anything further, noting the fleeting sadness in her expression before the veils encircled her again. It was that bloody 'specimen' she was thinking of, he supposed. No matter. It was not for him to judge. He let the silence work its magic for a few moments more before adjusting his tone and continuing: 'I guess it comes down to how committed you are to change – how badly you want it. We can all fill our lives with the stuff and nonsense we're told matters.' She looked up at him just then and her expression changed.

'I do want things to change. Me and everything. I just didn't know what I was signing up to. Forget about the small print – I didn't even read the large print. Didn't even realise there was *any* kind of contract.'

'There is always a contract, bab – the courts would have given you one – it's how these things work. It just takes a while to decipher, that's all.' Sensing she just needed to talk, he paused again, to allow her to continue.

'Anyway, there is one good thing that is occupying me. I've found myself a project!' Mick registered for the umpteenth time how every one of his more motivated clients seemed to have their own unique lingo for these kinds of things. Project ... sounded professional at least – not always a good thing – but Howra was most probably just overcompensating for her lack of formal qualifications. Bit cryptic though. What he said was: 'We can go with that. Tell us more.'

* * *

There had been many duds over the years, mass produced and machine-made in the twenty-first century even, that people had somehow thought were of rare provenance and value. Sometimes telling them the truth was like telling them they had an ugly child. Deep down everyone knew it, but who really wanted to be the one to say it aloud? Giles had enough sensitivity to manage these situations and always searched to find something to praise – often falling back on a florid turn of phrase, when something genuinely unique would hardly be in need of words at all. What was unrolled before him here was akin to finding a long-time hidden and unread parchment amongst a pile of free commuter papers; he didn't speak at all for several moments and just let his higher senses absorb all that lay before him.

The man-maid evidently had no idea what he was dealing with. He spread the carpet out before his mistress, like the market merchants in most Asian cities, who would happily unroll dozens upon dozens of rugs before any potential buyers – until the pile was the height of a small hill – only for the buyers to select the very first rug that they had been shown – which by then was gasping for air underneath the weight of a hundred sinful ancestors, begging now to finally be laid in just about any home, even one which contained multiple children and animals to run it into the ground. Giles controlled the urge to say something when the carpet was practically thrown in his direction, but as soon as he looked at it, all thoughts of hallucinogenic herbs and elevating heads left his mind.

The carpet needed no such pretence.

It was Mrs Luscombe who broke the spell.

'It was Al-Ghazali I believe who spoke of *the carpet of proximity* – and when I saw this, his theological exposition on the page just naturally came to life.' Giles was still too immersed to respond but did register somewhere that this particular proximity was not of this world. No. Not this world of books or letters or academic posturing – his reluctantly sometime inhabited world – the world where the object itself could consume you, with its infinite variations of designs. He wished he had been listening when she had told the story of her father and how he had acquired it. How could he bring her back to this?

'So … what's your assessment then?'

Giles was surprised. It was a very direct question – and it was rare for someone to ask anything at this stage – he would normally be left to imbibe the artefact and start with the questions himself. How crass to immediately be asked what he thought. It was the suited and booted one who spoke though, and who was now looking at him hard. Giles was resolute. He was there at the behest of his client Mrs Luscombe and no one else, and if she had the sensitivity to let him contemplate in silence, what was this strangely misemployed thug doing, even opening his mouth?

'That was the bit of the story I hadn't quite got to. Shirley has a bit of a vested interest in this you see, given the longstanding connection with Father.' Shirley … thought Giles. What the fuck. He suddenly felt able to meet Shirley's gaze, which had remained as fixed as a fundamentalist's truth. He felt a smirk of his own forming, but this diversion was taking him away from a genuine truth, one that would be at the very highest of Al-Ghazali's ladder of interim rungs. The carpet was magnificent.

'It was Shirley you see who was responsible for the safe carriage of the rug. It was Dad's final request while he still retained his critical faculties – and the dementia had yet to wreak havoc on his final designs on life.'

'Intriguing. *Shirley* – do pray tell me more.' Giles couldn't resist emphasising the man's name. Probably only due to the presence of and his familial regard for Mrs Luscombe did Shirley retain some professional courtesy. Otherwise he would probably have punched him.

'Of course, sir. But maybe then we could actually have your assessment?' Giles suspected he knew this question would rile him, so decided he would ignore it and just allow the man to speak. 'I've seen active service – in many places – but this particular episode dates back to Iraq in the '90s.' He paused and looked off into the distance, beyond Giles's shoulder and into the gardens. Giles wondered if the man was actually looking at something there or whether he was just reminiscing about this incident from his personal history. Actually, reminiscing was probably the wrong word – he didn't look at all as if they were happy memories that he was mining. Giles said nothing while Mrs Luscombe glanced up from the carpet and momentarily looked concerned.

'Take as much time as you need.' Her voice was low, and Giles felt his animosity towards the man dissolve slightly. He was a pacifist at heart, but Shirley was evidently still marked by whatever it was he had witnessed. It was then he heard a noise behind him, as if someone else was entering from the gardens to join them. He turned around and saw what Shirley had most likely been looking at: it was an elderly German Shepherd – elderly he knew as his back legs were going and he came bounding in with an awkward gait. He came tentatively up to Giles but seeing his mistress in such close and relaxed proximity to him, decided that there was no work to be done for him here.

Before anyone could react, he promptly settled himself down on the carpet.

'Coach – my goodness this isn't for *you*!' Horrified, she gestured for him to immediately return back to the grounds, and he surveyed her with that particular look of canine consternation that only dogs whose sole purpose is to unconditionally love and obey their owners can seem to manage. *I trust in you for my every need Mrs Luscombe*, was what that look seemed to say. *I always have and I always will, but I don't think I will ever understand you.* He then removed himself from the rug (after depositing a sprinkling of his own doggy fibres) and stared at the group of them for a moment more before obeying and bounding back onto the lawns. He turned and stared at them once more through the windows as if to say *you really have no idea what you're dealing with*.

Giles waited and watched as Shirley now took a seat at the far end of the conservatory and looked down at the carpet with a pained expression on his face. It was approaching early afternoon now and the shards of sunlight were hitting the glass panels with force. The carpet was one where the hues would be noticeably different depending on the direction from which it was viewed. Giles was tempted to walk over to the other end where Shirley was and look at it from his perspective, but he was unable to do so with the carpet spread out before him in this manner, without actually stepping on it. And there was no way he could do that. The dog may not have had any reservations of this sort but as a human – and a professor of antiquities specialising in textiles no less – this would have been akin to an act of professional heresy. While he still had shoes on.

Shirley was still silent, and Giles began to think through the information he had been given. He knew the carpet had an Islamic lineage, but although Iraq had been mentioned, this was not necessarily proof that this area was its origin – as he knew well how such ancient objects could travel both geographically and culturally – some even actively working towards being masters of disguise and duping the so-called experts of one era until those brave and dogged enough from future generations were able to mount some form of challenge – or even just open up a discussion.

'I'm afraid I am very ignorant as to the logistical demands of your work. Is it common for you to remove objects for further examination?'

'I am completely at the behest of my clients. Some are happy to release them temporarily into my care or via an academic institution, but others feel very differently.' Mrs Luscombe looked silently at Shirley then.

'Well, with the huge supposition that the carpet is actually worthy of your professional time, we would really prefer it to remain here.' Why the 'we', Giles wondered. Surely it belonged to her – and her staff should have no input into her decisions, but she then continued. 'But I am of course happy to accommodate you here in any way you need – and as long as required in order for you to undertake your work. As you can see, the home and grounds are welcoming and largely empty as I am essentially on my own here now.' She paused to drink more of her tea and again looked silently at Shirley, who was now looking up from his ruminations and directly at Giles.

'Of course, you will be busy with all manner of academic commitments, so an extended period of time here may not work for you, but I would nonetheless be very happy to receive you here at your own convenience.' Giles had had offers like this before, but they were uncommon. Even if the rug hadn't been such an evident specimen, he wouldn't have minded a return trip – or three – to this house, guarded as it was by the ancient forest trees and enlivened by the memories of a dead father. He realised afterwards that he had made his mind up at that precise moment. He was spending too much time in the city these days. In city buildings, conference rooms and lecture theatres. This was all well and good, but somehow his life had got out of balance – and with the current absence of any woman to travel with either, there was no sign of this changing. It wasn't just this though.

Before he left it had been his intention to ask to take a few preliminary photos, just to inform some initial stage work in exploring the designs. He had let that go though. As he walked over the gravel to his car a short while later, Coach ran up to him again as if to bid him farewell and he bent down to pat the dog. He was huge and his coat was as tactile as any rug he had ever encountered.

'Interesting family set-up you've got yourself here, boy, though I guess you must be missing your master.' The dog barked a couple of times then, but not with any excitement or malign intent. He just seemed to be agreeing in his own composed manner with what Giles was saying. As he somewhat reluctantly extricated himself from the dog and got into the car, he thought about the closure of the visit. He and Mrs Luscombe had begun speaking of the lecture series he had most recently been involved with – she was an avid listener of Radio 4 (of course) and this was Giles's first venture into recording a series for radio. Shirley had remained completely silent for the remainder of the visit, not even asking again for Giles's 'assessment' but as he was listening to Mrs Luscombe talking about a question she had posed recently on Gardeners' Question Time, he saw Shirley – with a gentleness he would never have thought possible – slowly gather the carpet towards him, then cover it with a piece of linen that had escaped Giles's notice previously. The man's huge frame then somehow crouched easily on the ground and his tattooed hands rolled up the carpet before tying it closed. He carried it in his arms out of the room – and just before he turned away and disappeared out the door, Giles was sure he saw tears in the man's eyes.

He agreed without hesitation to a return visit the following month.

7

The palace was a hive of activity, but there was only the one queen bee.
 Under the Sultan's direction there was a dedicated team that had presided over stage-managing the events to perfection. Firstly, the call had gone out far and wide through the extensive networks that threaded themselves across the kingdom. In fact, not just across this kingdom, as from the description that Roshni had been able to provide him from her dreams (there had been several more subsequently), he could have originated from several neighbouring lands. As an astute leader, he could see the possibilities for a mutually beneficial union if this was the case, and hopefully prevent any incursions into vulnerable border areas.
 It was to have been expected but the Sultana's reaction had been extreme.
 They had been sitting together in one of the many sheltered courtyards of the Sultana's state rooms. Each of them had a tiny glass in front of them, painted in fuchsia and yellow waves on the borders, and then

accented in gold leaf. There were also accompanying plates of sweetmeats and pastries. Roshni looked deep into the dark kohl-rimmed eyes that were so very similar to her own, the wide forehead and the full, heart-shaped face. After she had spoken she watched, transfixed by the thick lashes that were holding the tears in those deep, almost black pools. Once the banks had broken, she reached over to gently wipe them away – but was unable to do so.

'How can Allah, guardian of the lights of all souls work in such ways?' she had howled when Roshni had gently broken the news to her, but tears from this source were something that needed refined analysis; Roshni waited while her mother recited all manner of prayers in between her sobs – some of which she felt were of dubious theological origin, though this was completely the wrong time for any protracted discussions on religious discourse of this sort. She waited patiently as the tears slowly dried; the verses became vaguely recognisable and the wailing more intermittent. Eventually only the sounds of the crickets in the sheltered courtyard could be heard. Roshni realised at that moment how she had never paid them much attention before now; ever-present but never really heard, unless one was actively waiting for silence. The Sultana had not yet begun speaking, so while Roshni waited, she tried to see whether she could discern what these rarely seen creatures might be communicating. They couldn't be called melodious; there were no honeyed harmonies present as with the birds, no sole and solitary roar of command of any of the larger felines, nor the relentless banter and brawling of the simians. This was different. It made no claims to be noticed, so generally it wasn't. But right now Roshni felt that, in their own way, these understated crickets were maybe the only ones who were saying what was worth listening to, with their mantras that had no need of communion with each other, just for and of themselves.

She was unsure about her father's imposition of control over the process she herself had instigated, but as his daughter she accepted that this had to be the way. Shiraz was temporarily ensconced in a palace to the south of the kingdom – she suspected that this was to try and shroud some recent scandal he had been involved in – and the resulting threats to his life that had been made by the son of a minor deposed ruler with which he had fallen out. She hadn't spoken to him for several months now.

'Do not trouble thyself with drying thy wretched mother's tears. Thy path shall be clear from this moment hence, thy whole life chartered like the bears of the distant nations do to our lands – as if we had never previously existed. Let these tears, as they fall from mine eyes to my heart traverse their own journey, without thy undoubtedly well-meaning but ultimately futile intervention.' With that she stood imperiously and left Roshni sitting alone and disconsolate at the table, the sounds of the crickets fading back into her conscious awareness once more. Roshni briefly considered following her, but felt that it might be best to allow her news to sink in. Maybe in the morning she could have a further conversation?

Roshni was correct in this respect and a further conversation did ensue the following day. Though not quite along the lines she might have imagined.

The Sultana had taken it upon herself to remain in her chambers that morning, stating that she was indisposed due to a heavy burden having been placed upon her constitution (that of Roshni's revelation of course). Somehow the news had managed to spread like an attack of food poisoning in the night and Noura - who had never been known for her propensity as an early morning riser - had somehow managed to arrive while Roshni herself was still eating her *naashta*[17].

'Tell me about the dreams, Roshni! Was he handsome? Tall? Was he wild - or serene? And what was he doing in thy dreamworld - the ultimate place of carnality and sin? Roshni! Thou dost hide a veritable trousseau behind that oft-purported demure light of yours!' Roshni looked at Noura in despair but was not altogether surprised.

'Must thou lower thy tonality to the level of a sweeper's broom? It is of no consequence how he doth appear in body, it is his soul that visited me in the most holy of nocturnal hours. Verily, I can barely recall the exact shade and shimmer of his visage - all I know my dear sister-by-remove is that once his spirit is before me, I shall know that it is he.'

'Shade and shimmer? Shade? Roshni! Before thou throws any more shade at me, and thy candle turns inferno and burns all in the vicinity down to the quick, thou hast better at least illuminate whether he be of the countenance of a bear. How shall my exalted uncle reconcile this, if that be so?'

'Noura, I beg thee. If it is his spirit that I have seen, what bearing shall the outward form of a bear or anything else have on my decision?' Roshni watched Noura's fingers curl themselves round the glass in front of her, but not actually lift the vessel to her

---

17. breakfast

lips as she carried on speaking. Roshni slowly tuned herself out. Or in. Noura's voice was fading by the instant, but Roshni kept her focus on her cousin's hands, which had now unfurled away from the glass completely and were pulling at the tiny, bejewelled charms on her bracelet in succession, slowly rotating them round her narrow wrist. At this rate Noura wouldn't be drinking even a single sip of the tea, let alone helping her to finish the substantial pot that sat before them. Roshni drank steadily from her own cup as her eyes homed in on the tiny elephant, now between Noura's thumb and forefinger, and then she immediately filled her cup with more beverage.

'Steady, Roshni, thou shalt be fuller of this beverage than anything else - verily, even thoughts of thine impending nuptials are ripe to be consumed.' Noura had still not taken a solitary sip.

* * *

Hakim usually avoided such places but he had been on the road for several days now, traversing the dusty arid plains en route to the city. He thought he could perhaps soak up some of the local flavours, and hear what was happening through the olive vine. He did not doubt that the abundance of rumours and speculation would be causing the boughs to bend and sway, the fruits delectable to those of unsophisticated palates. He too was having to resist the urge to spit out the odd one that had made its way past his lips. It repulsed him if the truth be known, as if he was akin to one of the uncouth passers-by who would routinely send their dark red spittle hurtling towards the pavement after a mammoth chewing session on the betel leaves. Yes it was mildly intoxicating – as was all gossip – but the after-effects were nothing edifying. So much better to not imbibe it in the first place, than having to find some way to purge yourself of its both seen and unseen stains that was not an affront in itself. As his horse approached and the sounds of drumming and reed flute from the tavern grew in volume, he seemed to slow as if to say to his master, *in there? Really?*

'It be so, my noble friend. It is not for us to judge.' He dismounted and smoothed his robe before walking nearer. It was part shack, part desert sand brick and sheltered by a cluster of palms. The trunks of these had been wound with all manner of charms, random items of jewellery, slippers and of course the obligatory folded-up pieces of paper in their midst: the hopes and desires of the local or travelling populace, transcribed with care and laboured over, preceded by formal prayer or scribbled in the throes of rapture. He wondered how many had been prompted by the news from the palace.

But first, he was going to have to find a way in, past the giant *gulab jamun*[18] on the door.

There was nothing sweet or syrupy about this guy. His head resembled one of the largest of Hakim's sweet of choice possibly ever seen, but this was somehow balancing on a yet larger one, his body an enormous oval of what looked like solid wrestler's bulk, and not the fluffy sherbet interior that one might hope for. A makeshift red *benarsi*[19] turban was wound round his head in an elaborate configuration, and a black

---

18. a very sweet dessert of round fried dumplings
19. textiles made with intricate gold and silver brocade and embroidery on fine silks

eyepatch covered his right eye. All he needed now was
a sprightly simian perched on one shoulder and the
ensemble would be complete. Or a mynah bird. However,
Hakim knew this wasn't the time to be assigning him
a wise-cracking travelling companion, fit only for a
formulaic journeying tale. He needed to focus all his
energies on sweet-talking the *mithai*[20]-mountain of a
man. He stood imperiously with his arms crossed in
front of him, barring his entry. Hakim noted then how
comically small they seemed in comparison to his body,
as if the mound had taken in all the muscle available
from the remainder of his limbs and then left them with
what would have been more befitting of his monkey-
mate. Had he indeed had one. Anyway, he decided he
would employ his usual manner of courtesy, no matter
what the doorkeeper's demeanour was suggesting.

'Salaams and salutations, my friend. Be there room
for one more at this worthy establishment, for my
heart be weary and in need of supplication?'

'That's as may be – but there be no friends to any
man until they have succeeded in passing this here
threshold.' The man's voice was low and deep and his
solitary visible kohl-blackened eye was unwavering.
Why did such monstrous men wear the accoutrements of
womanhood with such lack of abandon? There were also
at least half a dozen gold chains of varying length
adorning the man's neck and chest, more than most
brides would wear. At this thought his mind wandered
of course to the mahal and brought him a renewed sense
of focus. Putting all thoughts of this man emerging
from behind a purdah in full *lehnga*[21] regalia, and

---

20. sweets, confectionary
21. ankle-length skirt (with a matching fitted bodice and
    shawl) worn on formal occasions such as weddings

shocking a prospective groom into an early grave rather than a marital bed aside, he decided upon a change of tack. Why did his mind take him upon these tangential tracks whenever there was solid work that needed doing? He discreetly unsealed a pocket of his robe, touched the precious object and silently began the mantra. He immediately felt the power permeate from his fingertips and travel up through both arms, but he ignored the sensation and pulled it clean out with a flourish, dangling it right before the man's eyes, both shrouded and revealed. Hakim would not have thought it possible if he had not seen the effect many times before, but even so he could never predict exactly what might happen.

The man's eye became fixated on the object in front of him, and the spindly arms uncrossed themselves and slowly began to reach out. Hakim was ready for this and carefully kept the talisman at a distance, where it could exercise its power and demand its due reverence, but not entice the man to actually make a haram-fisted grab for it. He then walked the man slowly away from the doorway, and towards a fire that was burning just a short distance from the side of the dwelling. He heard the man's low voice regress into the higher and altogether sweeter tones of his boyhood, as his eye brightened with both the guidance and the approaching flames.

'*Babaji*[22], when can I eat my *noogdai dhanai*[23]? I have been waiting such a long time,' came his pleading voice. Hakim strengthened and deepened his own and adopted the temporary tone of the fakeries of patriarchal authority.

---

22. a respectful term for father
23. a snack of small fried sweets, often sold by street vendors

'Very soon, *bettah*[24]. Very soon indeed.' He then circled the small fire three times, the man following him at a steady pace now. Hakim could hear the sounds from the tavern clearly above the man-boy's murmurings and, once he was sure they had reached the required position, he stopped and held the object aloft much closer to the fire itself. In a gesture of final submission, the man sat on the dusty floor and gazed deep into the fire, his previous yearning for the prayer beads now forgotten, yet as Hakim continued moving the beads between fingers and thumb, his own internal mantra gradually spoken aloud by the man before him, back in his adult voice now, he knew he was safe to leave him a while and enter the tavern. He walked slowly back to the main building and turned back briefly as he replaced the beads in their pocket. It was as if the giant jamun, having been placed before the open fire, had melted into a pool of *sheerah*[25] before his eyes.

His eyes smarted with the smoke from the sheesha pipes as soon as he walked in. If that were not a giveaway sign, he didn't know what was. He suppressed a coughing fit, not wanting to draw undue attention to himself as a disapproving stranger in these unfamiliar surroundings. It was dark but the red clay illuminated by the odd lamps and candles afforded him just enough light to see what he needed. The place was full. Full of bodies which were crammed in some corners but freer in others, though largely it was full of energies. The spirits – aligned, unaligned and indeterminate were in more intimate proximity than in any carnal

---

24. son
25. syrup

activity that could be imagined, sometimes welded to each other, sometimes overlapping at the edges and sometimes wholly climbing inside and consuming each other in an extraordinary visual battle of virtue and vice. And there was not a single woman in the place. There never was. Hakim wondered if this would change in time, but then had his own preconceptions immediately challenged. The smokers who were dotted round the establishment were largely silent in their private, hazy reveries, their unseeing eyes focused only inwards while whatever events unfolded right in front of them. In one corner where there were many communal wooden tables and stools, a series of debates (or arguments) were going on and the odd words and phrases floated into the air and hung there like speech bubbles, floating away from the mouths of those who had conceived them. Hakim watched as the *Urdu*[26] lettering with the odd word of Persian in their midst traversed the space, mingling with both the spirit-bodies and the smoke to form new phrases and arguments of their own, battling it out in the unseen ether. He couldn't help himself at this point; it was his one and only concession to an indulgent use of his God-given powers.

He reached out and pulled one such fully formed word towards him through the air, and quickly scanned the room. He saw the recipient almost immediately, as the sound of the bells on ankle bracelets was a constant background noise in the tavern. He tried to shake the thought from his mind that for a *khusra*[27] he certainly

---

26. language spoken in modern day Pakistan and parts of India
27. a castrated male, often born into poverty and forced to beg or work in various forms of entertainment to earn a living

had a most feminine body, highly accentuated by the tightly fitting kameez, like an embodiment of one of the sheesha pipes, as he danced and spun for a crowd in the centre of the tavern in perfect unison with their clapping and pounding of a drum. Of course his face was veiled in a bizarre nod to modesty, as that would most probably have given the game away with its sundial shadow. Hakim quickly reprimanded himself for his near lurch into lechery, and immediately dispensed the word in the man's direction. Then waited. Sometimes these things took a while. As it reached the dancer, the word conjoined with the man's rotations up above his head before bursting into a tiny explosion of stars and showering the man's clothes with yet more jewels, but rarer and more precious than those in the possession of the Sultana herself. He immediately stopped, though the clapping continued, and he then tore off his face veil with a dramatic gesture. Those in the crowd near him cried out in horror and one or two even ran for the doors, knocking some of the smokers to the ground in their haste (they didn't notice) followed swiftly by a stray dog in a corner who had been watching the proceedings and who now howled in distress.

It didn't stop there as to the audible gasps of the crowd the man ripped open his kameez and two large pomegranates were torpedoed into the air. A thin young boy, young enough to have quicker reflexes than the intoxicated masses, narrowly dodged their trajectory, but was evidently so shaken by this near-miss that he too ran straight out of the premises. Hakim was relieved. This was no place for minors. It was looking like a mass exodus was on the cards, though the debaters were only momentarily distracted from their arguments, and the smokers would not have been roused had *Shaitaan*[28] himself wandered in and asked them for a puff.

'No wonder we have a *bhadnaam*[29] with so much of the community ...' An elderly man seated to Hakim's side on a rug on the floor opened his eyes at this. Hakim had missed him upon entering but now saw that he had been deeply immersed in *zikr*[30] before Hakim had spoken aloud and somehow disturbed him. He couldn't abide the descent into general debauchery that he observed around him, as if a female impersonator made the men's lustful desires any more legitimate than had the dancer been an actual woman ... The old man got to his feet and Hakim noticed the man's extraordinary height and gait. Despite his wearing of his advancing years on his face and hair, his body was that of a young man, possibly a *pathaan*[31] though Hakim couldn't be sure. The one thing he was sure of though was that the man was a knowing spirit of some sort. He felt the hazel eyes upon him, and a shrewd appraisal undertaken that made him shiver. Despite – or maybe because of – his advanced state, Hakim knew that pride of any sort at his station was a sin, and wondered if it was this that the old man was observing in him.

'I am guessing you are a reader. Otherwise the spoken words would not have manifested in the physical

---

28. the devil
29. of poor reputation or ill-repute
30. a form of devotional, meditative practice where worshippers rhythmically and repeatedly chant various names associated with God, silently or aloud
31. a member of the Pashto-speaking community from the mountainous regions of north-west Pakistan and eastern Afghanistan

realm for you to appropriate.' Hakim was shocked. Yes this was his specialism but no one had ever directly observed him doing it before. The man continued. 'I know you have high standards and that is commendable. But beware of any shades of judgement creeping in. We serve no one while this lives on in our hearts.' Hakim was unable to speak, even to clarify that he no longer read books of any sort, as the only true learning he now felt resided within. The man was ahead of him though. Of course. 'This was written by a friend of mine many, many years ago. Take it. It is not a narrative to be read from cover to cover and understood by the mind – I know you understand this much. It is a series of parables and revelations to be opened and consumed as and when the need arises.'

With this he handed Hakim a loosely bound manuscript written in a quite beautiful calligraphic hand. He could do nothing but take this silently and bow towards his unexpected benefactor.

'You are correct in your view. We are each the living embodiment of all the canons, but the written word still has a purpose, if only to reinforce or provide a previously lacking framework. Pay heed, Hakim, pay heed and you shall not falter.' Hakim met the man's gaze again, while his hands felt the roughness of the parchment. He was momentarily distracted though, as there was some form of nervous energy emanating from a far corner. To cheers and applause a group of men walked in from an entrance near the back and took their places on a small, raised dais covered in rugs. There was a series of instruments laid before them: *tablas*[32], various larger hand drums as well as flutes,

---

32. typically a pair of small hand drums

and even the most vociferous of the debaters now quietened down slightly in anticipation, their words and phrases literally left hanging in the air with nowhere now to go. When Hakim looked round again, the old man had left the premises, so he carefully placed the pages in another pocket of his voluminous cloak. He then saw two slightly smaller – but only marginally so – gulab jamuns purposefully take their places at either side of the dais. He couldn't imagine why – if there was going to be trouble it would surely be in one of the many debauched 'dancing' establishments in the vicinity. One, with his oriental features and wiry physique, was clearly from lands slightly further east – nothing too unusual there – but the other had most definitely got himself lost on some form of pilgrimage – or pillage. He was foreign-looking with what looked like thick bronze-coloured hair and a matching beard, and he somehow reminded Hakim of a bear. In a most unique style, his beard, rather than being loose and in various states of grooming, was plaited, like the hair of the most faux-modest courtesans – and interwoven with all manner of trinkets too. He was even dressed in some kind of furs as the nights here could grow unexpectedly chilly at this time of year. Almost all the men were wearing thick shawls or even blankets over their *kurtas*[33], some even covering their heads. Before he could give it further thought the musicians began warming up their instruments, whether they were the tangible lovers on the rugs in front of them, or the incorporeal vocals residing within.

It was immediately apparent who the lead player was.

---

33. a loose collarless shirt or tunic

He was a well-built man, devoid of any beard but with the kind of luscious inky black locks that many a princess would be envious of. Even before a *Qawwali*[34] had been started, Hakim could feel the familiar vibration at the base of his spine, the sign that the experience would be one from beyond. The whole entourage had taken great care with their appearances, and were bedecked in raw silks and matching waistcoats, or robes over their kurtas, and for some reason it pleased him to see this. Why don the fake robes of poverty if you had actually been blessed? No need for extravagance though, just a respect for their position and calling. After a few more seconds of refinement and retuning, the intro to a familiar lament began and the crowd cheered their approval while the unfinished words of the speakers now too morphed into tiny stars and – after a brief series of gentler explosions – left a polished sheen on the proceedings, even overpowering the smoke of the sheeshas. The smokers themselves began to rouse, and some of them began to sway in time to the music or tap the sides of their pipes in a not very skilful approximation of the beats of the tabla players. Those who were deep in a purer form of zikr, however, appeared on the surface to remain unmoved.

The extended musical intro then quietened. The lead singer now sang one sustained note that he drew outwards like a beautiful chiffon sari being swept away by the wind. A note that grew, expanded and remained in pure faith, until it was sure it had permeated the hearts of even the most hardened religious theologian

---

34. a form of devotional music that expresses the mystical Sufi practice in Islam

114 The Prayer Rug

(unlikely though that there were any on the premises) before it shifted with extraordinary fluidity and ease into lilting vibratos.

I have you now, my friends. Your hearts belong to God and God alone, so let your imperfect minds quieten down or do what they will. You shall never escape this.

It was more powerful than Hakim had ever experienced before and he felt tears immediately form in his eyes. The players started up again and the full force of their musicianship conjoined with the vocals from beyond. Hakim felt the power reverberate around his body and more tears form. But he didn't care. Real men *do* cry. But before they could fall, he felt something entirely new. Instead of falling down his face, they popped clean out from his lids, leaving them completely dry, and then they formed two pools right in front of him. They started out as the same shape and size as his actual eyes, but then gradually grew until he was facing two large concave mirrors, suspended in the air in front of him.

He was now aware of a small section of the crowd starting to get to their feet and whirl on the dusty floor. He looked round quickly but it appeared no one else was aware of the double looking-glass that had presented itself before him. He was suddenly consumed by fear. What was he needing to be shown here? He quickly dismissed this though. Fear, unless it be born from reverence to the divine and acknowledgement of the majesty of Her power, was not a legitimate emotion. There was obviously a message for him here; first the gift from the old man and now this. He garnered his courage. He would have to take a look. Now … which side first? It would have to be the right. He would approach the left afterwards. He took a couple of slow steps forward and peered in. At first all he could see was a distorted view of the actual scene in front of him, of the musicians on the dais, but he was aware of the sounds slowly fading back out. He focused and looked harder, and saw the permeable pool now transform into an actual mirror and reflect what was actually behind him – a few seated men swaying to the music, the stray dog that had apparently re-entered the premises once it was sure the khusra would not be returning, and the odd hanging lanterns dotted around the back wall. There was one thing missing from this scene though. Before he could ponder this, he was brought right back to reality. Both pools then simultaneously contracted back to the size of his actual eyes before completely disappearing into twinkles in the air and he was returned to the world as suddenly as he had left it.

They were getting a bit too close. That, he surmised, was the main reason. In their ecstatic trance-like states, a couple of them had leapt onto the dais, and the smaller of the two bodyguards had swiftly but very sensitively intervened, leading them to a corner of the tavern where they could whirl themselves into oblivion if they so chose. The bodyguard was even ignoring the encouragement to dance along from one of the stage-invaders who had grabbed his tunic and was trying to implore him to whirl along too. He swiftly extricated himself and returned to his former position guarding the stage with the minimum of fuss. Unfortunately, as these things tended to go, once a couple of them had made this attempt, they were immediately followed by a few more. It was literally raining down riches. One of the men started throwing wads of his cash from under a shawl at the stage (he would probably regret this tomorrow as they usually did) but it was how the now almost beatific singer was taken out that was most terrifying. If Hakim had not seen it with his own eyes he would have thought the man was just delivering, for him, a customary extraordinary performance, his vocals generating new levels of rapture amongst the assembly with every chorus. But what made it even more astounding was that he delivered almost ten minutes of the final Qawwali with the full weight of the original gulab jamun on top of him while he tried to wrestle with a couple of the invaders. He had burst in through the entrance and Hakim was momentarily shocked that he had been able to leave the fireside so quickly, but also that he might come after him seeking some form of vengeance. He needn't have worried as he was evidently in need of a proper altercation.

A good proportion of the crowd were oblivious to the ruckus on stage as the singer's masterful vocals were entirely unimpaired, but while Jamun was rolling around and knocking over the tablas to apprehend the overexcited audience members, verbally it was the blond bear who was the sole object of his ire.

'*Bhaivacouf, tu kya khurrah*[35]!' he roared, but to no avail. For the man from the most foreign of foreign climes was away with the music in his own unique way. His blond locks swept back and forth like an approaching desert storm as he head-banged repeatedly to the rhythm of the hand drums, his right

---

35. "Moron, what are you doing!"

arm distended with a clenched fist – but with just his index and little finger extended in a gesture wholly unfamiliar to Hakim. He supposed it was some form of mystical sign in that part of the world from which he hailed.

This foreigner couldn't possibly have understood the unique configuration of Urdu with the odd inflections of Persian and Punjabi – could he? Hakim surmised it was most unlikely, but of course there was no need to understand the lyrics. The bear-man was reacting to the one and only transcendent language. That of music. That of the human soul. With the miscreants having been summarily dispatched, the Head Gulab grabbed the bear by his immaculately woven and decorated beard, immediately jolting him from his reverie. The furry one was not impressed and Hakim could see the musicians hurriedly scatter – with their instruments following them – as the music came to an impromptu end. The two behemoths began to circle each other slowly on the dais, doing another familiar dance, but one of the type that rarely leads to anything revelatory. Unless you were talking wounds and internal organs.

'Two tickets for the price of one *yaar*[36]!' A happy punter next to him piped up, slapping him hard on the back. 'Music and mayhem, top *tamaasha*[37]! What more could you want from a night out?' From out of nowhere it seemed, the bear had found himself a helmet. It was solid and looked as if it were made of cast iron and wood and was keeping his wild mane in check. The jamun began to remonstrate vociferously at this, engaging a

---

36. colloquial, friendly form of address for a male e.g. mate, bro
37. a performance or spectacle

small section of the crowd in his corner and pointing first at his own purely decorative turban then at his opponent's helmet. He was especially affronted at the two prominent weapons resembling curved horns that were growing out of this. 'Animal cruelty yaar look, the *beasharam*[38] bear has been slaughtering our precious baby elephants, robbing them of their lives and their baby tusks to attach them to his already illegal helmet, as even more illegal weapons!' Hakim sighed at his new friend. The horns certainly resembled tusks but he wasn't feeling the remnants of any animal energies from them. He suspected they were just carved from some other material. The man's furs on the other hand … The smallest of the three men quickly sprang into action and placed himself in between the two, both his arms outstretched towards them in a placatory gesture. He spoke in a low soothing voice but, with the sounds of the crowd now either actively baying the men on to fight or making their displeasure at the premature halt to the music known, Hakim could not make out a single word the man might have said. What he was surprised to see was Jamun starting to back off slightly, while the bear then stayed where he was and didn't attempt to encroach on his new-found territory.

Jamun then turned and with a ferocious roar – which could have rivalled that of the original owners of his opponent's garbs – tore the turban away, revealing in complete contrast his own perfectly bald brown head. He then began pounding this with his own fists, to the rhythm of the drum that had started up again, and the crowd now slow-clapped along in unison in

---

38. shameless

the background. With the recent hasty departure of the musicians, Hakim looked to see who it was who was now beating this, and could just about see the scrawny adolescent boy, who had earlier bolted from the premises, now seemingly recovered from his recent trauma. He had apparently taken inspiration from the oriental master and wrapped his shawl over the lower part of his face in an approximation of a ninja. The original ninja seemed to have had enough now, his attempts at mediation looking in vain. He walked off the dais. If you couldn't stop them, you definitely didn't want to be in their way.

'You look like a *sahib*[39] of impeccable judgement yaar – I mean sahib.' It was his new (and enterprising) friend again. Hakim could see his thoughts, but unusually there were no words or images forming in the air in front of him; there were numbers. Numbers and various other symbols. Of course, the man was evidently a quick thinker and was going to run a hastily assembled book while there was still time. Over the ever-increasing volume of the drums, he began shouting out various odds for the possible outcome of the fight, then wrote them in the sand in a corner that was not covered in rugs, using a stone. The book had been opened. A few men were already jostling around him, eager to get their bets in quickly, and predictably several minor scuffles then broke out in the vicinity as Hakim could see the same men who – just moments earlier – had renounced their worldly possessions by throwing wads of cash and other precious objects on their person into the air, now scrambling around desperately trying to retrieve

---

39. a respectful form of address for a man, sir

these. Hakim looked despairingly at the scene in front of him and prayed for guidance from his divine Mistress as to what it was She wished him to see. As he looked around him, his eyes alighted on Jamun's head again. At the sight of this, Hakim had to work hard to quell the old familiar cravings for a real gulab jamun (oh to be that size too …) from his mind. He was annoyed. Why was he being dragged backwards and being reminded of his former sins of gluttony and greed? Immediately then he knew. They weren't former sins at all. He didn't even know what the man's real name was but the odds were pretty high that it wasn't Jamun. Faced with the manifestation of his own pestilence like this, Hakim felt like running from the tavern, getting back on his horse and returning to his hometown, abandoning the object of his quest entirely. He knew though that this wasn't the way.

The man formerly known as Jamun now turned round and faced the men who had hastily assembled in his corner. He gathered round them in a huddle and the crowd too suddenly began to quieten. The mood had changed and Hakim could sense the collective spirit of the tavern pause with the growing air of expectancy. Even the smoke seemed to hang in the air. There was now barely a sound to be heard.

At a sudden loss as to what to do, he slumped on the floor and looked at the numbers written in the sand. He was half tempted to just place a bet himself; how about 3 to 1 for the bear winning by a submission through a triangle choke? It was then that he knew. He quickly got to his feet and started searching in his pockets. Damn this robe, just why were there thousands of the things? The small crowd who had been queuing up to place their bets now turned their attention to the array of random objects that Hakim now proceeded to pull out from his pockets. Firstly there was a large feather, then an old manuscript, then a real-life monkey (who immediately ran up to the man formerly known as Jamun and jumped up onto his shoulder). Ah, here it was! Hakim's fingers clasped his old familiar friend, his unfailing go-to whenever he was floundering and he pulled it out with relief from the manifolds.

'Hey, nice necklace yaar, a bit on the feminine side for me, but each to one's own you know.'

'This is not a necklace! Just how ignorant can you apostates be?'

'Ooooh! Keep your cloak on *bayaah*[40], he was just having some fun.' Hakim immediately regretted his hasty comment as voices from the crowd continued to assail him; one small tear in the seams was all it took and then all manner of djinns queued up to take residence. Full of remorse, he took himself off to a far corner where he could see none of the unfolding events, and began his familiar mantra to the movement of the beads. What is it you need of me, my Lady, he murmured.

'Just who is he to call anyone an apostate … He is even addressing the Almighty as if He were a female …!' Heavens, how had he been heard? He knew though he was deserving of these comments due to his earlier double slips of both the mind and tongue, so paid them no regard and especially knew not to argue. This was not a time to inform those who were so dogged by dogma that male and female were nothing more than the temporary cloaks of the soul, so what did it matter if the

---

40. colloquial, friendly form of address for a man, matey

Almighty were addressed in either the one form or the other? Neither were actually sufficient. Fortunately, with the myriad of distractions, no one paid him further heed. The scene was degenerating further and further; a place for worship – idiosyncratic in its conception yes – was starting to rival the absurdities of the literalists in how far it was descending from the pursuit of pure union. The words of the old man came back to him just then … we serve no one when this lives in our hearts …

It was then it began.

At first it was if a spirit (though one in possession of a child's immature hand) had decided to paint the tavern with an illegible scrawl. Still continuing the mantra, Hakim looked around him and saw brushstrokes of white light writ large in the air, but just as soon as they appeared, a few seconds later they dissolved again – though only to reappear in some other formation just after. There was undoubtedly something coming through, but he would need to apply his finest attention now. He looked again and in that moment it was as if a giant glow-worm, with a much steadier hand (or tail?) had appeared and this time left a trail of two parallel columns of light, suspended right in the centre of the scene. And there they remained. Hakim knew it was only he that could see them, so there was no threat of any impending mass hysteria. But what was he now supposed to do? He left his place in the corner, and with the prayer beads still in hand walked closer to investigate further.

Unlike the mirrors of tears, the two columns looked solid, neither reflecting what was before them nor distorting what lay behind. To either side and in between he could see the goings on in the tavern, the boy still beating the drum, the dog now entranced by the bear's furs and sniffing incessantly at them, but Hakim paid no real attention. The columns shimmered like a condensed Milky Way of stars and Hakim was possessed by an overwhelming urge to reach out and climb inside what looked like everlasting space. It was far beyond anything he had been bestowed with to date; he had no reference points from the – not insubstantial and constantly expanding – personal library of mystical experiences he had been gifted, nothing to draw on here, no parables from the scriptures he had read, no guidance from the others on Their Own Paths he had met. No. This was down to him now. He walked closer and marvelled at the tiny, almost microscopic, planets he could see, some particularly brilliant, and he wondered if the esteemed Sultana herself could ever be greeted with such a sight upon the opening of her ceremonial jewellery box. There were two things that perplexed him though: firstly how on earth could he settle upon a single star with the dazzling array that was greeting him here, and secondly – as he looked around the growing raucousness of the scene – would he ever be able to return to complete his designated work if he made the choice to leave now?

He knew he was going to have to place his faith in something way beyond his own pitiful human attempts at logic and rationalism here. They were indeed poor masters. He replaced his beads carefully back in their rightful pocket, closed his eyes and then reached forward into the space of the two columns with both his outstretched palms. It was out of his hands now.

The first thing that he registered was the quiet. After the multiple auditory assaults of the night, any reduction in volume would have been welcomed but this silence that enveloped him now – even his deepest moments of zikr – could not compare to the warming infusion of nectar that seemed to flood directly into his veins, permeating all his senses and stilling all the remaining agitations of the monkey-mind that – even at his elevated station – occasionally came to the fore. He wanted to savour this. He knew not what would greet him upon opening his eyes, so decided he would keep them closed – just a while longer. His arms were back by his sides now, but he found he could no longer move. Not just his arms either; his entire body seemed in the throes of paralysis – though there was no accompanying sense of panic. It was not the unrelenting dead-weight of being pinned to the ground by the bulk of say Jamun (sorry, 'the man formerly known as Jamun') either; there was a glorious lightness of being that accompanied the waves of blissful silence that now washed and cleansed his body. How long could he remain like this? Hakim realised that if he indeed did have a choice he could easily stay like this forever.

Gradually, he became aware of a faint but persistent presence around him, and it was growing by the second … He quickly slapped the back of his neck – it was a *dheet*[41] mosquito of all things. How could such a worldly irritant have managed to accompany him to the realms of an outer dimension such as this? The *haramzaadah*[42] must have been hidden in the folds of his robe somewhere. He realised then that with this bodily disturbance, and resultant encroachment of the

---

41. irritatingly stubborn
42. obnoxious male, bastard

distractions of the mind, his ability to move had been returned to him – and he felt sorrow at this. He now heard the light buzzing around his ear and swiped the surrounding air. Suddenly it felt as if his precious vial of honey had been broken open, and the resulting spillage was attracting all manner of insects. He could feel the humming growing and circling his head continuously now, as if a whole legion of ghost gnats had been roused from their nets and bloody deathbeds of walls and skin, and were intent on feeding on him and his sickly sweet sin. He waved his arms round desperately now, trying to somehow swerve away from the hungry hordes in a bizarre reconfiguring of the dervish dance of ecstasy. He could feel them conjoining together in their growing frenzy, their circular flightpaths creating a cordon with which to bind and restrain him before they could take their fill and feed off him and his essential energies for as long as they pleased.

'I understand you, my Lady! Forgive me, please!'

Upon his exaltation, he had involuntarily opened his eyes.

There was no galaxy of stars. No other world – not even a haze of angry insects.

He was still where he was. In the tavern. And there were the same characters populating the same scene he had left.

But it was quiet.

No one was moving and in fact everything and everyone …

Was. Completely. Still.

Even though Hakim now knew that the power of bodily movement had been returned to him, there was some reluctance to exercise this. For a few moments he stood largely confined to the spot – and it was a spot. Another shimmering window into the celestial world had seemingly opened up, right beneath his feet, while the former shimmering columns had vanished completely, leaving him with an unobstructed view of all that had unfolded. Well, firstly it didn't appear that he was in any danger of falling down into the heavens through this perfect square of a trapdoor. He could feel solid ground beneath his feet, though what would happen if he tried to move from here he wasn't at all sure. He invoked one of his backing mantras, and then with poise and purpose stepped deftly from his place and back onto the surrounding rug. For some reason the square was perfectly centred within the geometric pattern of the rug, and with his footsteps some of the stars from the other world came through, as a tiny army of lights, and began traversing the swirling lines of the patterns, slowly illuminating all the threads and fibres. They crossed over into the other smaller rugs that surrounded it, in the far corners, again just to gently follow the already drawn designs, no matter how crude the original workmanship. Not content with this, the stars then left the boundaries of the rugs completely and delved into the microscopic particles of sand, sawdust and spit (as well as other unidentifiable substances) until soon the entire floor was bathed in a silvery light, and the original doorway could no longer be discerned. Hakim found this new moonlit carpet highly reassuring and – no longer frightened of his next step – started walking around the scene.

Everything and everyone was imbued with the thoughts and actions they were currently engaged with. Expressions were easily read and the people looked alive, more so than when they had actually been animated – the colours more vivid, the faces writ with everything from spiritual ecstasy to unrestrained rage, the furs and textures almost begging to be touched and caressed. As he walked up to the dais, Hakim had a sudden (and wholly inappropriate) urge to run his hands through the thick golden locks of the bear … He quickly chastised himself knowing that if he wouldn't have dreamed of attempting to undertake this action while the man was aware, he should absolutely never do it while he was in this state of – whatever it was …

As delicious and welcome as these experiences could be, he deftly brought himself back to the apple core of a question: what was it that he was really being shown here? Yes, he was being asked to pause and reflect, so the environment itself had duly yielded to the divine will, making itself conducive to this state by offering him no further stimulus until he had processed what had already happened. If life could always be so accommodating, how many debacles might then be averted? He wove a steady and regular pattern through the crowd, taking great care not to inadvertently touch or otherwise disturb the surroundings in any way, lest that cause a giant rend in the embroidered structure of the scene and result in a cosmic rupture of the fragile space-time continuum. He reasoned he was most likely worrying for nothing; if he did knock a lantern or erase some odds in the now silvery sand, he was sure any genuine accidents would be patched up seamlessly by the ultimate guiding hand. To wilfully seek to manipulate events now, that was something he knew better than to even try. These days. As with most things though, he had learned the hard way, and shuddered when he recalled the events of many years previous at one of the Festivals of the Friends … In fact, his shudders almost made him career straight into the dog that was semi-obscured in the light, for some reason taking on the silvery hues himself: the canine-chameleon of the cavern, though none of the humans had been able to do this. Looking at the dog triggered another thought within him, and on a whim he decided to leave the boundaried rationality behind and head straight out the doors.

The first thing he saw was the palm tree, but this far inland, on an isolated dust track and generally devoid of any breeze or passing personage, he couldn't ascertain whether the outer world too had stopped to aid his reflections. There was no white light illuminating the desert sands here though, that much was evident. He walked round the palm and saw the tied amulets and prayers were slowly fading into the bark and in their place he saw a patchwork of faces appear – either the originators of the prayers or the recipients – or maybe even those who held the ability to implement the longed-for changes in their power. Hakim wasn't sure but it immediately revealed itself without room for any doubt. The faces themselves then dissolved too into the now familiar shimmer of the silver threaded light that wound itself around the bark and lit the palms above with its resplendence. Hakim carried on walking and decided to return to where Mohti had been tethered, what seemed like days ago now.

The lead lay coiled on the ground and the horse was nowhere to be seen. This was most irregular, but before Hakim could run the risk of breaking this fragile new reality by engaging in old patterns of conscious thought and deductions, the universe intervened again and his attentions were diverted once more. It was the fire. It was still burning with a powerful flame to the side of the tavern and he was drawn to it once again. The heat was a welcome refuge for him now, not bedecked in furs or heavy shawls of any kind. He realised now that most of his provisions had been left in Mohti's care, so if the horse too was now travelling another path, some other fortunate rider would have been gifted his modest but life-enhancing luggage. He gave it no further attention and allowed himself to focus on the crackle of the fire. He breathed in deeply and, instead of the vague nausea he commonly felt, he smelled beautiful aromas rising from the flames. He barricaded the windows of his eyes and his mind, and just let the one true sense unmediated access without the competing diversions of the others. This was when he felt the gentle patter of the whirling sands surround him and he knew he was being elevated to a new place. And one – as usual – that he felt entirely unworthy of.

'Forgive me, my Lady. But your humble servant begs you for a pace I can cope with.' She was immediately responsive. It was instantaneous. He reached out with both hands again, yearning for the divine embrace, and he opened his eyes. He saw the fire burning in a perfect circle, which seemed far, far beneath him – a galaxy beneath him even, but the fragrances were still making their way to him and he gratefully imbibed them. Greedily almost. His fingers grasped a thin silver cordon, so fine and delicate he felt it couldn't possibly withstand the clumsiness of his human touch. But it held firm and with every growing second he felt the hidden strength make itself clear to him:

The Prayer Rug

I may look composed of lightness itself, but lest this deceive you, there is not a force on this earth that shall ever break Me. So be assured, as long as you remain with Me you shall always be safe.

'Forgive me, my Lady' he begged. 'My errors repeat themselves, eternally, over lifetimes.' The cordon was glowing brighter now and as he clutched it tighter he felt a sudden movement to his left. As if he himself was now an integral part of this giant interplanetary sundial, he felt the shift in every cell in his body as every cumulative second that he had ever lived coursed through the very fibres of his being. On either side of him now, as far as he could see, there were large silver orbs attached to the cordon and with every shift to the left he felt himself buffered on either side as they moved in a steady circular motion around the circumference of the cordon. He started off by counting the movements, and with each one heard the familiar vocalisation of his own mantra that he had worked to refine and finesse over his life. He recalled the words of a sage he had once had the privilege to meet in a meditation: 'At first you pretend to do the zikr, then you do the zikr and finally … the zikr does you.' Here he was, many years later actually understanding the true meaning of those words. Nay, experiencing them in fact. He had given up counting (his Lady was no auditor, cataloguing Her infinite jewels, so why would he?) and just let the whispery intonations carry through the wind currents around him. He had no fear of falling – though he had no real understanding of where he was now – and if he were indeed to fall, where it was he would now land.

As they moved around the circumference, he looked down and saw that the fire was gradually being obscured by the dark veil of the night, being pulled right across the glowing embers – and to see this caused him no end of agitation. Who was this demonic force that had dared to cloak the manifest and created beauty of the sun? He shouted down at what he now saw but, despite his uncharacteristic howls, his ears could register no sound coming from his fury. The winds held firm and resolute, though his anger was showing no signs of abating. Forgetting where he was, he relinquished his grip on the cordon and reached down as if to rip the veil away and cast it aside for ever into a billowing black hole in the galaxy. This was a mistake. Despite what he was being shown, his perceptions were still operating as if he were on the worldly plane, so of course once he let go there was only the one place he was heading back to. He realised his error immediately. 'Even to beg Your forgiveness is not fitting for the worthless slave that I am …' As he looked up, he saw the semi-formed crescent moon above him and was consumed with remorse for letting go, for letting his anger consume him, and for trying in his arrogance to take already ordained matters into his own hands before the full cycle had been completed. The universe responded. Yes, the sun was veiled but just around the edges was a faint corona; more defined in places than others, it was undeniably still present. Whether it could be universally seen was not his issue. It was there, and that was all that mattered, and no amount of black matter could dull its primordial presence.

 He awoke to the sensation of sand, possibly dirt and other unmentionable debris being flung over his body.

132   The Prayer Rug

He quickly opened his eyes and tried to move. This was worse than life itself – he was alive but presumed dead and was being buried in an unknown and unmarked grave in the middle of nowhere! His panic station was then overridden by a customary coughing fit and he realised that the power of movement was still very much his own. He opened his eyes and tried to adjust to where he might now be. The eyes that greeted him were large as if they belonged to some kind of giant, and seeing (or maybe testing) that he was not in fact dead – or even particularly injured – he was given a sharp kick in the ribs.

'Owwwwww! This be no way to treat—'

'That be enough. For verily this one appears in the throes of intoxication prior to even entering the den of the divine.'

Clutching his throbbing head, Hakim looked up and saw a huge turbaned doorkeeper on one side of him, then another to the other side who looked like a cross between a buffalo and a *baloo*[43]. In between them though he saw his assailant. It was Mohti who had been desperately kicking sand in his face in an attempt to revive him after some kind of fall. Unfortunately he had been slightly too close with the last one. The two giants pulled him to his feet and dusted down his robe, returning various objects to him that had tumbled to the ground, including a set of prayer beads, an old feather and a small monkey that had been anxiously perched on the shoulder of the turbaned one, waiting for his beloved master to regain consciousness. As Hakim got to his feet, he thanked his two kind ministering angels and, seeing

---

43. bear

the black patch covering the eye of one of them, decided to gift him his simian companion as a gesture of his gratitude.

'He seems to be more befitting of your company. I have a long journey ahead of me and it may be best if we part ways at this juncture. No need for sorrow for I feel sure we shall meet again.' At this the bear removed a helmet adorned with horns of some kind from his head and as his flaxen hair blew in the wind (it looked ready for an approaching sandstorm) he began to sing some ancient and entirely foreign sounding lament. To Hakim's surprise, though he could clearly understand none of the words, his companion removed his turban (revealing a most impressive gleaming bald head) and began to weep. The monkey looked at his former master as if to say, *Listen yaar, even if the journey is a long and arduous one (and aren't they all?) not totally sure I really want to stay with this lot here … too long … you know?* But anyway, he was a monkey so who knew what he was really thinking, so once the singing and crying had settled down, he thanked his two unlikely rescuers once more, declined their kind invitations to sit a while in the tavern and prepared to get back on the road with Mohti.

'*Rhuko*[44]!' cried one of them as they were about to depart. With his turban back on his head and his tears dry, he ran up to them; then the monkey reached out from his new home on his shoulder and handed Hakim a loose-leaf volume of papers. 'This fell out of one of your pockets too.' He took the book and surveyed it curiously. There was only ever one book he actually carried with him (though he had owned many libraries

---

44. wait

worth over the years) and he could feel this still in its rightful pocket. Then, as if impatient with all these diversions, Mohti took matters into his own hooves and trotted away before Hakim could say another word. The two giants then headed off and when turning back momentarily, Hakim could just make out the vivid red turban now sitting atop the blond mane and the horned helmet – slightly askew – on the head of his bald companion as their arms locked across the backs of each other's shoulders (as large as continents) and they returned to the tavern.

8

Howra knew she had work to do, so had sat down that morning with the express intention of only reading until her cup of tea had runneth dry, regardless of where she was in the chapter. Of course, once she began she just continued, as it seemed rude to stop like that where she was, just like pausing the events of the tavern, but due to her own whims, and not those that were divinely ordained to show her something. The waters of her immersion certainly had not runneth dry. This was not a diversion or a piece of recreational downtime – this was as much work as anything else – and possibly even more so. It was just our fucked-up world that valued tasks and bucket lists to tick off, rather than any meaningful exploration of why these things were even desirable. Anyway, just who was she to talk? She had run round consumed by action, leaving miles of dead ends of half drunk (and spilt) beverages and abandoned books in her wake. She was never letting this one happen again. No. Things would now take whatever time they took and this was Officially Okay.

She put the book in her bag for later and decided to make herself another cup – just to slowly compensate for the ones she had managed to miss out on over the years, you see. She sat down in front of her computer (which she had given ample time to wake up this morning) and resumed her task. The memory stick that had masqueraded as a snail's shell had been dispensed with now – luckily she had managed to copy the entire contents onto her hard drive, as shortly afterwards it had completely broken apart and there was no chance of it ever being functional again. It was of no consequence, however, as the information itself was still accessible and that was all that really mattered. She briefly considered the possible moral implications of unexpectedly being party to it in this way, but a quick scan of the file names had told her there was no need for her to even open any of these – they were a mixture of other work that the professor had been involved in, and while it may have sounded interesting, she was not here to fall prey to any diversions from the task in hand, unless she was specifically instructed otherwise – and actually it really wasn't any of her business. There were only two that held any interest for her. The first was of course the PowerPoint presentation of the slides from the recent lecture (everything was clearly titled and dated) and then there was an accompanying word document which was most probably an aide memoir of notes and references for each slide – she'd not yet had an opportunity to actually open and examine either, but in the absence of actually managing to speak to him in person, these were most definitely the next best things and could possibly be even more revealing than the specifically chosen words of the man himself. Okay. Here she would start. She took a long sip and let the hot liquid work its magic, replaced the mug carefully to one side and opened the presentation:

The first slide was just the title of the series and his specific lecture with his name, so she clicked past to the following one and began her repeat odyssey into the world of ancient textiles. There was no further text itself in the presentation, just images as the professor had known that any accompanying words would only distract from the visuals on screen, so had left any exegesis to his oral storytelling. She worked her way through them relatively quickly, as she knew the one she wanted was towards the end, so she allowed the colourful designs to dance their dance before her eyes, leaving her feeling vaguely nauseous. She did stop once though, at the one that was the reason for her tracking this man in the first place, and she thought again at how his impeccable academic credentials hadn't prevented him from the fundamental error he had made in his assessment of its lineage. Strangely though that wasn't the one she really wanted to look at. It was slide 24. 'Her shawl'. The one that had no worldly value in terms of the quality of its weave, the finery of its workmanship or any cultural meanings of its patterns. It just happened to be what his yet-to-be wife was wearing the first time he saw her. It looked as ordinary as it had the first time she had seen it on the large projected screen, but for some stupid reason she reached out and touched the monitor as she let the slideshow stop there, as if this would do anything. Well, she felt as much static as she might have done from the real thing, but that was about it really. She looked again and decided to open up the accompanying word file to see if there was any more there in the body of the text about the mysterious woman in the shawl ...

* * *

Giles had had a busy month of it, but the nature of the busyness was not entirely to his liking. The recordings for the radio series were largely completed now and had gone well. The first couple had been aired to understated but positive reviews and he had a final one left to do, but there had been an uncomfortable episode with the recording process for one of the earlier ones that had nearly made him walk away from the whole project – and that was not like him to do. The series producer, who was hugely experienced and respected, had been unwell that particular day, so he had asked a junior member of his team to stand in for him. Unfortunately this man had no interest or even tolerance for the subject matter, and spent most of the time making just about audible comments at each break in the recording – 'who gives a shit about a pile of rags ... bloody hell, you can be a professor of this stuff can you?' Giles made the decision early on to ignore him. He was being interviewed by a knowledgeable museum curator; a series of intelligent questions had been scripted for him to answer, and beyond the timings and structure and generally overseeing the technical aspects, this wholly ignorant man would have no actual input into the final episode.

'Ignore him. There's a reason why he's still a junior. Technical wizardry gets you nowhere in the end. If you can't feel affinity with subject matter outside your own narrow range, that's where you'll stay.' Giles knew his collaborator was right, but for some reason his reaction was entirely disproportionate. He was consumed by a rage that he was only just managing to keep in check during the course of the afternoon – a big mistake right there – when what he should have done was to either dissolve it into the ether like an unwanted stitch in time or, failing that (as this was largely beyond him), said something immediately and snipped it from the loom. His whole evening and the next day were largely unsettled because of it, and he found himself more irritated about his inability to manage this than the comments themselves.

'Look sweetie, the world and his dog have their own interests. My boys had no interest in my garden – and I know you don't either – so let the man say what he wants. Our passions are our own and, so long as we have them, who cares whether we have another to share them with? Let the world stew in the fat of its own ignorance.' Katrin was consoling him a couple of days later over a cup of tea.

As if that wasn't enough, a series of lectures he was due to give had been cancelled, due to a high-profile benefactor of the hosting cultural centre being subject to some form of criminal proceedings (he didn't wish to know the details) so though not a natural fan of this medium, the decision to abort would of course be impacting on his pocket. A further irritant was that he had somehow lost a chunk of his work that was on a missing memory stick, though an arduous trawl through his hard drive had revealed most of the work was still there in some form or other. 'It's probably the mercury,' said Katrin. Giles was baffled by the comment – what did the weather conditions have to do with anything – he knew he wasn't a gardener and never would be, so maybe she was no longer listening to him and was making a comment about something to do with the change in season affecting her plants? Maybe it was him that had lost the thread? She took another sip and then added, '… in retrograde.' She then looked at him expectantly as if this would explain everything, but if he was confused before, her further comment had just compounded this. 'Anyway, what are you complaining for? Look what you've got looming.' She was right of course. By the time it came to pay a return visit to Mrs Luscombe (and the unlikely Mr Temple) he was practically counting down the moments.

It had been an early start that morning, as he wanted to make the most of the day – and it was a fine one too. The traffic had been as clear as could ever be expected at that hour, so he hadn't even found the drive too onerous. As he approached the gates this time, they opened automatically and he drove through the alley of ancient trees, now looking even more majestic than they had on his former visit. He wondered absently if they were redwoods. Did redwoods even grow in England? As he parked and got out his car, he saw the familiar figure coming towards him. Unsure as to what reception he would get, he had already decided upon an attitude of respectful but aloof neutrality. Giles knew (and the incident with that dick of a programme producer had merely managed to highlight it) that he could be the king of composure most of the time, and the world largely had no idea that he would dearly just love to land one in its face. Just the once. But there was something about that Shirley that made him feel the man was reading him better than most. He most likely would have known what Giles had really thought of his immediate demand to know his 'assessment' – as if they were on an episode of bloody *Antiques Roadshow* or something, and of course the fact that he just wanted to plain laugh out loud at the man's name. That too brought back a former memory. He had once been asked to appear on an episode that was being filmed at an old abbey – now a hotel. They wanted a visiting expert on textiles. He had several objections to this. Firstly, that the bloody format always required a quantifiable sum to be given for what the object brought in by the public was worth – the final denouement which he just thought crass. And secondly he had once spent a couple of nights there with his former wife, and it was so soon after her leaving that the thought of a return was just too painful.

'Good morning, Professor. It is good to have you back.' Shirley was all professionalism as he was at the start of their first meeting. Maybe all had been forgotten? Or it had just been in Giles's own head? He shook hands with the man.

'Please. Just call me Giles. The professor is just a piece of baggage that the world requires I carry, but trust me, it's a relief to leave that at home.'

For the first time Giles thought he could detect a hint of a smile, then just at that moment a much more demonstrative greeting came his way. 'Hey boy, how you doing?' Giles dropped his bag on the gravel to concentrate on fussing the dog, who was now leaping up at him excitedly. He then picked up his bag and followed Shirley into the house again, with Coach to the side of him. This time he was led past the room where he had been left upon his first visit, when the delights of the garden were too much for him to resist. Here Shirley gently shoed Coach back outside, and they entered a room a short distance away at the back of the house. The room was spacious and two of the walls were lined with bookshelves from floor to ceiling. In one corner, facing a wall with its back to the garden, stood a desk. On the floor was the carpet – well he supposed that was what it was as the linen covering lay on top of a raised mass in the centre of the room.

Shirley motioned Giles to a brown leather sofa.

'I can't imagine you would have eaten much at the time you left, sir. What would you like for breakfast?' Giles thought he would give up on asking the man to just call him Giles – evidently the background in the forces was just too ingrained. The offer of some breakfast sounded good though. When Shirley had left, he settled himself down onto the sofa, and thought he should wait until having eaten before uncovering the carpet. He took a notebook from his bag, and scribbled a few lines about unrelated matters that had come to mind on his drive, and then put it down. He began pondering the wisdom of having a desk facing the wall like this. People tended to fall into distinct camps when it came to things like this, with one feeling that any stimulation in the environment was to be welcomed – if not actively sought after, and the other feeling that work could only be focused and productive if all such distractions were minimised. This room was no cell, however. Not only did it have a window (actually doors as well leading outside) and a personal library of books, but the remaining wall space was almost filled with various paintings – predominantly miniatures that looked like they were depicting either Persian or subcontinental portraits or scenes from nature. He stood up to take a closer look at them and saw that amongst them were a few where the ornate gauze costumes were very subtly parted, just enough to reveal that the otherwise perfectly composed subjects were engaged in having sex.

Giles could hear that someone had entered from the front door and was walking through the hallway. He quickly sat himself back down, not wishing to be found gawping at the dirty pictures by Mrs Luscombe, even if they were flagrantly on view. Surely they couldn't be hers, could they? Maybe they were some heirlooms that had been left by her father? He guessed this was a private study of sorts. Wondering why he was being such a prude, he waited for his client to enter the room and thought about what he might say – if anything – but no one entered the room at all until Shirley appeared with a trolley that would have been befitting of silver service, with his full English as requested. He was again left to himself and found himself enjoying this solitude before his day's work began proper. If only every working day could commence in this manner. Though he most probably wouldn't get much work done if it did. The food was cooked to perfection – the eggs exactly as Giles liked them – and he ate at his leisure as it all remained hot. A while later he was washing it down (with coffee this time) while Shirley had disappeared off with the now largely empty trolley. He stood up again, this time with the intention of exploring the books. The contents here most definitely looked like they had been owned by several different people, over generations and with varying tastes. He reached for a slender volume with a spine so disintegrated that the title could no longer be discerned, hoping this wasn't too rare or valuable, when he felt a sharp pain in his neck. He was instantly reminded of his previous visit and the glass stone from the path that he had mistaken for being stung by a bee – except he was indoors right now, in a study not a sensory garden.

The book managed to glide to the floor with both speed and grace, landing with its front cover clearly visible now. Giles, however, didn't get to see it as he collapsed in a heap, his fall being broken by the linen sheet and the rug beneath him.

He was swiftly repositioned at the end of the rectangle, and with brisk adept movements, he was rolled up before being carried out of the room.

* * *

142   The Prayer Rug

When the room was empty and I could sense the coast was clear, I made my way in through the garden doors and, after an obligatory sniff of the dead cows so cruelly (I thought for the millionth time) stretched upon the unnecessary seating area that my esteemed mistress insisted upon having, I felt momentarily confused. I nudged that stick that was entirely useless as a bone that humans liked to hold in their hands, occasionally shove behind their ears but stupidly hardly ever in their mouths and it fell to the floor with another piece of sacrilege – a tiny but unmistakable part of a desecrated tree, again bound by the skin of my bovine friends. As if to further taunt her death, the wisdom of her years had been replicated not through the circular rings that quietly wound their way through her life-giving trunk, but through dead straight lines that humans in their continuing lack of reverence would make entirely incomprehensible marks all over. If one of my feline foes had ever used their (entirely natural I might say, though undoubtedly vicious) mark-making and despoiled a piece of human creation, in some homes they would most likely be banished forever. Yet did *we* ever banish our so-called masters from the natural world? Could we?

So what was going on? He was here just a second ago. I knew my poor master had lost some of his (admittedly very limited) human abilities as he had got older but I wasn't even that old – and anyway, whoever heard of losing your specifically canine faculties just because you had got older? I know my eyes are not my strongest sense but that fella who had first shown up weeks back – he definitely wasn't here now. I had seen him from the garden while being engaged in a well-deserved back rub from the massage path my mistress had kindly laid out for me. It was a shame she had gone so overboard with those particular plants though. Just because you lot can't smell anything. Inhaling anything too much round there was positively intoxicating for me. Oh shit. Maybe that was it? I had indulged myself just a bit too long on the highway to heaven and was so out of it from those plants that I had missed whatever had gone on in the house? Right. Let me try and recalibrate and get my bearings. With a brief prayer I jumped down off the cow carcasses and that's when I realised my favourite carpet had gone too. And it had definitely been there earlier that morning as the walking tree-man (but with just the two branches) had brought it down from the attic and most impolitely shoed me from the room. I had watched from the doorway as he then covered it carefully with a sheet. I felt sad just then. It reminded me of what they did to my master when he had died. Had the carpet once been alive then? I was really losing it if that was the case as I had never even realised. Alternatively it could just have been that he was having a nap I supposed, hence the sheet? It came to me all of a sudden then. That guy, he must have had us all fooled! He had wormed his way into the house (no offence to worms, just a turn of phrase that) and then for reasons known only to himself had nicked the carpet. I had to sound the alarm. It was better late than never.

'What is it, boy? And what are you doing in there anyway – you'll be disturbing the professor. Professor, I do apologise – I've just got here from—'

As if to emphasise the point, I jumped back on the cow hides again and back down into the centre of the room and barked as much as I could. My mistress stopped and stared at me and then scanned the room before quickly disappearing out the doorway. I was going to follow her but there was something nagging at me. There was still something off about the room and I was at a loss now as to what to do. In the absence of anything concrete, I dispensed with the barking as I was giving myself a headache, and on top of the already accumulating events, this really wasn't what I needed. No, it was a clear head right now, with no sensory distractions whatsoever. I knew what I had to do and how much I would hate it but there was no choice. I ran outside again and briefly marvelled (as I always marvelled) that there was so much room out there and how good it felt that the sun was out. The walking tree-man (but with just the two branches) was somewhere in the house and I could hear the sounds of my mistress and his anxious exchanges. I didn't need to understand their language, though I did think it would be much more convenient if they could just occasionally understand mine. They were humans though and over the years I had learned to adjust my expectations accordingly. Anyway, who was I to talk? I had just let a thief walk straight into our home and disappear with a precious object – and I had liked the guy as well. Anyway, this was not the time for self-recriminations. I ran straight across to the other end of the garden, where there were no sensorial delights to detain me, and immersed myself straight into the one that I absolutely hated confronting.

* * *

Shirley was all action and had immediately sprinted outside, but when he saw that Giles's car was still on the premises, and that there was no sign of either him or the carpet, he stopped in his tracks. He walked now, slowly round the side of the house and to the gardens at the back, as if he thought he might somehow catch him there. He was just in time to see Coach – who hated water with a passion – jump straight into the pond.

* * *

It was a poem. A love poem of course, she might have known – but not being well versed in this area herself she had no idea who the poet might have been. It could even have been the professor himself as far as she knew, but she doubted that, as the odd lines did sound half familiar, as if she might have once been paying attention in English one day in school and, despite the best efforts of her nomadic attention, something had actually gone in. She was trying to imagine what the audience's reaction might have been if, once having announced the shawl had belonged to the ex who had left him, he had then read the poem aloud. No – that would have been too much. He had disclosed it to perfection, with just enough of a fleeting detail to wake people up, without them worrying too much on account of his possible deteriorating state of mind.

* * *

The palace had organised things to perfection. Or so they thought.

There was of course a process of filtration, as the numerous helpers in the palace kitchens could attest.

Before any *dhal*[45] dish could be prepared, there were commonly more stones than actual lentils that needed to be sifted through by hand, and had any of these got through they would have all but ruined the rich and (proudly) unclarified tastes, enhanced by the added tempering of the onions. Ruined in texture – as there was little worse than having to extract a hard stone from one's teeth during the course of eating – and also in flavour. Indeed the process was so very onerous that the women who undertook this would regularly implore the heavens for forgiveness for the selfishness of humanity, for God had once decreed that rice and lentils – ready prepared and seasoned – be sent down to earth daily for the nourishment of all. Alas then, that people being what they were (and still are) they soon complained and demanded a more sumptuous diet, as their birthright. And so that was the end of that as the complimentary meal was withdrawn from the divine canteen henceforth, and the hungry hordes continue to be tempered – along with the onions.

So after the pronouncements regarding the princess's dream-vision, the Sultan in his wisdom had entrusted a few of his most valued advisers with some identifying details from his daughter's dream. As expected, most of the men who had approached the palace had been courteously (and occasionally, necessarily discourteously) turned away.

Events were progressing now though and with the rapidly diminishing numbers, the remaining few men were now to be granted an audience with the Sultan himself alongside his vizier, for the final filtering.

---

45. lentils

For the first time the women themselves were now involved, with Roshni, the Sultana and Noura now ensconced behind a specially assembled purdah so the unfolding events could be witnessed. Roshni would have preferred to have been there alone, but there was no way she could have asked her mother not to be present once her heart was set on this. She was also ambivalent about the presence of her cousin, but Noura had been so persuasive, and seeing as the only person who had been privy to her dream in its entirety was Roshni herself, she didn't see that it could cause any harm. It had taken her a while to choose a sign though.

'What bearing can it have, what thou choosest, Roshni, for who shall even see it?' Noura had been with her as she had been surveying the items in her treasure chest, and that familiar feeling came over Roshni of wishing she was alone. With a timely intervention her ayah had stepped forward and discreetly gestured to one of the pendants, and immediately Roshni had smiled and known that this was the one. The women were now sitting behind a carved wooden trellis screen that surrounded the full perimeter of the chambers, so between them they had ample room to both walk and view between the carved and carefully cut away leaves and flowers. They had arrived several minutes prior to the first man being invited though, and upon the Sultana's orders various foods had been prepared on tables behind the screens, should the proceedings provoke a suddenly ravenous appetite. Roshni was sure she wouldn't be able to eat, however, and just sat quietly in one corner, while Noura was trying to find the best vantage point to view the unfolding scene. The Sultana was engaged in a continuous pacing, reminiscent of one of the birds she had tried unsuccessfully on many occasions to free; and after many years of having dispensed with them, she was also choosing today – of all days, thought Roshni – to return to wearing her ankle bracelets. It was of no real consequence, as from in front of the screens they could most probably not be heard, and after so many years of their constant presence – followed by their silence – it was almost strangely comforting to hear their steady rhythmic jangling again.

Roshni could hear the heavy and slow tread of feet entering the room now, mingling with these more obviously advertised steps. The Sultana stopped just where she was then, but Noura now rushed to Roshni's side.

'How thou remainest so composed!' In actuality she was anything but, but saw no reason to disclose her nerves to Noura. Anyway, it was only her father and Feroz, his vizier, who had entered the chambers and seated themselves down. She could hear them speaking in voices too low for her to discern the actual words.

'What need be there for such hysteria in these matters …' she murmured to herself. Then, as if to confront her own fragile equilibrium, she felt a wave of anxiety flood through her body. Oh Lord forgive me, maybe I could feign an illness and be excused from this? I could tell father that it has all been a terrible mistake on my part – I allowed the influences of the poetic forms that I had been reading recently – far in excess of what could be deemed healthy – to overtake my senses and this, accompanied by the changes of the seasons, has led to my haste …

It was Noura who was the one who screamed. The Sultana managed to stay calm, almost unnervingly so as the invisible spirits decided to choose that exact moment to commence their game of dominoes from above. It was the screen nearest Roshni that fell first, clattering to the marble floor, but due to their placement it knocked the one immediately next to it at the same time, and so the circle of destruction began. The women and men too were left motionless now, staring at each over the scene akin to the felling of the forest, more stunned by the noise than seeing each other in unfamiliar mixed company like this. All bar one. He ran quickly and nimbly from his now exposed hiding place under one of the tables of food – his neck festooned with a silk fuchsia scarf that could either have been gifted to him or that he had at one time procured, as he clambered up his newest adventure playground right there.

'Damned monkey!' cried Feroz who would have said more, had he not quickly realised he was in the physical as well as the auditory presence of not one but three ladies of the palace; hence he checked himself before anything further escaped from his lips. He was startled then, looking at her directly like that. It had always been rumoured she was preternaturally beautiful but he had never given it much thought. Despite the circumstances, she returned his look. The Sultana was the one who regained her sense of decorum first and quickly ushered the younger women out of the chambers, leaving the capture of the monkey to the approaching staff who were now arriving. Roshni was now clutching her shawl around her heart as if that might steady her pulse, as they returned to an inner courtyard.

'That be an omen, my light,' said the Sultana in such a low voice that she could have been speaking to herself. She then looked shrewdly at her daughter, though spoke no further.

Noura had excused herself and, despite the two of them now being alone, Roshni didn't feel she had anything to speak of. She tried to rationalise her nerves. It was a life-changing decision so it was no surprise that her fears had manifested in the tangible world in this way. What if she didn't recognise him, or even worse, chose the wrong man? It would no doubt be better to abstain completely from any course of action if this be the case, but how then would her parents respond – particularly her father – after having gone to these lengths to help her find him? She suddenly felt foolish. She either had to have absolute faith in the process or suspend it completely now, while there was still a tiny fragment of time. Blessings be to that monkey – even if this was nothing more than a temporary reprieve, it was still a welcome one. It was very unlike her but she then felt a sudden craving for sweet. Anything with honey would suffice – even downing it neat – and so she called for her ayah who duly obliged and returned a short while later with a silver tray. Roshni took a piece of almond and sherbet cake and, rather than chew, held it in her hands and sucked the sweetness from it first, ignoring her mother's hard look.

'Thou beest sweet enough,' she murmured, but Roshni felt that had all the sugar cane in the world been growing in fields around her, it would not have been enough to satiate her needs. She began licking her fingers, as there was no way to eat this stuff with any decorum. Even if she was a princess.

A short while later with the screens reassembled in their customary manner, and the renegade monkey banished to the animal's enclosure (which he didn't mind) but deprived of his beloved scarf (which he had fought hard to keep), there was silence again in the chamber as the first man was escorted in. After all the preceding disturbances, the Sultan and vizier were again in their seats, and the ladies duly sitting too at their respective vantage points behind the screens, peering through the cut away holes. There was a hook discreetly hanging on the outer side of the screen, from which Roshni had instructed that her chosen amulet be hung from a long chain. From her position behind the screen, all she needed to do was to use one of her embroidery needles to nudge the chain and, on the other side, her father would be able to clearly see the swinging of the amulet behind the back of the man seated before him. And he would then know what it was he must do. Noura had been dismissive. Firstly, not a single precious jewel lay encrusted in the design – just coloured glass – and even the setting itself was a common metal. But this was all overlooked by the Sultana. Her derision had been reserved for what the pendant was actually depicting. Of all the stunning animals in the royal menagerie and the wider jungles themselves, of all the mythological beasts of yore that peacefully coexisted in their treasure chest of a home in Roshni's chambers – yet the one chosen by her daughter? It was universally regarded as the most stupid of all of God's creatures … and who in their right mind would have even thought to have this committed to a solid form? She didn't wish to know how such an object had found its way into her daughter's possession, but here it was being used as a sign for the most important decision of her life.

The Sultana was still consumed by her own thoughts, and not even looking out into the reception when Noura let out an audible gasp. Roshni wished (again) that her cousin could somehow refrain from being quite so demonstrative with her feelings. The man bowed low to the Sultan, while he waited patiently.

Feroz had been vizier and chief confidant for a long time – almost as long as the Sultan himself had been ruler. He looked at his esteemed master and tried to gauge his reaction to this greeting. He was a man who commanded respect and this was largely – and inevitably – attached to the position afforded him by the destiny of his birth. However, what was more precious to him (unlike many of his predecessors) was that he be respected as a man first and the position itself was arbitrary and almost – if the truth be known – a distraction. As much as he loved his Sultan and his loyalty was unquestioned, Feroz had privately often questioned this view. It seemed to him to be a luxury afforded by the position itself – which would always give him worldly rewards – that he wanted to be respected so much as a man first and foremost. Obsequiousness never resided well with him though, and he watched and waited to see his reaction.

Roshni saw this first man prostrate himself before her father, and as she looked closer, she saw the gradually forming view confirmed by looking through a series of other holes. She silently rued that she had to do this as the breaks in her vision were not helping her to form a cohesive picture, and it had been a while since her dream now. Could they not conceive of a material that would afford the looker with an unobscured view, while still preserving their own anonymity? These cutaways were no more than a hindrance, but she made the best of it she could. Next the man stood straight and Roshni was momentarily confused, as what the man was in effect doing was not purely a reverential gesture – if at all – he had in fact been unrolling a carpet onto the marble flooring directly before the Sultan's feet. The unhelpful view had evidently hidden the fact that he had been carrying this with him when he entered. She longed to see the designs on the carpet, which looked thick in texture but intricate in their composition. She was then jolted by a sharp pain under her right breast and had to clasp a hand to her mouth to prevent her from crying out.

'What view dost thou form?' Noura was now brandishing her embroidery needle as a weapon. With her eyes now watering she held her rib cage. Fortunately there were no traces of blood seeping through the dusky pink silk of her chemise. 'Forgive me. I did not intend to harm thee – but what view formest thou?' Roshni removed the offensive weapon from the hands of her wholly unskilled cousin and – at a loss as to where to place this – decided to absently push it through the refined nest of a bun that her tresses had been wound into.

'I cannot discern clearly yet. Please, distract me not but allow me time to look.' If Noura was not enough, Feroz then decided at that moment to step forward right onto the carpet itself! Surely this was not proper etiquette … Her father was standing to the side and was directly facing the man, and once he was upright, the Sultan walked a few short steps to sit on a dais and gestured to the man to join him. If this was not intolerable enough, Feroz then took it upon himself to begin slowly pacing – just within this confined space – hence making it even harder for her to discern any features of the rug itself. She would have to be contented with the fates hopefully affording her a more detailed glance later – for now her father had begun the gentle line of questioning in which she had instructed him herself. It had been in the palace library that they had met to discuss the form the meetings might take. She had taken the opportunity to spend the entire morning there and was engrossed in a poetry anthology when he had swept in. Unlike her mother and her jangling ankle bracelets, he had no need of any formal announcements of his entry into any part of the palace, it seemed. Roshni could go days without physically seeing him, but would then somehow know that he was due to sweep past with all his imperial rigour. And that was the case then, as she remained in solitude at the large round table under the sky-gazing window in the dome. She had roused herself from her reading, allowing herself one final poem and then stopped, stood up to replace the book (she was most fastidious about the ordering of the books, though to her mother's chagrin she cared much less for any similar system for her jewels) before sitting back down. She was right, as within seconds her father appeared. After the formalities of greeting each other, they swiftly got down to business.

'Father, I beg thee, the situation of being in thy presence and within the hallowed inner chambers of the palace be enough of a trial. For there be but one open question that I wish the men to be asked on my humble behalf. I wish them to speak – without prompts or interruptions of any kind – on their personal treatise of love. That is all I wish to hear. From this

154 The Prayer Rug

I am sure that I shalt know who it was that visited my dreamworld.' She didn't dare add the following thought – and wove a spell upon my heart – though she knew that this was what had happened. However, her intimate knowledge of the subtleties of decorum made her keep her counsel carefully. Day by day she was struggling to keep a lid on the aromas; having been marinated since her dream, she was now starting to cook in her own juices and she was sure all was evident to those around her.

Back behind the screen she looked to her side now and heard the hushed tones of her mother and cousin appraising the man's gait and bearing – so altogether oblivious to her boiling away, like all the other chickpeas in that poem that had described her particular plight. The man was speaking now. She registered somewhere that his voice was deep and he spoke quickly – very quickly – but the flavours were bland and suited to the restrained palates of the ascetic and not the regal banquet to which she was accustomed. No. He was not the one. She shook her head at her two companions and the Sultana signalled discreetly to her husband by a series of stamps of her feet. He allowed the man to finish and then asked the visitor to speak. Thank goodness Feroz had shut up now. The situation was stressful enough without the vizier deciding to take up precious cooking time with his own entirely uncalled for recipe. All three of the women had been shocked upon seeing Feroz so close up. Roshni was merely reacting to the debacle of the collapsing screens she felt she had created, whereas Noura's reaction was more of the thrill of the unexpected. She privately thought it unlikely that Roshni's chosen one could be anything close to as attractive as this man … already in the royal court … From thereon, the situation improved dramatically, as he stopped posing upon the visitor's carpet as if it were his own personal podium too. Roshni stood at that moment and, taking her seat with her, rushed to the other side of the perimeter. Then, placing the chair down, she carefully climbed onto it. Her head was still below the top of the screen and she leant forwards to see through one of the slightly larger carved openings at the top, clasping the fingers of both hands inside the holes of petals that too had been chiselled away. This was it. The treatise of love. And it had begun with that carpet. To this day she could tell you nothing of what the man said, and the only real detail of his looks she could recall was the voluminous dark cloak, giving the appearance of an aubergine. Her mind was empty, but she was immediately intoxicated by the seasonings that swirled themselves around her. As if God Herself was holding the ladle, first it was the fire of the chilli that started in the base of her spine before radiating up her back: not a subtle or refined feeling – she struggled not to gasp in rapture – but it was what it was. Next she felt the turmeric – tingling still, but running red through the veins in her hands and up her arms until it reached her heart. A more composed elation befell her then. It seemed like there was a side dish, nay a mere accompaniment, that had made itself onto the menu just then. The cooling lashings of grated cucumber and yoghurt were now relaxing her head, as if her crown itself was being massaged by gentle fingers, attempting to comb themselves through her hair but finding themselves encumbered. 'Yes,' she whispered and pulled the embroidery needle from her bun and in her haste her long tresses came tumbling down onto her shoulders. Just as she wished.

'Forgive me, Your Serene Highness. I know those screens have been erected for a reason, but your modesty does not reside in your hair, your face or your physical presence. I feel sure that you will understand. Your crowning glory it certainly is though. Now that preening imbecile has stopped, I hope you may be able to see the manifestation of my spirit more clearly.'

What? He couldn't possibly have said this aloud. From this vantage point she could see the carpet clearly. It was the colour of a golden lion and had a lotus at its centre, with various designs from budding and semi-formed flowers to individual petals emanating outwards. Around this was a waved border, again of petals and abstracted natural designs, followed by a much harder and straight-edged border, before the fringes of the rug at the two ends. Rather than being left loose, these had been carefully knotted in a series of patterns that were almost as intricate as the weaving itself. And they weren't yet complete. The far side fringe was only partially knotted and it was then that she knew.

She climbed down quickly and hurried back over to the other side. Noura, still engaged with checking out the hot vizier paid her no heed, but the Sultana immediately registered her haste and her flushed cheeks. She touched her daughter's arm.

'By the light of the inner sanctums, there be several other men to see! It is not obligatory to form any decision before the sun doth set on this illumined day - thy chosen sign was but a possible means of alerting thy father, but that is all.' Her words not so much fell on Roshni's deaf ears as floated in the air – and, hitting the tangible body of her intellect, just evaporated. Could her mother of all people really be urging caution in matters of the heart? How had this role reversal occurred? She shook her off and with tresses loose and embroidery needle in hand she hurried to her original look-out post to nudge the chain of her trusted talisman into action.

9

It had sounded like an owl, but as it was the middle of the day and she had managed to doze off right after finishing the chapter, Howra reasoned that it must have been a pigeon. That was one good thing. There was the odd tree to both the back and front of her block that were preferred by the birds, so she was often serenaded by a personal chorus (she liked to think) just for her. She checked the time and saw that she would have to hurry now, to make her way to the professor's next engagement. A few moments later she was boarding a bus that had luckily arrived on time to take her to her local Tube station. As she took her seat, she wondered what line of demarcation lay between her particular actions and those of a stalker. Well, she was neither in love nor had the intention of causing any harm, so that was the main criteria right there out of the window. If someone had asked her though what her actual motivation was, she would have struggled. This was the difficulty. She could speak to Mick about these things and he understood her completely: maybe not the detailed context but certainly the intent. It would have been a struggle to explain this to anyone else though. She thanked the heavens for the millionth time that she had been assigned to his caseload for individual support, and not been referred to some form of group support programme. She hated groups. How on earth would she have coped with that? She would have either shut up shop or refused to go after a while, and where would that have left her?

No, as long as she had Mick she knew she would be okay. Her reporting times would be reducing again soon. She knew that and didn't like to think of it. She knew it was right. It was the system after all, and it was a sign she was making progress if she was being allowed to attend with less frequency. The only way she might be able to see more of him would be to reoffend, and she knew that was total stupidity – even at the time she knew it was a massive transgression. There was nothing there in her previous life to indicate any pattern of behaviour – it really was a first offence and she knew that with a community sentence she had got off lightly. It hardly felt like a punishment though, the external process. All offenders will eventually be physically released, but it's much harder to be discharged from the endless film reel that was running in your own head. That was the real sentence.

It was a tiny museum and she nearly walked past it, mistaking it for a coffee shop as the entrance was just to the side. She walked through the glass doors, waited in line as there was a short queue, and gave her name to the young woman with the tablet. There was time before the talk was due to begin to explore the show, and she was momentarily torn between settling down with her book in the coffee shop and wandering some more. No, she'd had enough of reading for today. She needed to take advantage of where she was and the book could be read on her journey home. If her wandering mind would let her. It had no real connection to the professor but maybe it would do her good to go off track a bit?

She walked into a dark studio space and saw a series of eight large screens arranged in a line on the wall. Each screen had matching embroidered backdrops of wall-hangings and flooring, and seated on a variety of stools, crates and boxes were eight different street musicians – some with instruments and some without. A woman in one of the central screens was singing and playing the guitar, while in the other screens the remaining performers were turned to face her and were gently swaying or tapping along.

A conjoined but also separate series of virtual performers – and an attentive audience in one. It looked like one of the woven backdrops had made its way out of the screen and into the centre of the dark viewing space, as there were a series of crates and large cushions where a few visitors were sitting down and enjoying the musical performances. She thought the professor would definitely not approve. Nothing rarefied or of beauty about these creations. They were just coarsely woven and rough to sit on, though they did the job of covering the floor and recreating the feeling of an eastern marketplace well enough. Nothing could detract from the music though. She decided to ignore the rug and sit on a colourful dais to the side, close her eyes and just listen.

To begin with there were various intrusions. The cushion behind her was lumpy, and she couldn't relax until manoeuvring it – and herself – several times. No sooner had she got herself settled by pummelling it into submission and shutting her eyes again, than she became aware of a draught. It wasn't a momentary gust of a door opening and then closing but a slight yet persistent irritant most probably coming from an air vent above or something. It was no good. She was going to have to move. She knew there was more space at the other end – and hopefully this would be outside the trajectory of the draught. She had been fidgeting around so much she hadn't looked up at the screens for a while. The song was continuing but the screens were all empty of the musicians now, with the woven rugs taking centre stage, their harsh horizontal lines provoking a sudden pain in her temples.

It started on the top left. It was like an invisible hand, just off screen, had found the end thread – and for reasons known only to itself had started to tug at this. The rug very slowly began to unravel and behind this there was nothing but a black-and-white snowstorm. Howra forgot everything: everything she was there to do, wondering what the tea in the cafe would be like, her hopes of finally speaking to the professor, what would happen next in the book. Instead she found herself rushing up to the screen. She started by sliding her hands in the opposite direction to the gradual disintegration, trying to reverse the inevitable. Nothing was happening to halt things though, so she thought she would have to push harder in order to overpower this invisible hand. Some hope. It was as if it had accomplices now as she saw the rug was being tugged at from several directions, up and down, then left and right – at some points partially disappearing from the screen entirely – and the unravelling – well, it just continued, as now the bottom right of the rug was being subjected to the same thing and she saw how she was powerless to stop this. Howra began to cry. She flung herself at the screen, just desperate now to try to cover it herself, now that the rug was looking like it was unable to offer any resistance. The unwound yarn with all its kinks and snags was being wound round the screen itself now. And around her too. How was that happening? She felt it digging into her skin as if it was a fisherman's rope – around and around and around ... gradually though she began to feel no sensations ...

* * *

She knew that the winding had continued for a time, and after a while she just gave up trying to fight. Short of having a knife on her, there was no way she would be able to free herself from these restraints, and there was always the possibility that this might have injured her even more. Even more? Injured her in yet another way maybe. And what would a child be doing with a knife anyway? With neither fight nor flight at her disposal now, there was only one way to protect herself. It was a flight of sorts, though not a physical one. The cords were tight round her now and she remembered the lesson from science in school. Had she been tested in class on this just a week later, she was sure she would have had no clue. Her page would have been filled with either her customary doodles or a likely highly imaginative – but wholly factually inaccurate – answer. She wasn't being tested in a classroom though. And it wasn't her teacher's voice she was hearing either. The strains of acoustic guitar and female vocals had segued to another performer. She could now hear accordions and tablas and what sounded like a faint accompaniment – of bells? She couldn't be sure, but it didn't matter as these were merely in the background now – reassuring enough and taking her away from what was happening with the rug – as it was the narrative she was listening to.

But why *his* voice?

Well, who else was there that could lend the subject matter the necessary quiet but unquestionable authority? The gravitas from a lifetime of detailed observation, in order to achieve one thing and one thing only – the truth of life itself, no matter how humble the creature living it.

162   The Prayer Rug

... For many creations of outstanding beauty must start their journeys in the humblest of circumstances.
And before the journey can commence ... the conditions must be absolutely perfect.
It needs the onset of the warm weather for the white mulberry trees to come into leaf but, once they have done so, this tiny egg, no larger than a peppercorn which was lifeless before its food was ready, begins – finally to live. The hatched caterpillar nourishes itself upon the mulberry leaves until, when it has grown larger, it undergoes a process of moulting several times, until it finally emerges pale and naked. And then ... of its own accord, it spins silk from its tiny mouth around any intruding twigs until it has made a narrow cocoon.
In which it buries itself.
Thread by thread she slowly weaves her cocoon, for she knows this is as necessary as it is inevitable.
For this shall be her home and her sanctuary ...
During this most vulnerable of states, the cocoon itself provides a vital layer of protection while the pupa remains almost entirely motionless.

Howra knew she was safe now. She just had to stay in her cocoon and she was safe. It was her body – a body – it was not her. She was safe. So she kept weaving and winding (and bleeding and binding) until the entire rug had been pulled apart by these multiple, invisible hands.

... Yet the natural world is full of predators.
Even in the cocoon the silkworm must be vigilant to any potential threats. Though what it can do about them is almost nothing.
For there are many reptiles which will feed on the silkworm, given half a chance.
The most pernicious of these... being lizards ...
... and snakes ...

It seemed like she was rushing through the exhibits and that wasn't like her. Oh, she was back in the other exhibition now was she? The one with the

The Prayer Rug 163

yards of hanging textiles from ceiling to floor, and meticulously researched information about the regions the designs hailed from. She had been resolute in not attending this one so maybe ... she had changed her mind? She wasn't at all sure about the layout. It seemed like she was running through a life-size plan for an electric circuit board and every time she brushed past some fabric she received a resulting shock on her skin and felt her hairs stand up. Speaking of which ... without thinking she grabbed the nearest passing roll of material and threw it round her. Yes, like a toga, that the Roman goddesses all wore. That was decent, wasn't it? That was dignified. She didn't want the unsuspecting public thinking she had left home without *any* thought to her appearance. She might be a silkworm but she still had to retain her modesty if she was out in public like this now. But that wasn't right. She was supposed to have transformed into a moth by now, hadn't she? If she was out? Had she escaped prematurely? What would that mean? She started to wonder if perhaps it was quite loud in there for a museum – and quite smelly too if the truth be known. And dirty. Maybe there was some kind of film playing – yes, that would explain it – one of those interactive exhibits. It was a shame that kind reassuring voice from the sky had stopped speaking to her though. She had liked that voice. She had felt safe when she heard that voice. It had given her a story you see. A story to make sense of the world. Her world. We all needed stories. Humans were entirely stupid and egocentric, thinking that storytelling was the preserve of them and them alone. How many of them could say as an objectively verifiable truth that they had heard the voice of God? Yes, there would be a few who might claim this – and fewer still of these would be genuine (and those who were would actually know the higher intelligence of the animals) but it was within the animal kingdom you see, where this could happen en masse, with no hysteria or weakness in spirit and where for the most part it was heard, it was revered, but then we all got on with our lives as ordained.

    Not for us the distractions of ambition and accumulation. A silkworm was a silkworm. It knew what its role was from birth, and from thereon in, its whole purpose was to fulfil this. It didn't expect accolades for spinning a cocoon larger than its friends, with a finer silk or in a more desirable neighbourhood of mulberries; it had no cognisance of this. A cocoon was a cocoon. It was a temporary abode for the minutest speck of time and after that it could be brushed aside. A silkworm was not a honeybee or a water lily or a magpie. It was attuned to its role from birth so the roles of others held no envy for it.

But just who was she?

It was just then that she sensed danger. The hairs all over her body stood on end again and this time there was no stimulus of an electric shock, either. She felt eyes on her.

They were the reptiles.

She kept running – though it felt like she was crawling. There was someone who would help her – who had brought her here, from when she was that tiny peppercorn-sized egg that the divine voice had reminded her of. Where was she? She would know what to do. She would understand the predators for she was a much larger silkworm than she. On her hands and knees now she crawled. The floor seemed like a fine dirt or sand rather than the smooth texture of the leaves she was accustomed to living amidst, and at occasional intervals she would come across a truly repulsive puddle of sorts. The hairs seemed to be picking up this dirt the more she moved and she had no means by which to shake this off, her arms and legs appearing to have become incapacitated now. The thought of the accumulating dirt and foul fluid was somehow more distressing than how she no longer appeared to have control of her limbs. Her skin was thin and porous. How could she help but imbibe this rather than the nutrients of her food of choice from the sacred tree? She was a silkworm. Her job was to spin the most beautiful vestigial yarn around her, but how could she now do this if she was contaminated? Any woven output would be severely impaired – and this was if she could even weave at all. Her cocoon would be nothing more than a discarded – or maybe even entirely crushed – shell of a snail that had unwisely crawled out from the leaves after the monsoons – and then been flattened by an inattentive monkey. And she would be no more than a red stain on the ground, slowly being washed away by the returning rains until no trace of her ever having lived would remain.

After the numbness came the pain. For pain is an inescapable part of metamorphosis. She knew the one who brought her here could not be found, for she herself was nothing more than a larger silkworm than she, with no functioning cocoon of her own, let alone a fully realised transition into a moth. Her limbs had grown back and though she could now feel herself returning to where she was, she was still momentarily unable to move them.

Run.

It mattered not where to. Just to run was enough.

She was aware she was colliding with people, but with her hastily snatched and assembled armoury around her she felt she was safe for now. Surely nothing else could happen. She was running up a waterfall of cascading colours and designs that were making her tail spin. What – her *tail* spin? She really had no idea of who or what she was now, just that she had to get out of the bazaar and find her mum somewhere. All these grown-ups and none of them was her mum. Or anyone's mum. Why was the market always full of snakes and lizards working on these stalls? It would only ever be women buying the bangles and ribbons and yards of fabric. If she had spoken the language better she would have asked for help. But she was a human (and a girl) so she couldn't speak reptile – and even if she could, they wouldn't have listened.

Just keep running.

And that's when she saw it.

The stall was at the end of an alley and several times the size of most of the others in the market. When she saw it was both a dead end and there was no sign of her mother still, she was going to turn back around and run again. But something held her attention.

She slowed down and walked closer.

It seemed as if there were hundreds of them. Some were round and fringed, others rectangular with no fussy borders or ornamentation to distract from their pure functionality. The largest were spread in the centre of the entrance, piled high, but there was a customer there who was obviously interested in one near the bottom of one of the piles. Howra wrapped her toga round her more carefully, now that she was no longer running. She

166   The Prayer Rug

didn't want to be seen, so covered both her head and lower part of her face with the expanse of material, leaving just her eyes. Yes. She was completely invisible now. She then had a sudden impulse to cover her eyes too, so she wrapped the material tightly around her head as well. Her toga was evidently very special, for in addition to rendering her completely invisible, her sight was not in the least impaired by the material substance itself. She walked up to the solitary customer and it looked like solitary vendor.

It was the customer who was intriguing her. With his sandy hair and western clothing he was obviously a stranger and she was worried that he wouldn't be able to communicate with the vendor. Maybe she could offer to help? She quickly dismissed that stupid thought. She was finally in disguise and here she was immediately drawing attention to herself. She drew closer until she was just behind the customer and clearly in the sightline of the vendor. He paid no attention to her of course, but quickly proffered the man a seat and a chai, as if sensing that a significant sale might be on the cards. A European was always a great opportunity to potentially treble the takings – or even more. The customer took a seat on a wooden stool to the side, and a young boy – perhaps even younger than Howra – now appeared with a small silver tray, a teapot and two cups. He actually could have been the same age or even older, but he was so slight and gaunt it was hard to tell. He set the tray down on an even smaller wooden stool to the side, and then jumped up to assist the stall owner with displaying the wares to the customer. Howra began to realise that the customer was indeed able to communicate in a basic form of Urdu, but there still seemed to be an impediment to him making himself understood.

'*Bhai sahib*[46], he's as deaf as a *dhenda*[47].' It was the boy who was now pouring the chai into one of the cups, and handing it to the customer. He took it with a smile and indicated he would just have to shout – or gesture at him. The boy then poured the tea into the second cup but left it there on the tray as the vendor was now talking loudly in an animated patter about the carpets in their midst, while simultaneously untying one from a

---

46. polite form of address for a man
47. post, stick

rolled stack that Howra presumed were the most precious. And the most pricey. He removed a white linen covering from the top and she saw a dazzling silk weave displayed before them. The customer had had the cup in his hands and was inhaling the flavours of roses, cloves and cardamom before he sipped – the fragrances were so strong that Howra could smell these too, despite all her senses being cloaked – but he now hastily put the cup down. He slowly got to his feet and walked round the perimeter of the dais, piled high with the other rugs beneath this, as if he needed to verify what it was he was seeing. He then leant forward to gently touch, just the edge, of the material and then seemingly made his mind up very quickly, grabbed the linen covering and replaced it on top of the carpet. The vendor smiled and Howra saw his betel-stained teeth clearly for the first time. She guessed they were going to haggle now; this was what usually happened in these places. Prices were never fixed, despite what any (rare) signage might say, and she had seen people very adeptly bring the prices down by almost half at times, pointing out any real or imaginary faults or defects in the goods they really wanted. This was going to be a prolonged and interesting shouting match she was sure. But no, her expectations were confounded once again, as the customer agreed to the full asking price without batting an eyelid, and pulled a small wad of notes from a jacket pocket. The vendor's smile grew even wider – and even more stained, if that were possible. He curtly summoned the boy to start rolling up the rug again but she saw the boy hesitate here – just for a second. The man's smile quickly vanished and she had a horrible foreboding of what that might mean. Luckily the customer quickly diverted the man's attention by rolling up the carpet himself and handing over the money, and once this was in the man's hands he seemed happy once more. He even stood up and offered to tie the carpet back up again, so it stayed rolled and easy to carry, but the customer was barely containing something himself now. He swatted the man's hand away before he could touch it again and carried it away in his arms, out of the stall and back through the market.

The last thing Howra heard was the boy's voice calling out to her.

'You didn't drink your chai, sister – that cup was for you. You didn't drink your tea.'

The boy had seen her.

This was too much for the man.

The last thing Howra saw was the large stick in the man's hands, his face contorting as he beat all the rugs that were hanging up, clearly on view, the dust being violently expelled deep from within the woven fibres with every strike.

This was the open door to her freedom.

* * *

'They call it *loo*[48] over there. You'd think that the breeze would give respite from the heat, but all it does is move the blazing hot air around – like a fan in a furnace. Some stillness in the air would be more welcome.' I felt her hands all over me, penetrating deep, starting from the top of my head, across my shoulders and down my back, as if the extraordinary heat itself was not sufficient and it was only the addition of her touch that could have the ultimate healing effect. It felt so good that I willed it to go on forever, though to my sadness I knew that it couldn't. No matter, I would just enjoy it while it lasted and forget about all the stresses of the day. I had no idea what she was saying – I was barely listening and they were random words as always – not just with her but with all of them, but combined with that additional sense we have been gifted, you could put it all together. If you really wanted. The sweet or sourness in the voice – no matter how well disguised, their physical movements or facial expressions were nothing compared to this. There were also the fragrances though and I could tell that great care had been taken with those. It smelled of roses in the room – real roses – though I couldn't actually see any. In fact it smelled more of roses than any actual roses I had ever encountered. I was sure that all the roses I came across these days – though they looked as beautiful and delicate as they always had – were somehow devoid of their fragrance. There were even some I had seen that grew without thorns – can you imagine? Give

---

48. very hot, dry summer wind that blows over plains of northern India and Pakistan

me the aromas and I'll take the possibility that they may draw blood too. You can't have one without the other. Well, apparently you can but in no way could that be called the real thing.

So yes, they all added to the picture but it was no more than a confirmation of what I had already discerned, and if there was any conflict here I knew immediately which sense it was I would trust, my go-to whenever there was dissonance. *Don't stop now* ... She had momentarily removed her hands – she could stop talking if she wanted but I didn't want her to stop touching me.

When she started I thought the noise would have disturbed me. It didn't exactly add to the overall ambience if you know what I mean. She had taken me upstairs, and although I thought I knew the building well after all this time, it was a room I had never been in before. I felt like I was in a hallowed inner sanctum. It wasn't just anyone that would be allowed in here, I sensed, but we had been together for a while now, we had. If they could do something about the noise it would have been pure bliss – but it didn't detract from the overall experience. How could it? It was a sensory delight from start to finish, and after what I had been through there was no one who could tell me that I didn't deserve it – *need* it even. The only thing that came close to her touch was the softness of those towels around me – I could have buried myself in those for a while. Actually I wouldn't have minded being buried in them for real if that were a possibility.

Anyway, there I was, completely immersed in the experience and there was only a knock at the door wasn't there. I mean – what? This had better be good. She looked across and I wanted to tell her to ignore it – whoever it was would just go away soon enough. Short of the building burning down (and given the heat in here we would barely notice – that would be a way to go) there was nothing else that would count as a bone fide emergency in my book. Of course, she left me where I was and headed over to the door. Given my current state I decided not to follow her. I heard a male voice speaking to her and recognised it. His voice was low but there was agitation in the air; I could sense that much, though what the exact cause of this was escaped me – and I didn't much care. A few seconds later it sounded like the conversation had come to a close, and I heard his heavy footsteps walking away. She didn't immediately come back to me – and I thought about calling out to her – but even this seemed like too much of an effort now. I decided I might as well take a closer look at my surroundings, but it was too much to contemplate. I closed my eyes, and in the absence of her healing hands just let sleep take me instead.

* * *

Coach was asleep when I came back in and I looked at his sandy coloured hair which was gleaming now. He had better not be getting any ideas that he could stay there, but as there were other more pressing matters to attend to now, I just left him where he was, went over to the basin to wash my hands and made my way downstairs.

 He was still very unsettled. Given his line of work, I would have thought he would have been able to take this in his stride, but evidently not. He was standing still in the hallway at the bottom of the stairs, watching me as I fixed my hair as I descended. This was annoying me – I hadn't pinned it up properly and it was impairing my sight. I was having to constantly toss my head around, like an angry mare that hadn't been broken in, to be able to see what I was doing, but after a while I just let my hands feel their way and do the work. I was going to tell him not to worry, but prior experience told me that he needed to work through his agitation in his own time. It was fortunate I knew him as well as I did. We'd been together for years now. To any casual observer he would have seemed quite composed I guess. But it was there nonetheless. It was in his face. Like the flutter of the wings of a moth that had managed to fly right under his eyelid, it was his right one that would start its involuntary blinking – normally not more than a few times in succession. It was his personal hazard warning light for those around him – though most people seemed largely oblivious. It was good of him to have developed one though. With others it was always a question of uneducated guesswork to begin with. Some would either have no visible 'tell' at all, and would just bleed all over the carpet whenever their own internal threshold had been crossed, and with others it would be so subtle that only the most observant could see it. And then, seeing as it was only the first stage, the entry point into the psyche of another, you had to know what to do. Or more tellingly, what not to do. I wondered whether that was an innate skill or just one I had developed by necessity – I had never been too sure. Anyhow it was immaterial; his was a clear one and I knew him well enough to know what not to do. I paused on the first step as otherwise it was impossible to reach him.

'I thought you'd have gone back to your good woman by now, Shirley, what are you doing still hanging round here?' As soon as I touched his cheek, the moth immediately settled down, as if resigned to its fate, its wings still open but no longer desperate to escape. His eyes narrowed and I moved closer to him now as I was at the bottom of the steps. Closer but somehow further away. He took a polite step backwards and to the side so he was not obstructing my way, and followed as I walked into the front room. He waited until I had sat down before doing so himself and I wondered (as I always wondered) how such a gallant man had managed to be born into this particular era. And not a self-serving form of gallantry either. It was who he was, pure and simple, and you could disregard the outer shell for what it was too.

'You're right here, ma'am, so there's nowhere for me to be heading.' I allowed him his default of excessive formality – as I always did in times of trouble. He seemed to find it comforting: a source of steadiness in a volatile and uncertain world. The clearly delineated verbal boundary wasn't replicated anywhere else though. I was sitting on an armchair at an angle to him – on the end of the sofa. He was easily within touching distance. I reached out and in the absence of any hair – sandy or otherwise – to run my hands through, I held his face as if it were a precious crystal ball and leant forward to kiss him on the forehead. It wasn't really what I wanted to do. I wanted to kiss his mouth, breathe his air and give him my own. To my sadness, I hadn't yet been able to do so. It was too sensual – okay too sexually laden a gesture for me to contemplate. If I ever did, it would have to be when any flares of that most obvious of attractions had subsided between us. The gesture would then be pure and could not be misinterpreted. So now really wasn't the right time. I disregarded the implication in his response and continued.

'Just to add to the other events of the day, I have no idea what Coach was doing. All the years we've lived here and he's avoided that pond like it was the harbinger of death itself. And today he goes and jumps straight in.' After Shirley had met my eyes, I continued to hold his gaze for a few calculated seconds, and then let go of his head and moved back into my chair. I knew how finely calibrated these things were.

'He must have known something was about to happen. It was his canine way of attracting our attention, to do something totally out of character like that. And people say dogs are creatures of habit. Yes, until the habitual itself is no more, then it all goes out the window. Or into the pond.

'Well it was nothing a bathe and blow dry couldn't fix. I thought he might have objected to the noise of the hairdryer, but he didn't actually seem to mind. Taking him upstairs was the least I could do. Under the circumstances.' Shirley glanced back at me then, but like the consummate professional that he was, he not only quickly averted his eyes but also got to his feet. He began pacing again and staring out of the large windows which overlooked the gardens to the front. Other than the muffled sound of his steps on the thick carpet and his barely perceptible breathing, he remained silent. And so did I. I sank back into the cushion as I let the high-backed armchair do the job it had been created for, and mould into the frame of my neck, shoulders and back – though I'd have preferred his hands to do that job ... I let my gaze become soft before I slowly closed my eyes. I had learned this from a sadhu back in Rajasthan, oh so many years ago ... We all had our own ways – if we had any sense. I had mine. And Shirley had his (and I dare say Coach had his ways too).

I was briefly aware of the ticking of the clock ... and then my own breathing – before even that too faded away. I couldn't have told you how much time had elapsed until the words formed from somewhere and I received the guidance of what it was that we were to do.

* * *

Giles recalled a conversation he had once had with an unofficial matriarch of a desert tribe. It was through an interpreter, of course, as he was completely lost when it came to these regional dialects – as were even most native city dwellers in these lands these days. The gist of it had been her unwavering belief that everything was recorded. Forget CCTV or your digital fingerprint – that meant nothing in this context. She didn't mean minutes of meetings, or testimonies from friends, or anything that was tangible and somehow therefore more 'real', she meant every thought unsaid, every desire suppressed, every word uttered in private, every deal sealed behind closed curtains; it was all recorded in the eternal and never-ending tapestry of creation of the universe. He watched her own brown and bony fingers working away, as her sparkling eyes darted constantly from his to the young man's who was translating, never once needing to look down at the work being produced, as if her faith was enough now and her technical skill just a mere detail. He asked the young man to ask her, if she was so sure there was a great plan being woven as we all thought and desired and regretted (and whatever else we did in our lives that we hoped no one else would ever know), what was the role of her own prolific work? Surely this was then redundant?

As soon as she had been asked the question, her face broke out into a prolonged but gentle smile. She carefully placed her work down to the side of her and paused for a few seconds before she spoke. Giles waited patiently for the man to speak once she had finished. She was so expressive in her words, it was as if she was willing him to understand her, beyond the shackles of their respective tongues.

'The master weaver is the creator, the producer, the fashioner. He has the template or the pattern for the tapestry, but all of humanity has a share in its production. It is up to each of us which patterns we choose to embroider, and which we leave as faint outlines, and then how we choose to embroider – with a deft light touch, with shading and colour, as directed and in unison with the other patterns around us – or do we override these, stitching across our boundaries, using our needles as weapons rather than tools of the beauty of creation? No matter what we do though, rest assured that whatever our pitiful, human contributions, the ultimate creator, She shall always be aware of who took what share in both its production – and its desecration. This shall be so, regardless of what the world and its minions choose to see. Everything is thus being recorded, whether we choose to accept it or not.'

He had no idea why this largely suppressed memory had chosen this inopportune moment to make itself known again, but such were the vagaries of conscience. But was it conscience though? Surely he had had no choice in the matter? This was a section of the tapestry that had been filled in by a hand most definitely other than his own; he was just the one reaping the possible temporary rewards. And any future consequences. He had travelled as fast as he had dared. As he pondered the lady's words from easily a decade ago, he tried to do a rough summation in his mind: Well, he was no saint, and he was sure there would be many who would judge his chosen occupation in the world of women and their handicrafts as niche and indulgent at best, and not befitting of serious academic consideration (and more than a bit weird) at worst. He had done no great harm in his life, no serious addictions – well maybe a few but nothing that really counted on a rockstar scale of things. He had loved and been loved, though that all felt a long time ago now. Another random memory chose to rise to the surface at that moment. She had been a colleague from another department, and they had been doing some cross-disciplinary work. How siloed the world of learning had become, that this was seen as something irregular – *dangerous* even. An aberration rather than something to be encouraged. Her faculty had been science, and she had wanted to undertake an in-depth analysis of the fibres of one of his most recent, but simultaneously most ancient, acquisitions. They had ended up taking their interfaculty project a bit too far though. It was right after his divorce.

It was her habit of just dropping in curios at moments when he might have preferred some silence.

'Did you know,' she said and he could feel her hot breath in his right ear, 'that the tongue of the woodpecker is three times longer than its beak.' He then felt the soft, wet trail of her own tongue and lips, traversing his neck, then his chest, then his abdomen …

'And when the woodpecker hits the bark at ten times the force that would kill a human,' she continued, 'the tongue wraps around the brain and cushions it, so the woodpecker can do the woodpecking …'

So no, there was nothing really heroic in his life.

He was pretty sure no one would think back to any encounters with him and feel anything beyond a mild affection, but he was no murderer, he loved his work with a quiet but enduring passion, and would occasionally buy a cup of coffee for a beggar on the street – so he wasn't a bad man. Absolutely not. So why then was he now so anxious to desperately pull any records from his memory banks, of just how far from being a bad man he could reasonably claim to be? Was any even modest good now to be unstitched before his eyes, by the actions resulting from a moment of madness?

None of the previous rules seemed to apply now. Neither the relatively minor ones – such as any semblance of adherence to the Highway Code – nor the more serious ones to do with burglary, and the possibility of some form of criminal record as recompense for what he had done. The other rules he could barely bring himself to even consider right now, for while he took complete responsibility (he had to) for the originating act of taking the carpet, what then transpired was rather out of his hands. As if the transgression of this one rule had led to a break in the certainty of *all* rules to which he might be subject, so of course he hoped he would outrun the law, despite all the evidence that the beautiful Mrs Luscombe and the not-so-beautiful Shirley would have at their disposal.

To start with it was nothing like controlling any other car he had ever driven. Driving was just a very occasional inconvenience for him; he used public transport when this made more sense, and his manual car was really for occasional journeys not well served by any other means, such as today. He had no interest in cars beyond this, as symbols of his manhood – or anything else. He considered himself a good driver, had had the good fortune or necessary competence over the years to be able to evade several accidents, and the rare couple he had had were not his fault. This was an entirely different vehicle and he wondered who out of the two (both equally unlikely) potential drivers had taken it out the most? Of course it could have been Mrs Luscombe's father as this was evidently not a recent acquisition in the family, but it was hard to be sure. All *he* knew for sure was that he had never experienced anything quite like it.

176 The Prayer Rug

In no particular order, the collective lack of reference points in his prior experiences included (but were not exclusively confined to) the following: Firstly, he was no longer in the reasonably clearly demarcated boundaries of the ground, with its lanes, road markings and culturally accepted directions of travel and signage. Up here ... up here there was nothing. Nada. Nope – nothing to guide him whatsoever. As a consequence, once the carpet had tentatively hovered above the floor in the study and invited him on board, it had taken him quite a while to get going *anywhere*. Well, what it had actually done was formed a concertina effect of stairs from one end leading him up to a steady platform. He hadn't given it a moment's thought, hadn't engaged the limitations of his rational mind at all before stepping on board. Once he had done that, the carpet had stayed completely still until he had sat comfortably and cross-legged in its centre (he had of course first removed his shoes). It had then smoothly edged towards the garden doors and waited patiently until Giles had crawled over and opened them, before it made its escape out into the open air once more. It was slightly too wide, however, so had deftly rippled its outer edges to reduce its surface area, and on doing so, cleanly exited via the doors without damaging its precious surface in any way. Thinking about this, now they were miles away from the scene, Giles couldn't see how he could even be accused of theft. None of this had happened of his volition – if anything he was some form of willing accomplice to his own abduction, though how he could possibly explain this to anyone would no doubt be a challenge. Least of all to a court of law.

Once out in the open, the carpet almost began to exude a form of joy. Firstly, it went straight over to a part of the lawns where the sun was unbroken by the shade of the multifarious trees and then – still hovering a couple of feet off the ground – stretched itself out to its full dimensions (which now seemed to well exceed those of what it was indoors) ironing out any ripples, then slowly rotating 360 degrees as if to ensure the full effect of the sunlight on its face. Or body. Or whatever. On its way to the lawn they had glided past the sensory garden and Giles had inhaled the familiar, now almost intoxicating, aromas and he was perilously close to being overpowered by them as he felt his eyelids close, but he then (again) felt a sudden sting, this time on the back of his arm as a piece of glass hit him once more with full force. By the time he looked down though, the shard was nowhere to be seen and must have fallen back down to the path from whence it came. After completing its slow circle, the carpet then remained motionless before rising up high into the air. It was a steady trajectory so he wasn't frightened, but when he looked down over the sides and saw the tops of the trees of the arboretum surrounding the home, he did wonder how much higher they might go.

It was then that the carpet paused in mid-air. It was completely steady, even though Giles could feel the gentle currents of the breeze around them. Despite being completely open to the elements, it was somehow far more buffered against these than any light aircraft would have been. It was then he realised the reason for the pause.

The carpet was waiting.

For instruction.

From him.

This complicated matters somewhat, for if he had up till then convinced himself of being nothing more than a largely passive passenger, if he was now being charged with directing the carpet, it would be hard for him to claim to be an innocent – and somehow accidental accomplice. Anyhow, he decided that this was not the time for a philosophical interior dialogue on the matter, and thought about what to do. The first obvious difficulty was that there were no evident manual controls. Right. He would need to experiment. How about words? Open sesame and all that seemed to do the trick in all those ancient fables, so maybe that was the steer needed here?

'Err, straight ahead. Walk.'

What? Walk? This was a carpet and not a horse, though he had never ridden one of those either. Not that that would have helped much. He could almost imagine the carpet responding to him. *What do you think I am mate, a bloody horse or something*? Or *Master, I respectfully remind thee that I do not belong to any equine ... lineage.* Great. He was giving the carpet a personality now. He absently started to wonder if anthropomorphism applied to animals, why there wasn't an equivalent term that applied to inanimate objects, that had somehow evolved some highly animate properties? Objectomorphism? Anyhow, all these ruminations were not exactly helping with the matter at hand, and the carpet was still patiently awaiting instructions in mid-air. He tentatively stood and – similarly to the sensation of sitting – he felt what seemed like solid ground beneath his feet, as he took a couple of steps forward to the front of the carpet. To be honest he wasn't entirely sure it was even the front, as there was no indication in the patterns on the rug that there was a right way up, in any of the four possible directions.

Now what? His voice held no power or gravitas up here in the rarefied air, so maybe he could be less prescriptive – less depressingly human? He stood as near to the edge of the carpet as he dared, slowly put his arms in front of him at shoulder level … and was then immediately put off by seeing a cluster of doves sitting high in the branches of a tree to his left, all staring intently at him, it seemed. This was not at all helpful. He immediately felt as if he had stumbled into their living space, with no inherent rights of belonging, and even worse, was seeking to imitate what to them came so easily and naturally. The birds sat completely still on their branches, watching, waiting, and intrigued by the prospect of what was perhaps to unfold. This was too much for Giles and he decided to turn round and walk to the other end of the carpet, where there were conveniently no birds – or trees even – in his immediate line of sight. Still feeling stupid (though not as much as when he had an audience), he repeated his previous stance of his arms aloft … and then very slowly began to move them in sync, as if rowing with a pair of invisible oars, but in the incongruous element of the skies.

Nothing …

The carpet stayed exactly where it was in relation to the trees, but without warning, it suddenly dropped to the ground and the movement was so unexpected that Giles immediately lost his balance and fell backwards. The carpet was nothing if not responsive, however, and it immediately recalibrated, and the previous firmness that assured his footing made way to a softly textured cushioning effect, that ensured his lack of competence did not result in a lack of consciousness. Simultaneously it also managed to break the vertical descent just a few inches from the ground. This being quite a resounding sign that bodily movement (even without the comfort of tangible controls) was not the way, he knew he would have to think again.

He slowly raised himself back to his previous sitting position and, as he did so, the carpet very gently rose into the air once again. This surprised him but in the absence of any concrete knowledge of what to do, he accepted this gratefully. Okay, so he had no physical machinery at his disposal, no one else with him in the driving seat, the spoken word seemed to have been stripped of any presumed power and his trial of using bodily movements by extension had almost led to a catastrophe. So what did that leave?

With his tongue now silent and his body and mind still, the carpet settled on that moment as the instruction it had patiently been awaiting. It moved forward – with neither haste nor hesitation – and Giles saw the same group of birds in the tree – still staring – coming closer and closer. This was evidently a most unusual spectacle. As he looked harder, he saw more birds, some on their own flight paths and others in their perfectly coordinated groupings, heading for this tree and settling with surprising order in some form of hierarchy of species upon its branches. And he was mightily grateful that he didn't spot a single woodpecker at that point. He (or most likely his unusual means of transport) seemed to be the chief attraction here, and he suddenly felt himself to be the world's biggest charlatan. What had he spent his professional life doing? An aesthetic and cultural study of textiles of all kinds – primarily rugs and carpets. Yes, this was his passion, but despite his study and knowledge and appearances on the lecture circuit, the letters after his name and all the rest (it was a most nauseating thought now), what was it that he really knew? Yes, he had flirted around the periphery, but what was being shown to him now (in all its manifest though uncomfortable glory) was just how much more there was to know. The essential properties of these works of art were not to be studied from an appreciation of their weave or stitching, or the cultural nuances and narratives embedded in their composition, or even by sensory immersion through touching, walking or even shagging on them. They were not to adorn either floors or walls.

It was their essential nature that he had never once appreciated.

Never once been bold enough. Never been intellectually honest. Up until now.

There was nothing that resembled a speedometer as we might know it, so Giles was having to judge his speed by the other vehicles around him, but this was more difficult than he might have supposed. Feeling like an articulated lorry in a world of agile skateboarders, he realised quickly that he was going to have to write his own rules of the road, rather than conform to those of the birds around him. His first terror was of hitting the tops of any trees – at speed. But once he internally acknowledged this, the carpet was immediately responsive and began to weave its own skyway through the branches near the rooftops. They were now entering a dense wooded area that backed on to Mrs Luscombe's fast disappearing grounds. So now he knew. He just had to articulate any of his fears, clearly in his mind – with no caveats – and he would be protected. So the physical obstacles in his path went first. At that moment they were approaching a majestic oak, and as Giles looked down, the carpet slowed in response until they were hovering just before it. The wind was picking up and he could see the tremors of the upper boughs and leaves, and feel the breeze blow through his own hair and clothing. The carpet, however, remained steadfast and unmoved underneath him.

It was the wind that brought the question.

The question that he knew he had spent his whole life avoiding.

It was a deafening whisper that faded in and out of his hearing, as if there were a multitude of speakers on different frequencies, all transmitting together.

'What is it that you *fear*?'

'What *is* it that you fear?'

'What is it that *you* fear?'

The question swirled towards him, then around him, until the question became him.

He knew the answer. All the answers. So he told the wind but the carpet stayed still.

There was no living person in the vicinity, let alone within earshot. Even the birds had vacated his invisible cordon in the skies. The carpet was his own confessional. There was only a giant oak to hear his secrets, and he knew then what it was that he must do. He sat down once more and briefly held his head in his hands. He then looked down at the patterns on the carpet, and for the first time noticed what looked like the most quintessential of English designs, swimming with the currents of the wind across its perimeter. His first thought was whether reaching out to touch one of these apparently living organisms would disturb the creatures, and it was then he recalled a further instalment of his brief tryst with his interdisciplinary colleague. Her hair – though much shorter and severe than his former wife's – was embedded in his memory as he could always smell avocados when she was near. In fact, three years on and he still had that association, but this one he had forgotten. Until now.

Was that a shirt or a dress she was wearing? He had asked her the question as she had thrown it on, while he was lying still naked on his bed.

'A shirt dress,' she had replied and turned away from him to fix her hair. He surveyed the design as it took shape and cohered over her hips and stomach as she buttoned it (wrongly).

'Did you know that paisley print came originally from Persia? We think it all began with the young Queen Victoria wearing them from the town of Paisley, but actually the design travelled the length of the Silk Road on shawls and rugs, way before then.'

She looked searchingly at him then.

'You do say the oddest things ...'

Given her earlier comment about woodpecker's tongues, Giles thought she was hardly in a position to talk.

Anyway, as usual this was nothing more than distraction.

The wind implored him again and the patterns now swam at even greater speed around their fixed perimeter. He slowly raised his head and looked straight at the dense foliage of the oak. It was as if a forest of oaks had conjoined in the skies, though he was sure there was only the one solid trunk standing at the very centre. Giles had heard of underground networks of roots that offered joint sustenance to whichever tree happened to be in need, but he had never heard of (let alone seen) a mirrored manifestation of this unseen phenomena above ground level. The carpet appeared to be shrinking around him now, as it glided ever closer to the leaves. As soon as he was sure he would be forced to make a grab for one of the upper branches, or else tumble to the ground, the carpet stopped contracting at about a yard square and the branches parted, as if to allow him safe passage through. And so, for the first time, he gave the monologue he was supposed to. No auditorium – let alone visible audience – no distractions of projectors and the vagaries of IT – and whether there might be questions at the end, well that was anyone's guess now.

And with every spoken word, a branch made way before him.

* * *

'I don't know if there is an accepted protocol for this.

'God, I sound like I'm in a meeting or something – what I mean is, I don't know if there is a right way or a wrong way, so please forgive me if I don't adhere to what I'm supposed to. It isn't irreverence, just pure ignorance you see. I've held on to this for way too long now, and the one thing – and maybe the only thing – I can say with any sincerity is that it is time. In fact, it is long overdue.

'This was partly the reason why my career took the trajectory it did. I could have specialised in any number of areas you see. The most obvious would have been contemporary design. Plenty of my fellow students went into the production of their own textiles or for some well-known company – one even ended up designing the new moquette for the seat covers on the revamped London overground trains. It's a rare skill this you know. You want something that is instantly identifiable, but without being ostentatious in any way. Well actually you probably do know. Yes, I could have found myself a nice comfortable role at Liberty prints or somewhere – though in terms of lineage I would have preferred William Morris and Co. though the irony of how far this now is from Mr Morris's original lofty socialist ideals is not lost on me. It's just so you're aware that I did have other options.

'I didn't have to choose this obscure path of antiquities.

'It wasn't ordained.

'Anyway, it was back in the mid-1980s. I had completed my first, first degree (I have many of these useless markers now) and had spent a number of years afterwards doing an odd collection of temporary jobs, as the lure of a permanent position in design wasn't quite strong enough – even then. At the time my one real interest was travel – and specifically around Asia.

I think the first seeds of my future passion were possibly sown at this time, though watered by the experiences that then transpired. Looking back now, I think I saw myself as some kind of Bruce Chatwin-lite (though I only found out about him many years later). That I needed to stretch my wings way before it became a de rigour rites of passage for middle-class kids – who actually knew what it was they wanted to do even before they got to uni.

'I can remember that trip. I had managed to get some work teaching in an English-speaking secondary school. Don't ask me how. I'd never taught before then and had no experience of it, nor interest in the education of adolescents no matter where in the world they happened to be. I think they just saw I had a degree and was from a conveniently located country and that was all it took. Anyway, the job wasn't onerous. Early starts but the school day ended by two pm, leaving me with plenty of time to travel around the city.

'Anyway. I don't need to give any more background than that. It's just peripheral really. I recall the day clearly enough. Though the temperatures were pretty much unbearable in the heat of summer, the winters could be distinctly cold too, with morning and evening frosts. There was pleasant, warm sunshine that afternoon though. I had finished at school for the day and made it over to explore an old fort and surrounding Mughal gardens that I had never made it to before.'

It was then that Giles looked down. Not only had the leaves been parted at this elevated position, all the way to the very lowest branches, but rather than seeing the forest floor he saw something else entirely. He had stopped his spoken monologue to try and discern exactly what it was he was seeing, and again, as if reading him, the carpet – now the size of a mat – obligingly floated earthward, so he could take a closer look. The clearing was now huge, with the former wrapping of the leaves being peeled back more and more, like a forestry version of pass the parcel – though lacking the incentive of gifts between each layer. It was a game alright though, but not one he had ever played.

Even as a child Giles had never really been one for board games. He had a rudimentary grasp of chess at best, and had on occasion played the odd card game, but that was the extent of it. So when he looked down at the giant maze on the ground, he had no immediate reference points for what he was seeing. So with the lens of his lifelong experiences colouring his views, he initially settled on a giant rug with an abstracted block pattern – not really to his taste, but heaven help him; who was he to argue with the interior furnishings of the Gods? He continued:

'There was a well-known bazaar a short walk away, and I decided to pay it a long overdue visit. I was well used to being treated like a curiosity on legs in the bazaars, tho assumption being that as a European I had access to ample money but little sense to apply to its safekeeping.'

The tiny patch of carpet he was on was gradually descending, and he knew now he had no need to continue his clumsily spoken narrative. For here he was, back amongst the sights and sounds of the bazaar itself, where he had drunk copious cups of tea, smoked various substances and picked up an array of stomach complaints in his youth. How could he forget that afternoon? That was the start of it all you see. It was easier to carry his bundle than he might have thought: more blessing than burden as it was securely rolled, so its internal beauty lay safely hidden from the world. But he always attracted a bit of attention in the bazaar, and what with this new piece of luggage, he found it slightly more cumbersome than usual to manoeuvre the narrow alleys and questioning eyes that now opened up before him. He wasn't even entirely sure where he was going, but decided that any closest patch of open track on the periphery would be good enough to head towards, rather than risk going deeper and deeper into the heart of the market, with no clear route in his mind to negotiate. He was sure he was being paranoid. No one was looking at him. The alleys were not growing ever narrower, and the contents and colours denser and more oppressive. How ridiculous, to be fearful of glass towers of bangles and bobbins of brocade, all dangling right in front of him, begging to adorn the wrists and blinding in their intensity. Right, his shades. Where were they? He clumsily leant the carpet against the side of a stall and fumbled around in his rucksack until he found them. The effects were immediate and he no longer felt like the market was a living, breathing monster and he in its bowels, desperate to trace a path back through its innards, towards freedom once again, through its ever-restless jaws. The alleys widened and he heard the sounds of car horns and rickshaws – usually akin to chainsaws – growing louder now, and also, somehow, comforting.

* * *

Where was she now? All this jumping from one world to another was exhausting. She envied those who had only to hear these tales (narrated so beautifully by the Voice in the sky) rather than live them out themselves. But she supposed we all had our roles to play. Well, she knew instinctively that the danger was past. She was no longer being haunted by the hanging silks in the bazaar, the vibrant colours and golden embroidery doing nothing to mask the grotesque shrouds in her midst that she had no choice but to run past, the unborn moths from the cocoons never being birthed, but being thrown onto the funeral pyre from where the silks were extracted for their material beauty alone, before their natural pristine whiteness was dyed into more 'desirable' hues. She was no longer running in fact. She hadn't run for a long time now, and it was even longer since she had crawled. Having been prematurely torn from her own cocoon, she was at least grateful that she had survived and not been thrown into the inferno, the place of no return. She wondered if this was some form of recompense for the suffering that had come her way, but it was immaterial now. She was where she was. But where was this?

The trace memories were always there. She remembered again the reptiles, those lizards with their rough scales and initial seemingly accidental movements, that were nothing of the sort. The sudden collisions when there was plenty of space around her on the branch of the mulberry tree – and plenty of alternative branches they could have darted across to get to their destination. She braced herself for what was coming and being dragged once again from her abode, and the invisible cocoon she would again have to weave around her. The first sensation had been akin to being unspun, like a tale that had somehow been told wrong at its very inception and then passed down through millennia, gradually becoming more and more distorted, picking up more and more dirt and debris from every subsequent generation until the original was barely discernible through the heavy veils of lies. Firstly it was dizzying. She was used to this by now. She was being dragged by force from her natural habitat so how could it be otherwise? But there was something else this time. It must have been the 'trauma'. She didn't actually know what trauma was but as the Voice had just told her so, who was she to argue? This was going to be interesting: she recalled one of the stories that had been told to her by one of the Elders while she was lying dormant in her hanging cradle. It was apparently this aforementioned 'trauma' that could lead to one of these experiences. Out of body they were called. Well she knew all about that one. She didn't even know what kind of body she did inhabit from moment to moment, let alone what she was in these other, all too frequent, episodes now.

... for of all of the transformations that the natural kingdom in its splendour has to offer, this alone must be one of the most striking.
 No matter how many times one sees interplay between the disintegration of the old and the emergence of the new, one cannot but help marvel at the beauty of what will slowly ... but inevitably ... unfold ...

It went just as the story said. One moment she was in her safe and familiar abode, her senses slightly impaired by the multitude of veils she had around her, but there were still some impressions of the sights, sounds and smells of the world, the movement as the wind blew through the branches of the mulberry tree and rocked her both gently to sleep and to waking. Her personal favourite had always been that liminal phase between the occasionally blinding light and then the encroaching darkness. It was here that she was both privy and privileged to witness her personal kaleidoscope of colour reflected on her own internal panoramic screens. She would often gaze at this divine display and wish she could tear the veils from around her and see it in its full glory. But she knew the time was to come. And to rush this would be folly. In the words of one of the stories themselves, 'lift the veil but do not tear it.'
 She was never the destructive sort, even when she had been violated herself, it had been too much for her to even draw attention to this, let alone physically tackle a whole group of reptiles on her own. So maybe this was

a form of 'displacement'? Yes – that was probably what it was. All that psychology she had unwillingly imbibed had at least given her a vocabulary for this – even if it frequently missed the mark somewhat. Or completely. So she had just been holding on to it for too long and, in the absence of an appropriate channel, it was seeking expression as release in the most visceral form it could. She felt the life force coursing through her body now, and it was this she used with a violence that until then had been largely unknown to her. Instead of hitting inwards with her self-destructive narrative of guilt and blame and shame, she did the only thing left to her.

She hit out.

With the first blow came ambivalence. Her body – once more – didn't feel like her own and she wasn't even sure with which limb she had struck out. Shit. This was so stupid. She was destroying her own personal screen no less, her one and only connection with the outside world, so how would she now be able to watch what was unfolding before her? Wait – this was odd. What was happening to the Voice? It was like she had inadvertently picked up another frequency, and tuned into a new channel, and the slightly muffled but undeniably authoritative tones that had always been with her suddenly took on an air of crispness and clarity. Well, she guessed, if she couldn't watch TV any longer, at least she would have the radio to keep her entertained.

But there was more. Having already inflicted a seemingly mortal blow to one side of the screen, she thought, what the hell, it would probably be beyond the repair of even a master spinner of yarns now – and she'd had to hear enough from that lot over the years. A mistress spinner might have done the trick, but somehow, it was none of these stories she needed right now. She hadn't been aware of her own strength with the first blow, coming as it had like an accidental hammer-fist. But she felt more oriented now. All she had to do was focus on the memory of those lizards again, who had forced her into this exile, and she was sure that would suffice. She could see where her cave, suspended precariously as it was, was vulnerable now. There was a small window to the outside world that she had broken into, and it was on its periphery that she would aim her next strike.

She breathed in deeply once more and took aim. The strange thing was she knew what she was aiming for – the upper edge of the gradually fragmenting hole that she had opened up before her – but what she was actually aiming *with*, she had no idea. Could it be that all this time she had been the reluctant possessor of an arsenal of weapons that had always been at her disposal? Surely not. But the facts seemed to speak for themselves as what seemed like a glowing protective shield now unfurled before her and broke through another, even larger fragment of her cell. This was still nothing. The more she brought through now, the more convinced she became that there was just as much still to come. The air was now streaming through and there had been a lull in the narrative from the Voice in the sky, but the comfort it dispensed was still very much in evidence as she inhaled the intoxicating aromas of this new, yet not so new world that had always been there, right before her. She needed to be completely free now. With the desperation of a lover eager to have her fill of her beloved after an eternity of inhibition, she tore into her veils, leaving them hanging, discarded – for ever more now on the branches of the tree, a few garments now falling to the forest floor and mingling with the leaves. And it was here that she hesitated. The world was not the world. The heat and the light of the sun, so much brighter than what she had ever felt. But if the world had been illuminated so, then once she was in it, she would be too, of this there was no doubt.

Suddenly mindful, she paused here, just on the cusp. Not to entice the growing breeze to take her himself now – for he could easily have done so – no, that choice was hers and hers alone. More to fill her own senses first, one by one, with what she was embarking on. She stretched her wings simultaneously to their full span, leaving her body exposed for the first time – in her own time – to all the elements around her, languidly letting them rest behind her now. They were almost translucent in this light, as the wind slowly blew straight through them, making them quiver. The time was now. Every creature around her was naked and fluid, except these strange behemoths, who occasionally lumbered past. She had to unlearn it all, that was all. Unlearn the shame that had kept her veiled and give it name and give it flight. She wasn't on her own now, in that prison of her own making, whose original use had long since been corrupted by a world intent on making light. As she flew, arcing her way to the next tree – the wind himself taking her in his arms – every beat of her wings forced his breath to make her rise but ten beats more.

10

After the extraordinary events of the day, a darkness had crept up on her.

An out-of-body experience was all well and good, but at some point we all return to the world of our making. She was on the ground now, and could see the odd flickers of fluorescent light in the air around her, hear a gentle humming of what she supposed were the multitude of beings existing in this world, that she had yet to make full and proper acquaintance with. There was all the time in the world for that. So here she was. She had vacated her cocoon and had no cognisance now of where it even was, let alone how she might begin to go about rebuilding it. She shuddered slightly when she thought of her wanton destruction, but then swiftly reminded herself that this had been of its own time and place, had served her needs perfectly but no more – hence to rue her actions now would be fruitless.

Ah, so she had moved house, that was all. No wonder the Elders had oft mentioned it was one of the most stressful events in the entire life cycle, rivalled only by mating and rearing, whatever these might be. She was in no hurry to find out. If there was one thing she was sure of, her cocoon, while bijou and perfect for her own not insignificant needs, could never have accommodated another silkworm in addition to her. This would have been a huge impediment to her own healing – and probably to her mate's as well, so she was glad she hadn't in a moment of weakness succumbed to this particular route. Even the thought of having her transmissions by the Elders, or her reading of the then veiled world, not least her ability to move – though slightly constricted – at will, impaired by another presence, seemed unconscionable to her now. She knew she had both taken the right route, and then upgraded when circumstances had demanded this, but it did leave her with one slight dilemma – for if she had left her previous abode, stripped and far forgotten and likely in an uninhabitable state, just where was it that she was now supposed to live?

In the swiftly diminishing light, she headed over to a bed of flowers and temporarily settled herself on a large, strangely familiar feeling leaf, while she collected her scattered thoughts. It was then that he made his approach.

'The show's over for this evening, I'm afraid.' She surveyed her new companion. He hovered just above a neighbouring leaf, before a landing both gentle and adept. She was vaguely relieved that he had not chosen the one she was currently perched upon, despite there being sufficient room. Boundaries you see were always important – and even more so when you were in both an unfamiliar world as well as an unfamiliar body. Talking of bodies, she tried not to notice just how impressive his wingspan was. And even in this dying light, those colours of his wings … what misguided teachings led us to believe that it was always the female of the species that were the recipients of aesthetic beauty? This world really left nothing to the imagination. She supposed it was a given that all creatures who had been granted admittance could see beyond their former carnal desires to something more expanded, and the last thing she wanted was to be expelled from the garden on the first night of her entry. Given how raw still, and arduous her journey had been, that would have been a fate worse than the oblivion of pure death itself.

'But the joys of this world are never far from us. Give it some time and the light show will dawn on us yet again.'

'It was always there wasn't it? It's just that in my former state I was in a self-made cocoon that only let in a sliver.'

'Don't be too hard on yourself. In our own ways we have all traversed the same path. It was as necessary as the night following the day – and it's not as if the cocoon was your first abode either. It's easy to forget all the life cycles that preceded this one, and at some point it will do you good to bring them all to mind. Maybe not just yet though … I myself recall a previous state where I spent most of my time buried underground and completely oblivious to the light, not even mediated through the form of a chrysalis.'

Her new companion continued in this vein, while she rested beside him and ingested his words. Yes, something new was definitely afoot here. As he spoke, she began to notice the vibrant colours of his wings starting to take on a different hue. It was not just that they were changing in relation to the external light around them, something was also happening from within. As the light around faded, he himself was starting to glow and become more and more luminous. And this spectacle was so very beguiling that she found this was all she could focus on. All previous idle thoughts of his wings – just inches away from her now – were not only seemingly banished, but her mind itself seemed to be fortified by a ring of battlements to prevent their future access. Long may they remain in exile.

He had stopped speaking now, and she was unsure just how long they had been there in silence. But even though she was no longer drinking in this glorious nectar, his silence did nothing to halt the growing shimmer of his wings.

'Come fly with me, just to the bed next door. There is someone there you need to meet.' With that he took flight and as he ascended she saw in his wake a trail of sparkles, illuminating the way for her to follow.

* * *

The large cushion was more comfortable this time round.

Howra saw that the installations appeared to have run their course. They must have been on some kind of replay loop, but had now been replaced by either blank screens with 'systems error' messages, or snowstorms. She had no idea how long she had been sitting there and now she was looking into the expectant eyes of a stranger, with no idea of what he had just said.

'I'm sorry, would you mind repeating that? I'm afraid I was somewhere else.'

'No, I'm sorry – I was saying that this isn't actually the full working display. It will be back on again tomorrow morning when we reopen. I really recommend it. It's a fully immersive audio-visual piece.' The gallery

192   The Prayer Rug

attendant was perched on a cushion next to her, and the room was almost in complete darkness and silence now. She was aware that there were the low and muffled sounds of conversations coming from a room next door, the light from which was enabling her to see the man in her midst more clearly.

'Thank you. Luckily I caught them earlier. I must have fallen asleep to the music or something as I feel like I've been here for hours.'

'That's the beauty of art, I guess, transporting us to a different place.' He got to his feet at that point. 'I don't know if you're interested, but there's a talk happening soon that you're welcome to stay for?'

'Oh, I will be – that's actually the reason why I came here this evening – these displays were just an unexpected bonus.' He smiled at this and she followed him to the adjoining room, where a gathering of people were sitting themselves down, some with drinks and some without. He motioned to her to take a seat, which she did so near the back.

Giles looked down and gently removed the protective shroud of linen that had been lining the carpet. He had briefly toyed with the idea of a more dramatic unveiling, a sudden flourish befitting a magician revealing what the audience half expected but still couldn't quite believe. But he had decided against this. This was no cheap trick. Gimmicks were unnecessary. The carpet could speak for itself and it didn't need him to add any extraneous gestures. He wanted it on display, in its fullness and entirety from the outset, as soon as anyone happened to enter. Of course, in the limited time he had he couldn't possibly furnish them with anything more than a rudimentary overview of its essence and qualities. But they had eyes. They had senses – and if their interest was genuine, they could spend as much or as little time gazing at it as they wished.

* * *

Well, it wasn't chequered in any way, but there were clearly defined markings nonetheless, with what looked like two parallel lanes crossing diagonally through a centre circle. Bizarrely it brought to mind the bird's-eye views of the newest pedestrianised crossings in large urban city centres. There was no traffic impatiently waiting at any red lights here, though, just the stylised foliage on the periphery, undulating as if gently swaying in the breeze. That's when an old memory resurfaced. Of course – he knew what this was now. It was the game of kings.

Its name had been Pachisi and many a sultan – rather than playing it at the level of a board game on a table – would invoke their (not exactly latent) megalomaniacal tendencies and have it played as a scaled-up version. Though not as you may find with chess and the oversized pieces that were the size of a small child, but a live version where the women of the harem were used to represent the counters and moved around the board – actually sculpted into the palace grounds or an internal courtyard. The sultan then, from his vantage point could direct proceedings.

* * *

She looked around her at the expectant audience.

If there was any kind of hierarchy in play here, she couldn't discern it; the leaves were graduating outwards at different levels, but this was mainly to afford the variety of insects in their midst a vantage point that all could see from. She was starting to feel more at home in her body and could sense she was: one, significantly larger than many others (she would place herself near the back and then she could spread her wings if she chose, without obstructing anyone else's view) and two, had been blessed with the ability to fly as well, so if there were not enough leaves to go round, she would be happy to gently hover and circle the proceedings. She observed with a smile how one of the caterpillars on a leaf near the ground was surreptitiously taking tiny bites from around the edges. She saw her fellow moth land nearby and open and close his resplendent wings three times in quick succession; and the darkness of the ground – far below – was suddenly illuminated by a series of overhanging pupa in the branches directly above. Ah, she thought, so this was going out as a transmission too and could be watched by others who couldn't – as yet – attend in body. Perfect and very forward thinking too. And humans thought *they* had invented technology and podcasts ...

The moth began his opening address and the audience all settled down.

'Welcome everyone to this special event – it is great to have you all with us. It's a fine night out there, so we do so appreciate you choosing to spend it here with us. And a particularly warm welcome to those of you not naturally of a nocturnal nature.

'Just a few fieldkooping rules before we begin – if all antennae could please be temporarily switched off or placed on silent that would be great.

'We're not expecting any forest-fire alarms, but those of you with heightened senses, do feel free to raise the alarm in your own way, and then all please assemble in the glade just in the direction behind me.

'And specifically to any birds in the vicinity, do feel free to tweet, using the following wingflag.

'So with that all out the way, it is my pleasure to welcome such an eminent scholar and arachademic no less, to speak firstly of the dazzling web within our midst, but also about the myths and stories we insects of all persuasions have used since time immemorial to make sense of the natural world around us that we call our collective home.' The assembled insects then signalled their approval through a mixture of stamping of multitudinous legs, beating of wings and gentle humming while the spider took centre stage, and the pupas directly above shone down a series of laser lights on to the web.

And so it began.

There was once a master weaver, whose skills exceeded those of all in the vicinity. There were many who attempted to emulate him – and just as many who failed. His webs were not the result of planning and formulation, but a simple and spontaneous expression of his need to create. And why did he create? Why, what drives any of us to create, if not the plain and simple desire to be *known*. So the master weaver had no desire for fame, no desire for fortune, but just the peace and enduring solace that came from spinning his webs. Unseen by others, what really marked him out was the time he spent in his preparation. But this did not mean in design, for his primary concerns went something like follows: Where was the hanging to be displayed? How would it be viewed in its natural environs? Would it be hung from branches of the trees or lie flat on the ground to be admired underfoot?

One early morning, just before dawn he awoke with a start (considerably before his natural waking hours it must be said) and felt the familiar urge come over him. He quickly staked out a space about a foot above the ground, where the surrounding foliage would do much to support the canvas of his new, burgeoning creation, and he set about to work. First he traversed the stem of a steady-looking plant, and then up to the first cluster of leaves and prepared himself for the process he had undertaken a thousand times, always under cover of darkness.

He began to move. Not just move, he began to *dance* and with eight legs at his disposal, my friends, this was truly a sight to behold. Dizzying, in fact, had anyone been watching him and, for him too, he felt the bliss rise inside him as the latent energies had again awoken and guided him to his new work. As he looked back at the initial outline of the path he had just traversed, he saw something he had never once seen before. And so startled was he by what he saw, all eight of his limbs then seized up completely in gradual succession. For despite his dazzling routine, the trail – well, the trail had actually left no visible markings in between the leaves behind him.

There was nothing there.

He had been expending his energies in the usual fashion but when he looked – there was nothing to show for it. No web. He stopped then, unsure about what to do next, for if he could no longer spin his yarns, well, what was his purpose then? The webs were lauded for being beautiful and, while he had no need for this, what he did have a need for was their dual purpose of providing him with sustenance in the world. How would he now survive?

It was then that he heard the quickening patter of the beating of wings. Soft and swift, the sounds rose in volume as did the insects to whom these wings belonged, for so entranced were they by what they had just seen that they were giving him a flying ovation. His prey ... were praising him ...

'Please, no I mean really, please – stop, do stop ...'

But his bewildered pleas were in vain as the applause just continued.

Once it had died down and the insects had returned to their respective leaves, he surveyed them hesitantly, still completely unsure as to what had just happened – and how best to respond.

It was in the very first row that he saw the first antenna go up.

'Err, yes?'

'An absolutely mesmerising display if I may say so. Who knew that weavers could be Lords of the Dance too ... May I ask, such a subversion of both form and content, with you opening up your hidden creative processes to your audience for the first time, rather than just presenting the finished article – and also freeing yourself in terms of movement by not being bound by your previous webbing. What was your inspiration for this?'

Fuck, thought the spider ... they actually thought he had done this on purpose. He quickly gathered his composure and – ignoring the question he had no real answer to – tried again. His legs came back to life and he continued his path as before, but this time with much more intent, as if he could actually will the web to come to life. He could feel the dew caressing the leaves underfoot, and the memories came back to him of how this would often bathe his own creations too, and he found a resentment rising inside him, of the indiscriminate ways of this early morning sparkle, as if it belonged to him and him alone. Anyway, the natural patron of dawn love was most definitely not going to be blessing him with her presence much longer, as yet again when he looked back there were no trails of his web to be seen. He could still hear the vague strands of applause, but the insects, as if realising that explanation was not his forte, were now just content to leave him to it.

He was tiring now and decided to rest. His impromptu audience had slowly begun to fade away, leaving him to contemplate his current seemingly impotent state. Was a spider still a spider if he couldn't make webs?

* * *

After the talk and subsequent Q&A, Giles gazed upon the rug with almost as much love as Shirley might have. He was reasonably pleased with how it had gone. Mrs Luscombe had given permission for it to be displayed now on a permanent loan, and the gallery staff had a backlit glass case prepared, awaiting the new arrival. Public speaking did always take it out of him though, and he was looking forward to an evening stroll on the river, to settle his papers as it were. He had arranged its handover to a member of staff, and was engaging with a small group of individuals who were milling round, either wanting to give him personal thanks – which was very kind – or had questions or comments that there hadn't been sufficient time for. And that was when he saw her. She was hovering around and looking at some of the other exhibits on the periphery of the room – but it was obvious she was just waiting for the final remnants of the crowd to clear, though Giles had most of his attention on what was being said to him.

Now that the moment was unfolding right before her, Howra realised that the oft-rehearsed scenario of her imaginings was not likely to have any bearing on how things were going to go. She stood just enough to the side to not be intrusive, yet close enough for it to be clear that she was indeed waiting for her turn. She watched as people went up to the professor and shook his hand, and she took in the gentle hum of conversation that wasn't quite taking the form of words she could clearly hear or decipher.

* * *

What with the soles being the first point of contact and that, people understandably (but quite erroneously) believe it starts with the feet and then works its way up from there. But they couldn't be further from the truth. It starts way before any bodily contact. Firstly there is the storage. Where are we kept and how are we kept? Some of us are rolled like the finest of Cuban cigars, but kept in corners harbouring cobwebs and dust, that no one could possibly choose to inhale. While others, of a perhaps finer disposition, are folded and kept on shelves or above wardrobes. Then there is the frequency and durations of our airings. Do we belong to those of an outwardly pious disposition, through whom God Himself could set the eternal clocks of nature, with the rise and fall of His sun each day? Or those for whom internal time moves to a different rhythm? One shared only with the Lord Himself? A time zone where even we may lie largely dormant, in our corners and shelves? But in truth our inception – and subsequent reality too – precedes our physical forms. So while we may have been conceived in a weaver's workshop in many a region around the world, our colours and patterns bearing some universal motifs – but some entirely unique once and our creation born either at the hands of one or two, or the collective looms of many, the needs which we serve in this tangible form transcend our physicality, and are but one – and one manifestation alone – of communion with our Lord.

The memories from those earliest of days are of course the haziest. We start as a jumble of string and cloth, before being stitched and woven into shape, much as the skin, bone and sinew, the individual features of human beings, are going through their own process. There is often huge care and gentleness, flowing through from our weavers unto us, and when we feel this the lengths of our silks become soft and compliant in their hands. No complexity is too much, no time spent here is wasted, no matter how quickly the rugs of others may manifest. But when there is harshness – or even indifference – when we are tugged and pulled as if we had no sentience in the world, we knot and tangle and snag. Our patterns may lose their symmetry and coherence, and even if they do perchance give the external appearance of a unified whole, that abuse, or neglect now permeates the length and breadth of the very fibres of our being.

I recall my own inception well. I was noble by birth – regal even. Originally made more for display than actual use, even on a cursory level. I was conceived I know by some of the greatest craftsmen of that era, and for more than one generation I was simply hung and admired. And for a while that was enough. If the truth be told it was actually everything to my ashamedly debased state back then. My colours retained their original hues and vibrancy, the quality of my texture – finer than the sands of the east and softer than the meadows of the west – remained preserved and untouched, unlike so many of my brethren, faded and bleached by the sun, afforded no protection and so threadbare in patches as to render their overall design almost indistinguishable. And this was initially much to my liking. Much too much to my liking to be honest. As while I remained pristine and untouched on the surface, so too did my deepest desires. True, I was not trampled into the ground, in taverns of ill repute, or exposed to the debaucheries of lustful bodies with their urges, but my rarefied existence was starting to suffocate me now. Even if I couldn't escape my high-born origins, I still longed for certain things. I was not a palatial wall hanging at heart, I knew. I longed to be taken from there and feel – even if fleetingly – the presence of humanity beyond a purely visual and aesthetic appreciation. All the rugs and tapestries longed for this. To be unfolded and spread out in all our glory, yes – but not just on display. To actually feel, first the soles of a believer, either completely bare or encased, followed by the gentle shifts in pressure as she moves her arms in supplication, and then finally prostrates. To feel then not just her soles but her hands now too, the lengths of fingers and the spread of palms, simultaneously with the skin and pulse of forehead. And while I may never have understood the words themselves, I dreamed of *feeling* the meanings, emanating from her heart and not her mind.

There were times when I felt oh so close, particularly in the very early days. There was a lady of huge refinement and nobility, so much so that the very movements of her feet, while sometimes almost too wild and ecstatic in nature, were accompanied by the chimes of bells as sonorous as the nightingales who occasionally adorned some of my fellow tapestries. It was her gaze you see. She had a look occasionally of pure adoration and, outside of all the usual protocols of prayer, I did occasionally feel her touch as, even suspended as I was, she would occasionally run a tantalising bare toe over me, gently tracing the outline of part of my designs or borders. But there was also a profound disconnection. Her spirit – beautiful though it was – could never fully surrender and she would swiftly move on to the next thing that happened to alight her moods. However, this was infinitely preferable to the attentions of the various simian creatures, who initially fooled me with the externally worn garbs of humans, but whose souls alas were not yet quite so developed. They would leap around frantically, often in a state of extreme agitation, while making incoherent noises for all they were worth. Indeed, these so-called courtiers and members of the Sultan's elite political inner circle were definitely the least evolved. But there was one very legitimate hope that I did cling to for many years. A spirit that was almost born wrongly into the world itself, and the particular milieu in which it found itself (though may God forgive me as He makes no errors in His infinite wisdom). Standing apart from the ties of her lineage, I bore witness to much of her struggle with the burdens of expectation placed upon her. I felt so sure she was the one. The one who would finally take me down from the walled mausoleum, through who I could finally attain self-realisation and facilitate her divine communion with our Lord. There was a steadiness about her that sadly was always to remain just before, yet still beyond the grasp of her mother, in whose image much of her spirit was formed. I could feel it you see. Even without her physical touch or hearing any formal prayers ever emanating from her lips, I could feel she was so close to the carpet of proximity – the metaphysical one that was. And I was so sure that with her I would actualise my one true purpose.

But even with her, something was amiss.

It was more than that; it was most irregular.

It was more than that even; it was against all possible royal protocol – forget royal – it was against every last drop of decorum from her culture and era, regardless of her supposed regal and elevated station. But she knew there was a precedence for this in a much earlier generation and even if there hadn't been, she was beyond caring now.

For she had found him.

Her other half.

The sun to her moon.

The one that would complete her.

And they sat together. And they drank together. And they spoke together.

There had been a specially designed purdah created for the purpose, for of course the princess and he would be spending increasing amounts of time together – that was indisputable – and the Sultan, probably because of the unconventional manner of their introduction, was keen to ensure that his daughter did indeed know what she was doing. So there was no need for the kingdom at large, or even a few beyond the trusted confines of the inner circles of the palace to know about the frequency with which they met.

And that they did so alone.

They were cut from the same cloth – and trust me, I should know – but just from different sides, so while the weave was the opposite and the dominant colours reversed, with the absolute skill of the Master Weaver, they could be worn either side on show to the outside world. It was material. Yet immaterial.

And while they sat and drank and spoke – and sometimes just sat, and other times just walked, the Master Weaver seamlessly conjoined the prize cloth of their souls back together.

And I could see that she didn't actually need me. She had her own path, where I would remain redundant. She wasn't the one. So alas this was all to remain yearning and supposition, as while the years turned to decades – and even beyond – my true desires were never once realised, but my shameful lack of faith at the time belied the true purpose I was actually to have in the world.

I remember The Day That Everything Changed as if it were yesterday.

But it wasn't the soles as I had once anticipated; it was the hands. And they were neither raised in supplication nor support for man's prostration. They had one purpose alone and that was to loot and to plunder. And while in time I came to accept my own fate, it was the fates of those less fortunate than I that I still to this day struggle to reconcile. Yes, many of us who were adjudged to have some monetary or aesthetic value in the world of men were indeed stolen from the sanctity of our homes; those that the most debased simians of them all could not find value for in their hearts, suffered a fate I can barely speak of to this day.

It was many years later after the deaths of both the Sultan and Sultana, and the subsequent physical freedom of the eldest daughter, who was the only child never to marry, from the palatial prison. It had been a long time coming, and while I knew it was inevitable, a part of me could still not accept it until it actually happened.

You see for many years the Sultan had been somewhat distracted.

The decision of his daughter – while unorthodox – could at least be delicately stage-managed so the outer kingdom was none the wiser. If she wished to live the reclusive life of worldly renunciation, with a Sufi mystic as a companion, and not as the wife of a prince, he could accept this. His eldest son – one of the aforementioned simians – was, however, always more of a challenge. Despite the promise his vizier had made to the Sultan on his deathbed, he was largely powerless to prevent the ultimate overthrow of the once mighty kingdom. And as a consequence of this, the marauding tribes that now roamed the region had their sights set on all the most visible manifestations of the former empire. For what is the most powerful way to attempt to destroy a civilisation than to first attack and then attempt to systematically erase all its cultural artefacts and artistic satellites, emanating from the very epicentre itself? So it was the palace itself that took the hit. It matters not what the particular ideological brand was that was espoused at the time – it never does – more so that it was born of such an insecurity it felt the need for an almost total annihilation of any of the symbols of that former era. But while you can destroy the entire world a million times over, what you can never touch is what resides in people's hearts. In a strange way this is where the slightly ambiguous nature of my origin saved me. Had I been a very obvious tapestry, depicting scenes of the human form in any setting, everyday bazaars to regal opulence, I am convinced I would have been convicted and punished with no opportunity to state my case. As it was, while not *obviously* a prayer rug, there was enough in my overall design to leave sufficient room for doubt that I could perhaps be fulfilling this function – though what I was doing idling my time away on a wall, rather than being put to this purpose was a detail that did not at all speak in my favour. For being in a state of leisurely observation of life was not to be encouraged. And for this 'crime' I was sentenced to a severe beating with sticks, while still resident on my very own wall, with such ferocity that minute particles flew off me into the stratosphere, and I hoped found a better home elsewhere. I was then – while still in profound distress – confined to a completely dark cell and held in solitary confinement at the behest of those who had attacked me in my own home. And they believed *they* were upholding the law …

However, my own fate at the time was nothing compared to what I knew had befallen some of my brethren. I was not alone in my need to be needed by an aligned soul – I knew this. There were many objects who harboured these desires, and there was one particular part of the palace where they tended to congregate, a place I had never been myself. It was rumoured that in this worshipful chamber there was a direct window to the heavens themselves – not an exclusive one mind, as these divine portals can manifest in the most unlikely of spaces, but one nonetheless. And when any of these embodied objects achieved a holy communion with another soul, they were blessed with a natural ascension. But of course there were such multitudes housed together, and such worldly distractions competing for the soul's attention in that palace, that some could lay untouched for a generation – and didn't I know this. And even if perchance one was taken down by the Sultan himself, it could just result in a cursory perusal, rather than a cover-to-cover reading. And then, even if this too had taken place, it was furthermore dependant on the abilities of the reader to engage with the text on a deeper level. They had time though – they were wise and in no hurry. Once they had been conceived, the *share's* [49] share of the work had been done. But the barbarians who broke into the palace had no such reverence for the abundant riches between those covers. And in a terrible way, it was the very fact that they had been housed together for so long, knowing each other so intimately, with the scaffolded support of the wisdom of former generations constantly available to all, these very means of mutual support and proximity, that were to tragically directly contribute to the speed of their demise. For had they been more collectively savvy, they might have diverted the enemy by being split off into different parts of the palace.

Some could have languished in the individual chambers of the respective members of the royal household, books of verse scattered in private dressing rooms perhaps, the weightier tomes of astronomy maybe stacked in proximity to the outdoor courtyards, or philosophical treatise abound in the more formal stately areas. The exact formation matters not, as with any prayer rug or so-called inanimate object we know we shall eventually be found by exactly who needs us and when. It was the Sultan's tragic desire to impose overall possession that was to facilitate their destruction. He needed them housed in one specific enclave, you see; he needed to feel that they were all there

---

49. lion

The Prayer Rug

in one place, ordered and catalogued by subject matter to his own personal satisfaction. Many he valued purely for their rarity as physical objects, alas: the finesse of the artisans who had illuminated the pages, the skins of animals who housed these works, the reputations – sometimes deserved and sometimes not – of their originators. And as such, he not only began to neglect their true overriding function – to be *read* – but also prevented access to them to most of the palace, let alone the kingdom. Alas, his was a double defamation. But for those bent on destruction, this was a perverse gift. They didn't need to expend energies in tracking and hunting down a succession of mercenaries or freedom fighters, dispersed throughout the palace: they were presented with them in a giant holding cell of the Sultan's own making. And while there can indeed be safety in numbers, there is also regrettably the stagnation and suffocation of the ghetto to contend with.

I was highly distressed from being first beaten, then forcibly removed from my home before being confined in a dark and dusty cell – my very first, though not my last, experience of solitary. And there is nothing that can truly prepare you for the initial horrors of this. It is one thing to voluntarily surrender oneself to a reclusive dervish, or to join a spiritual order that – while removed from some elements of the world – has replaced these with the unique joys and blessings of right communal living, but it is quite another to have one's textures torn away from the intertwining fibres of *any* contact. It wasn't the random beatings that were the worst though – not for me – though each one of us has our own personal hell that must be transcended. It was the horrors of complete sensory deprivation. At least mounted on the wall, while I might never have been used for the prayerful purposes I felt I was created for, I did at least feel the greater benefits of the rising of the sun each morning, and I was at liberty to hear the accompanying birdsong chorus. In solitary, I was barred from any of this. Rather than a growing reliance on my remaining senses, born of circumstance, darkness had the effect of dulling and then completely enveloping them until I was unsure if I even still existed. At least when I was beaten, the resulting pain was a form of bizarre reassurance I was still alive. And it was just when I had begun to accept my utter powerlessness that I was inexplicably granted a reprieve.

But immediately upon my release I almost wished for a return to my previous incarcerated state. For nothing in the world was as I had remembered, and I wasn't sure if it was I that had changed, or the world itself – or the both of us in unison so we no longer recognised one another, like former lovers, who despite once being so close, were reunited to find each was now nothing more than a stranger. The light that I had longed for – for so long – no longer illuminated this new world, and the birds now sang only mournful laments – occasionally interspersed by screams of portents still to come. Despite my release I felt an inexplicable sense of dislocation from my surroundings, as if I was not truly a bona fide inhabitant of this world any longer. I had no idea where I was now, though I knew where I wasn't: I wasn't being used as a prayer rug that was for sure; I felt no touch and communion with a human soul, and I wasn't returned to being a purely ornamental work of craftsmanship and displayed in any other location. It almost felt as if I was still physically in solitary and in my cell.

Until I realised. That was exactly where I still was.

I hadn't in effect been released at all, but somehow the extremities of my confinement and the harshness of the contrast between this and my previous life had initiated some form of disturbance in my perception, some kind of temporal shift in the space-time continuum. So once again I returned to my world of darkness, until the next episode.

And it was this time that I saw and heard it clearly. What I would have given right then to have remained anaesthetised to the fates of others, but we don't choose what we are shown any more than we choose the circumstances of our births. My companions – my brothers and sisters, all housed in their one enclave in the palace could withstand the encroachments of the enemy no longer. And I was powerless to do a thing about it, except through the intercessory powers of the divine to bear witness. The flames took no time to take hold, and the books remained shelved together as if their physical proximity could somehow lessen the hideous pain of the genocide that was befalling them. A few interlopers seemed to have escaped the shelves and lay scattered on the floor – no doubt tossed there by the invaders, seeing no value in any wider forms of knowledge or creative expression, failing to recognise that *all* was a manifestation of the divine – not just the obvious scriptures. But their singularity afforded them no further protection than the others had, for they were still all housed in the one enclave, still all made of the same paper and binding, equally vulnerable to the force of the flames. And this was the scene that unfolded before me. The smoke rose up to the domed roof that the Sultan and his eldest daughter considered to be a window to the heavens, where one could gaze at the stars and planets in orbit, all endlessly turning to their Lord and creator, mirroring what the hearts of the true believers unceasingly did.

After this I traversed many generations, struggling to reconcile the reality of what I had been forced to witness, with the belief in an interventionist Creator that had been embedded in my fibres since my inception. For what was the purpose of prayer if it remained unanswered, especially when offered in those collective moments in the depths of despair, when the entire library was being razed to the ground! Had those volumes not offered their supplications to the Almighty? Had they not lived lives of dedicated and selfless service to those of any open-minded as well as open-hearted human whose paths they crossed? Waiting with endless patience, while these same human souls immersed themselves in lives of decadence or denial? The older volumes even offered to willingly sacrifice themselves, if this could prevent the same fate befalling the newer editions. I had heard their prayers myself. And this also had profound existential implications for me, a prayer rug no less. Of course, prayer could be offered at any time and in any way, by any sentient being (which meant *all* beings) and my part in this process was by no means obligatory, especially if one didn't happen to be a human, but what then was the deciding criteria in terms of who or what would be answered?

Now I knew these were not the ruminations of a truly surrendered soul – and at the time I was nothing of the sort: I was in profound distress at my own incarceration, forcibly bearing witness to a mass slaughter, and then daring to question the essential righteousness of a divine decree. Looking back on it now, I deserved to be burnt alive for my irreverent ways – much more so than my brethren – so how could it be that I was the one, who despite languishing in prison, was somehow saved?

They had their stories you see. The stories that had already taken shape in the minds of their writers, and then been committed to a tangible form via the written word. Open to interpretation no doubt – especially the literary and poetic – but they knew their purpose and had lived it.

Yes, there were a multitude of physical bodies turned to ashes that fated night, but in the very fires of their destruction the spirits of their words flew out, free into the world – the stories, verses, dialogues, arguments, treatise and more, no longer dependent on the physical ability to read their texts but now open to whoever – pauper or peasant – who needed to be able to access their wisdom. Libraries are more than physical books and more than physical locations. Even the grandest ones 'owned' by the kings …

So it came back to story, and even a prayer rug needs a story – but as I had not yet uncovered mine I knew that the Omniscient one still had a chapter or two in store for me.

And so I was blessed.

* * *

Howra knew it was a ridiculous thing to be preoccupied with, given the wider circumstances, but such is the human psyche. So, as she waited, she found a bizarre place of solace from her anxiety with considering whether to address him as professor (too formal?) or Giles (too informal?) or should she just dispense with this all together? Well, whatever it was she was going to say or not say, the time was now: the last dregs of the audience had drained away and even the museum staff were nowhere to be seen.

And of course that was when it came to her.

'Mr Lewis? It's me. It's Howra.'

* * *

It was many generations after. I think rug years are like dog years. Or lunar calendars. Humans must insist on that most human of instincts of imposing their will on whatever they can – be that other humans, the natural world, the animal kingdom or even time itself. No reverence for its natural rhythms and ebbs and flows in progress. So a generation for a prayer rug is not equivalent to a generation for man. And a generation for woman is again entirely different in flavour too. So let's just say that with the passing of the seasons, their cyclical nature was matched by that of the rise and fall of empires, cultures, conquests and so-called civilisations, which were in fact anything but civilised. And I just saw it all, time and time again, not with the births and blooms of spring, but akin to winter followed by winter with each one seemingly harsher and more unforgiving than before. If the truth be told I began to quietly despair of humanity by then. And so in turn despair of ever uncovering my one true purpose. So imagine my surprise when I was used not merely for ritual prayer – which would have been everything at that point – but rather a form of deep-soul confessional. Transforming both myself and my 'passenger' in that one unique instant.

* * *

I had never forgotten her.

How could I?

It had been hard to place her at first, but that's always the way when you encounter someone out of context. She'd been a pupil in one of my classes, so seeing her in the marketplace that afternoon had just completely thrown me. And as for what I witnessed …

She completely disappeared afterwards. Both she and her brother, who was in a younger year group, were withdrawn from school at the same time. They had both arrived in the middle of the school term just a couple of years before, so maybe the family had just moved on somewhere else abroad again? It was all different back then. These days you have proper safeguarding policies and procedures; even in the university there are codes of conduct. But that was a different time. And a different culture.

The only solace I had was that I know I got her away.

But she fled from me after too.

I should have done more you see, should have informed the school, spoken to her, her parents, someone, about something, anything. But I never did.

And then she was gone.

Epilogue

Session Two:

[A woman sits at a table in a tastefully decorated, well-lit consulting room, with art on the walls and potted plants.]

It was the second time I had seen him. And just like the first time he was sitting at the communal table in the middle of the room. There were a host of small individual tables for two, running around the walls, but even if one of these were free he would always head for a seat in that central spot. Jo and I had just finished a clinical supervision and as usual it seemed to be more about her own issues than anything much to do with my caseload, but anyway, it was just after she had packed up and left and I was finally sitting there in silence with no one else's noise to interrupt my own. And that was when I noticed him.

The task he appeared to be engaged in – which was actually just a cover – was some form of transcription of a foreign text into English. But this wasn't why he was there. He could have easily sat in one of the numerous reading rooms if he needed to really focus, or was under pressure of some external deadline. The first woman was polite. Almost too polite. He had waited for a suitable cue – maybe a split second's eye contact or a pause in her own work, taking a sip of tea or something and then he was off. We all have our personal tipping points when it comes to this kind of thing, and they depend on a whole heap of other factors too.

It was more a monologue than a dialogue – a few cursory introductory questions but no more. And that's fine if that's what the mutual expectation is, if that's what you're paying for and what you need. But while he was adept at identifying the cues that met his own need to speak, he wasn't quite so good at reading those expressing someone else's need to actually get away. So to begin with, she smiled politely and nodded and made the appropriate right noises at the right times – but even if she hadn't, I don't think he would have noticed and would just have carried on talking. Anyway, after a certain amount of time – if you are not given to being direct and running the risk of hurting the feelings of a frankly just lonely and essentially harmless old man, you start to work yourself up to the non-verbal cues. Maybe starting to put away your laptop, retrieve your scarf from the back of your chair and start wrapping it around your neck. Maybe quickly downing the dregs of your remaining tea, all with the hope that your physical movements will be mirrored now in the verbal winding down of your new-found friend. But it didn't really happen this way. He was in full flow now and nothing was going to break his academic discourse – it would have been akin to sitting in a formal lecture in the middle of a row and then walking out just as the speaker was getting into their stride, and making everyone stand up in order to let you pass in the process. So what happens? We end up sitting through these things and taking courses we didn't even know we had signed up for. What do you mean you have no memory of enrolling on this one? Of course you enrolled – how else could you even be here? And you know what, you haven't even been charged tuition fees – this one's on the house. But right now, this woman is looking to drop this module completely and she starts being just a little more explicit – still smiling, still nodding, still making the right noises but on her feet now and actually saying that while it has been fascinating hearing about his work, she really does need to go as her mum is waiting for her. But of course he doesn't hear or see any of that. The poor man.

What's the most prevalent condition of our modern era?

Loneliness.

I wonder if that's what motivates people to become lecturers or public speakers as much as any passion for their subject (and some of them don't even have that): a desire to be heard and just have an audience – irrespective of whether they are even receptive. Or awake.

The second time was completely different. I don't know how long the monologue might have been going on for – as I said, Jo was subjecting me to one of her own at the time and even I can't listen to two of these at once. But from the expression on the woman's face, even if it had been just a minute, it had been a minute too long. In fact, so powerful was her need to expunge him and return to her screen that this was effectively what she did. The man bade her goodbye and, gathering up his papers and books, shuffled out of the room. I don't know. I felt quite sorry for him in that moment. But had *I* been the one immersed in my own work, I probably may have felt the same. Reacted differently maybe but felt the same. No – I'm afraid that unless you tend to be paid to hear the stories of others, most people these days just don't have the time for it. And even most of the ones who do get paid (and yes I'm one of them) don't always have the requisite skills. The letters maybe as N keeps saying, but not the full portfolio.

Apparently that's why a lot of men go to prostitutes. The sex is just a cover for what is much more embarrassing to admit – that they haven't actually got anyone to talk to. Of course it would probably be better for their psyches if they did spend that money on a psychotherapist, but I would say that wouldn't I … And you'd have to find a good one. Maybe that's what I should do, market myself as a high-class prostitute – but minus the sex work. Maybe that would be good for business?

Of course, if you can find someone to genuinely talk to – and I mean really bare your soul to – and wouldn't mind having sex with on top, you're probably halfway to heaven right there. And then if they feel the same – and with no money changing hands in either direction – that's probably as good as it ever gets. Without that you haven't really got anything. You can wrap it up in the shared life and kids, in the four-bedroom detached house with a conservatory, put a worldly contract of a marriage around it but what does any of that really mean? If you just spend it feeling lonely? There's no sex and no money that can compensate for that one. Who is it that staves off the loneliness – seek them out and then never let them go. Most people would probably exchange all the sex in the world if they could find that one.

Anyway. I don't want to be encouraging inappropriate attachments either. So I banish all thoughts of chatting to the old man myself, even if I do see him again and wonder if next time Jo might actually give *me* a chance to speak. Actually, seeing as I've only had a supervision in name and not in form maybe *you* might like to hear it, as an alternative? Don't worry – you don't need to be in possession of any specific qualifications here. Right now all I need is someone to talk to. You don't even need to talk back – let alone make any polite noises at appropriate times, or ask me any questions. You don't look like you're busy doing anything else much if you don't mind me saying. I can't see a laptop on your table, or another person seated here on your sofa, and the people next to you on the Tube all seem to have headphones on. But if you are by chance waiting for someone who just happens to be running late, or is always late, I do apologise. It's always good to meet in a cafe. I've spent enough time hanging round outside Tube stations and the entrances to public places to know how irritating this can be. But, I'm neither a lonely old man nor an unboundaried professional and have no desire to detain you against your will. I can see a mobile right next to you though, but as long as it's there just in case of emergencies, and you have to run off, and not as a major distraction, I think I can cope. It all depends on how much you've processed your own digital addictions. You know, when you realise the last thing you touch at night and then first thing in the morning is not a lover but your mobile phone. It's true you know. Most people spend more time touching an electronic screen than the people they love.

So anyway, I'm looking at you right now and thinking actually maybe this is exactly what I need: a pure witnessing and nothing else. But I leave it completely up to you. If you'd rather not, or think the subject matter might be too heavy, or cause dysregulation you can walk away right now. No polite and very British explanations needed. I'd rather get expectations clear at the very start. I must warn you, however, that I am not entirely sure myself what might emerge and how long I might talk for, so absolutely no compulsions here. If you do need a break just gesture at any point and we can resume by mutual consent whenever you are next ready and available. It's the very uncertainty in our temporal shared covenant that may give it strength: you don't know me and I don't know you. As far as I can tell we have never previously met – I'm doing a quick mental scan as we speak – or as I speak – of previous universities, workplaces, gyms, clubs, socials, lovers, and so on and your face isn't registering with me anywhere. A total blank. And that is just how I like it. No preconceptions about the past – as we have no shared past – and no expectations about the future – as we'll have no shared future either. Sorry if that disappoints you, but trust me, once I'm done – and if I've done my job properly – your overriding feeling may just be one of huge relief. And hopefully mine too. But while we're here and together – if you agree to this that is – I want nothing between us. No caveats, no qualifications, no excuses. The only possible concession I shall make here is a pot of tea – preferably a masala chai with oat milk, but I can tolerate a builder's tea if you must.

It starts of course – as all good psychotherapists know – in childhood, in our very formative years. But you see, this is actually a misnomer. It starts way before that, way before we are even born as you, or you, or you or you *[gesturing to audience]* or me or anyone else, way before we are even in the womb. Now for me to say any of this to my colleagues or to write it in academic journals would be absolute heresy you see. Complete professional suicide. That is why I've kept quiet. Until now that is. Right, so this is where I ask for some audience participation. Entirely voluntary, it's a mere request and not an order. Think of a baby: maybe the most recent baby that was born into your own family or in your social sphere – and it might even be one of your own. Do you believe that this baby was born pure? A living, breathing, blank slate for the world to make its marks on? And vice versa? And just hold that thought, just sit with whatever view you have forming in your mind's eye right now. I don't need to hear it – no one does, not unless you want them to after we part ways for today. Then you can tell whoever you choose, whatever you choose about not only your views on the innocence of babies but about this slightly deranged woman claiming to be a psychotherapist that you met today.

This is how I see it: we are all carrying the sins of the fathers – and the mothers – but also of all their fathers and their mothers too. But not just sins, you'll be happy to hear. All the virtues too: all the goodness and the glory and the enriching, life-enhancing sustenance. The fruits of the tree of life itself. So everything is on this endless continuum that stretches from us and back in time as far as it's possible to go, as well as the other way, forwards in time to encompass all of our children and their children, and their children's children and so on. And it doesn't stop there. This eternal vertical axis then branches out like a sideways growing family tree and takes in everyone who just happened to be alive at that time too, anyone who happened to ever have been alive, at any point in time, and anyone who is due to be in the future. In this beautiful and entangled web of the whole of humanity of who is currently living, who has ever once lived and who will ever live at some point, there are actually connections we can all access, if we so choose. Forget your limited family tree that a dogged relative keeps uncovering on ancestry DNA. We pathologise or attach to the closest of families ties to our joint peril and detriment. We are all connected. We are all family.

And it's not just people either – it's every single living organism too. Every animal, every bird, every piece of foliage and fauna, the cycles of the moon and tides to the meteorological changes in our weather fronts; nothing is random and by chance, there are no happy accidents – it is linked together by the one ever-pulsing, balancing, calibrating energy in the universe.

And that's why you see. That's why I have ended up with this part-time role at Her Majesty's Pleasure. And that's why prisoner N has ended up being referred to me. And that's why I have chosen to impose on you in this way. Though to be honest, it isn't me who has really chosen you at all, it's more that you've been chosen for me and you are fortunately kind enough to be honouring this. Same with N and I … same with N and I … we've been chosen for each other. I just hope that lovely old man finds who's been chosen for him and stops disrupting the good people of the members room in the British Library. As I said before, that's what we're all looking for really, someone to give witness to the fact that we were actually here, that we lived and we loved but most of all that we suffered. Like the oldskool graffiti you used to get on walls – now it's all gang names and tags – I woz here: I lived a life and I had a story but when I die it dies right with me as I take it all to my grave. This is why I'm doing this. Imposing on you in this way. I'll be actively relieved if we never meet again, if you know nothing more about me than this.

What you do with it then is entirely up to you.

Session Three:

[The prison setting. N alone. Even more piles of books.
Dr's notes appearing transcribed on screen: Session 2]

So how you been, doc? Busy doctoring? Sorry – bad joke that. If there's one thing I'm good at it's bad jokes. Busy ministering then maybe? But I guess you'd need to be a minister for that and you don't seem the type exactly. They all talk too much for starters. Would have been a great one for me that, thinking about it: a ready-made audience, the best venues, and timings all taken care of too. I could just have spoken each week to my heart's content – and everyone else's discontent most probably but you can't please 'em all. That's actually one I've been pondering on a while. What is it exactly that qualifies people to speak from that platform anyways? We can all read the scriptures for ourselves can't we – though on second thoughts maybe I shouldn't be so quick to assume. There's more than a few geezers in here that would struggle to write their own names and addresses if asked, and as for their reading ... can you imagine that? You probably can't, doc – you've probably read more books than I've smoked roll-ups, but for the unfortunates that can't, entire worlds out there that they'll never be able to access, because our impoverished school system couldn't even do the very *basics* for them before they left. So nope, I retract what I just said – we can't all read the scriptures for ourselves but I think I was on one of many side-tracks there anyway.

So what was I on about ...?

Oh yeah, so given a significant number of the congregation maybe *could* read the scriptures, what exactly are they doing up there anyway? So mister minister here has been to some kind of theology college and, to be fair, probably read a lot more books than most of us – maybe even more than your good self with having to get all your letters, and my not so good self, stuck in here for hours and days and weeks and months on end now, with books as my only real company. But even so ... what does he really know? What are his real-world credentials? As far as I can tell, from my own not insubstantial reading, most of the genuine sainted ones would tell their own stories first, and would ensure they had aforementioned stories as straight as they could. Whereas most of that lot stand on their platform week after week – nothing wrong with that itself mind – but just tell the stories of others. And only certain others at that. But what about *their* stories, doc? How do we know they really have what it takes to be telling us lot a thing, when we know nothing much about them at all?

Oh yeah, course, my apologies – we're here to be talking about my story, ain't we, not me sounding off about others and their lack of. Thanks for nudging me back on track, doc, much appreciated that You must have the patience of a saint yerself to have just sat and listened to me last time, not even taking much notes mind. Dead impressed with that I was. What's that? I'm sure you *do* have a good memory, doc. I ain't got no grounds to be refuting that.

Contracting ... what's that then? I guess if you're looking for someone to do your dirty work for ya, this would be the right place ... nah, I'm just joking. Don't pay no attention. Right, let me have a read through ... though you may just regret this, doc, I always have a million and one questions me, if I don't get side-tracked by one of my many stories that is ...

[Complete silence while he reads the contract]

Actually, I may have to take that one back too – I think this all looks in good order here. Shall I tell you the truth, doc? Well, even if you don't want it, you don't really have much choice with me, do ya? I'm not really bothered by what's in this contract here, the detail of it much. All the basics are covered: practicalities – time and place, though I guess neither you nor I have much choice about that one. You can't just be working in this place can you, doc – I guess you must have your clients on the outside too? I bet you have a proper nice office an' all, pictures on the walls, plants, soft lighting, some real thought gone into the kind of environment someone might need to feel safe and tell it like it really is for them. Not like this shithole here. Enough in the environment to be stimulating but without being distracting, 'cause no one's really there to admire yer taste in interior decor. Shall I tell you what, doc? If I did have a choice and so did you, do you know what I would go for? The outdoors. Not no consulting room, no matter how tastefully done, I would choose a walk in the park, followed by a cuppa – though listening to me is always gonna be far from a walk in the park for anyone. Youse probably end up running away from me if we ever did that and at least in here you gotta sit here and take it all in. For the time you're here you're as much of a prisoner as I am. Only the officers, the official, designated key holders can let even you in and out of this place.

There was something else I was reading about *[N's pile of books has grown even more since the first session, and another book is pushed towards the audience while the cover and title is shown on screen – Thinkers of the East by Idries Shah]* it was a parable about a man who was in a similar predicament to myself, he too being incarcerated at Her Majesty's Pleasure, but this being in some foreign land and of a time long past.

We all have a gift, you see, something unique, that we and only we can do for the people around us, so for example, for you it would be your ability to listen, and for my brethren here from a distant land and another story, his skill was metalwork. But anyway, I'm getting ahead of the story here, it really starts and ends with his missus. So our girl here, she's only been married a short time she has, barely out of their honeymoon they are when her fella gets himself locked up. As it happens the geezer's actually innocent, but as I'm sure you're aware, prisons in all countries and all eras have only ever housed innocent men and women. None of us have ever done a thing. With the exception of me that is – I confessed to it all. But actually her fella he genuinely was. And so she has nothing at that point, she really doesn't. Her family shun her, as if it's her fault her husband has turned out to be a miscreant, and his family shun her too, for exactly the same reason. Well, that place it isn't like prisons over here and in the twenty-first century – though there's enough feedback I could still give to any Home Office minister, so the whole concept of visiting rights doesn't really exist. And she can't even send stuff into the prison, let alone see him in the flesh. Me – if I could just be sent more books, that would pretty much sustain me for my whole life sentence, but over there, neither of those two were able to read, so books would have been out of the question anyway. So for a while, our girl here is proper distraught. What can she do? She can't get in to see him, she has no one to turn to and no means of communication. So she thinks. In desperation she turns to the Imam of her mosque but all she gets there is more of the same. A criminal man must be the result of a dishonourable woman, and when was the last time either of them had shown up to a sermon? Just another one of those – mind you if you think the ones on the outside are bad, you should see this lot they have in here – and of course she no longer has the protection of a man around either, despite all the officialdom of her legitimate marital status. Like she is the one who has left him and should be volunteering to spend her own life behind the bars of her village home because of it. Well, she's having none of that, but she does start to notice the looks of the young men in the alleys when she makes her way to the market or to gather water from the well. And no matter how tightly she wraps her shawl around her, she can still feel their gaze. Lingering. Always just a little too long.

Like the hordes of kids who will never really make it through the academic rigours of school, being apprenticed to a trade for the rest of their lives, there was only ever one thing she had been raised for, and that was to be a wife. And with everything that her world had told her this entailed – but no more. And her own mother had taught her well, she had, but what was the point of it? No one to cook for, no family to tend to – they hadn't had any kids yet. One night she sat outside their tiny cabin, looking up at the stars – always a dangerous thing to be doing – her head aching from all the thinking and the closed doors and the sheer pain of missing him. She turned to the one thing she had always excelled at, though fuck knows what good it was gonna do in practical terms, but you know, sometimes the very worst thing we can do is try and think ourselves out of a predicament. So with an oil lamp burning beside her, she lets her fingers dance to their own tune, one she can't actually hear in her head, but can feel in her bones. And that's the main thing innit? Neither her nor her fella had ever gone in for the formalities, the visits to the mosque (except for their nuptials) but of course as her mother had taught her well, she'd been schooled in her designated prayers at set times at home, but if she was honest she knew that she never really felt much while doing them. Her fella was more with it, having dispensed with them altogether and just immersing himself in his metalwork when needed, but we all have to live and learn these things. But that night she sat and let her fingers embroider as her mind became still, or maybe as her mind became still it was her fingers that then embroidered, but whatever way round it was, was immaterial as she had the material – she just didn't know it. So for the first time in her whole life probably, that night was the first night that she had truly prayed. Not with words – that'd be you and me, doc – but in her own way. And as these things usually unfold at their own pace, like brewing a proper tea that can't be rushed, to begin with she had no idea what she was creating – but actually it didn't matter as it gave her what she needed, a way of communing with something bigger than herself. And in her own way.

So, this became a nightly ritual for her it did. She would sit under the stars with a view we would never have these days, what with all the light pollution everywhere, and just keep at it. Once she was immersed in her work there would be nothing that could distract her attention from it. With the exception of just one thing. If the night was ever graced by a passing meteor shower she would lower her needle and raise her eyes and allow them the freedom to follow the light show unfolding before her. And she knew it was stupid – she did – but she liked to think it was just for her. For who else would be sitting out there night after night and embroidering of all things? You might get a few travellers and ne'er do wells up at that time – I should know – done enough of both I have, though not embroidery sadly. Here, doc, maybe you could put in a recommendation for an embroidery class for us inmates and see how that might go down? I know what they'll say – sharp implements and enough rope to garrotte each other – you are joking? Or hang ourselves with I guess. Though I've got no personal need for that one, me. I just need to carry on talking. So the travellers would most likely be looking up at the stars (as how else are they gonna find their way?) but the other lot will most likely be looking down into the gutter. Again.

So this continued night after night until after a time she looked at her handiwork and just knew it was finished. It didn't need a single knot or stitch more and she knew had she added one it would have ruined the whole effect. A rare skill that one is. Actually knowing when to stop. So the next day, armed with her story, she decided upon a plan of action. She would go to the local ministry for justice – maybe she might be granted a sympathetic audience with a minor official at least. Having no idea of the accepted protocols for this type of thing (sometimes a blessing in itself) she decided on the direct approach and undertook the short journey to the government offices and, to her surprise, was admitted inside immediately and without question, let alone any trace of hostility. She sat in a small dusty waiting room until she was greeted by a tall and imposing elderly gent who asked her what was the nature of her visit.

And that was all the invitation she needed. A captive audience right there. Is there ever any other kind? But I guess, doo, you could terminate this session right here as per this line in the contract right? Not that I have any intention whatsoever in behaving in a threatening manner, but our girl here, raised to be a wife and skilled at all wifely arts couldn't have been threatening if she'd tried. But she didn't need to be. All she needed was to tell him the story of her husband, but from her point of view. What it had done to her and her life and now the role she had been raised for her entire life was suddenly no more. The man was silent and just listened – probably as good as you, doc – and at the end he asked her one question and one question only:

What did she want? What did she want?

It was a prayer rug.

She had woven it with her own hands.

If it was within his power, could he please see to it that it be delivered to her husband?

And that was all.

She didn't ask for no retrial – as hubby didn't really have one in the first place – or for visiting rights, or financial support for herself or none of the things that we might ask for today.

Just to make sure – if it was within his power – that the prayer rug got to him.

What's that? Oh yeah, the contract, sorry. Course I should look at it a bit more closely – you're totally right, doc.

What's the next one here – confidentiality ... sharing of information ... I guess that's all part of your profession innit? What do I have to lose by you sharing my story? The more people who hear it the better, as far as I can see. I know what you're saying though. It's about being transparent about this process here innit? Professional supervision and safeguarding is one thing, but you won't be going home and telling your fella all the ins and outs of your caseload, will ya? Or gossiping with your girlfriends about this sexy beast you get locked in with to spend quality one-to-one time with every week.

I wouldn't mind you doing that.

Session Four:

[A bare room in a prison. N and Dr sitting facing each other across a table.

Dr's notes appearing transcribed on screen: Session 3]

N: I knew it, doc, I knew you'd be back for the next instalment. Like a good boxed set I am, hopelessly addictive.

Dr: It's all Netflix and streaming these days – sorry, that won't mean a thing to you.

N: No worries, doc, now where were we – the prayer rug!

Dr: Ah, the prayer rug of course – I *am* very interested in that story, but actually I was more intrigued about the goings on in the forest you mentioned, *[looking at notes]* ... a couple of sessions back now? How about we save the prayer rug for your encore – as it were?

N: Encore eh? Certainly know how to sweet talk a fella don't ya, doc? Well, as you know, I'm full of stories.

Dr: The Prayer Rug's been downloaded, and we'll press play at some point in the future. But for now let's go back to that evening.

N: More than happy to oblige, doc. And this is what I asked for, wasn't it? After all these years.

Dr: So you were distressed, you felt the forest was your refuge but you also felt that in your distress you had ...?

N: You know, some of the geezers in here will do anything to avoid seeing a shrink – even if they look like you – not me though. Not now. I'd be seeing you if you looked like Medusa.

Dr: Well we wouldn't get too far if you were turned to stone.

N: Guess not. You'd be more like one of the sirens, I reckon.

Dr: You wouldn't want to hear me sing.

N: Oh what – really? Me on the other hand—

Dr: *[interrupting]* Tell me more about the girl. How long were you seeing her for?

N: I knew it, doc – I knew you'd be interested in her. The signs were all there when you wanted to write something in that first session, remember?

Dr: Is there anything else that comes to mind about that whole episode?

N: *[pauses]* It was the blood.

That's what I remember. The most *visceral* memory as it were. It was the colour. I'd never seen so much of it, I guess. Course I'd been in enough fights over the years – in school, at home, on the streets, all over. Cuts and bruises here and there. But nothing to compare with this.

[suddenly panicked] Listen, doc, I don't reckon there's much there you need to be exploring, you know – not that I'm trying to tell you how to do your job like—

Dr: *[gently]* Tell me about the blood. It's okay.

N: I couldn't tell what it was at first. Nothing seemed quite real that evening. I just thought it was part of the forest, like the moss that grows in any space it can find, any crack and crevice. Like the demons that find a way to root out any painful memory they can and capitalise on it. Blackmailing ya for all they're worth.

Dr: *[as if to herself]* Like a bad psychologist maybe ...?

N: You know, I keep calling you doc, what's your name? I don't mean Dr Kahlil. Nah, you won't be allowed to tell me, most likely – not 'professional'.

Dr: Do you trust me, Noel? I may be here to help excavate your past, but I'm not one of your demons.

N: Trusted you from session one I did. Believe it or not. I don't go round telling my story to just anyone. Even if I have a rep for never shutting up. It's what I always left unsaid amongst all the bullshit.

Dr: Then you don't need to know my name. What happened next?

N: It wasn't moss though, and it wasn't a premature covering of dew neither. But it was a part of the forest still. It was the innards, the guts, the gore that I had spilt with every kick and punch I had landed in my fury. Can you believe that? That giant oak tree that could have felled me with one casual flick of a branch just stood there and took it all? When the whole time it had always been there for me? But even now I'm not too sure you see, whether it was blood or if it was tears. It was definitely green though, no mistaking that one, and it was fucking everywhere – droplets of it like Chinese lanterns hanging from the boughs, flowing into pools on the forest floor, mopping up the leaves in its wake. And all over me an' all – on my bare knuckles and the knees of my tracksuit bottoms, and in the midst of it all I distinctly recall thinking how the fuck was I going to get it off my new trainers? And what would my mum say? It didn't take much to start her off ...

Dr: *[as if to herself]* Blood or tears, yours or the trees – what would be the difference ...*[then gathering herself as if she shouldn't have said that out loud]* Sorry, so despite this all happening, the almost supernatural elements, with the green, er – substance – you were still aware of things like your stained trainers, your mum's reaction?

N: *[carrying on as if he hasn't heard her question]* I read about that somewhere you know. Did you know that trees – even those of different species – have interconnected roots? All us thick bastards see is what's there from the ground up – the different barks, shape of the leaves, whether they ever flower – but below the surface there's a whole other support system going on, and if a tree's in need, the surrounding ones – instead of going all Darwinian and fighting for their own survival – actually fight to feed *that* one first, not picking it off, like the fucking runt of the litter, like we'd do.

Dr: *[puts down her pen, pushes her papers to the side and takes off her glasses and then there is a pause.]* So there was a lot of this green – definitely green – er ... sap, tree blood? Tears?

N: *[quietly]* There was a lot. More than there should have been. More than I would have expected even a mature oak could have held, as its lifeblood, you know? But that was way before I knew. Way before I had read even a single fucking book from cover to cover, let alone about biological ecosystems and trees all being interconnected. It was like some portent, an omen. This isn't going to be the last time you hurt someone – I mean a tree like—

Dr: [*reassuringly*] A tree, of course.

N: It will happen again and again, and this is the measure of it. This is the measure of the amount of blood – or tears – you will spill. But of course back then, I couldn't understand it, had no idea what it meant, what the universe was trying to tell me. That was my mistake you see. I didn't know how to keep quiet. I ran home – more freaked out by that point, by staying in that forest, than of anything my mum might say or do – and told 'em. Her, my brothers, sisters, kids on the street. And I kept seeing it you see. If I opened a tap anywhere it would come out gushing – and green. If it ever rained, the drops would have a – subtle, I give you – but definite green tinge to them. Even taking Tiny out for a walk, the first time after the episode, when he pissed against a tree, *that* was green too.

[Dr's notes appearing transcribed on screen and said aloud on stage via a recording: I won't ask him if his own piss was green too.]

But there was no *evidence* you see, you'll have read my files, doc – there was nothing green on me, not on my hands, not on my trainers, just raw and bruised knuckles and bloodied shins and muddy shoes. They didn't believe a word of it and I thought by insisting they would eventually get it, but that made things worse. My family had already written me off as half-baked but saying it to everyone in the unit got me properly barbecued … nah, nah *[puts his head in his hands and shakes it]* that was when the real trouble started, where it all started going wrong. If only I had shut the fuck up.

Dr: That was the first one? The episode?

N: The first episode in the sorry boxed set of my life. Yeah, the first *psychotic* episode that went down in my file after the unit referred me to CAMHS. And after that I had no chance. Couldn't overwrite it, couldn't understand it. Until now that was.

[pause] Why are you a psychiatrist, doc? Why are you even here?

[Said aloud by Dr via a recording: No one's ever asked me that before.]

Session Five:

[Dr by herself now, still in the prison setting.]

Dr: No one's ever asked me that before. Trust it to be a client – and a prison inmate at that. Technically I'm not a psychiatrist – I don't dispense any drugs. Shouldn't really be in a prison as I'm not even a dealer. My doctor credentials are just through being over-educated. So why am I in a prison ...? Why *am* I in a prison?

People often ask me how I feel about the work I do – sitting with the damaged and deranged, the total outcasts of society who will never really be given absolution, even if they do eventually get released. Well I didn't actually plan it this way. I was more than comfortable with my practice on the outside, as it was. And it was precisely that which was the problem: it was comfortable. For me and my clients both. My comfortable office and consulting room, with my tasteful John Lewis furnishings – well, if I had no reason to decorate my own home in this way, I figured at least my clients could get the benefit. I'm not imposing a hierarchy on human distress and suffering, and who is more or less worthy of intervention, but there was definitely a gap, in me and out there. It was only ever those who could pay, those who had in some way identified a need – even if incorrectly – and then had to make the commitment to actually show up regularly. And after a few years, this was what I started to feel: it was me just operating in my comfort zone.

And it was then that I started to make some enquiries. I was never intending to completely shut down my practice in the community, but things definitely needed to change. And looking back now I don't really know why it didn't come to me sooner. Of course it had to be prisoners, who else could it be? Given my history ... If there was anything that was going to take me out of my comfort zone, it would be this. You see, there's a lot to be said for the external conditions, the furnishings, the artwork, the tea brewed in a pot with leaves (with a choice of non-dairy alternatives) and the clients having the freedom to come and go and commit as they choose. But if you really want to test your practice you've got to take it right out of that space. Getting the letters after your name – if you even choose that route – is the easy bit. And it's from right here that a lot of the self-delusion in my not so esteemed colleagues stems. Your actual apprenticeship is then doing the work and proving to yourself that you are genuinely worthy of the job title you have got for yourself or given yourself: professional, clinician, teacher, mentor, whatever. And that's only the beginning. Even if you've been practising for decades – until your actual retirement even – you may never have grown beyond this probationary phase. All the articles in journals, all the headlining at conferences, all the leadership responsibilities – they don't actually mean a thing until you genuinely progress to the next level. It's only then that you legitimately, in your heart, have the right to call yourself what you and your world may have erroneously been calling you for the best part of your life.

That's how it was for me. I was never one for research or public speaking anyway. I supervised a few colleagues over the years and ran a team for a while, but that was as far as it went. I just wanted the real work. And the created professional bubble of my peers just didn't do it.

And I knew, you see. I always did. It was prisoners.

But not just that.

It was that specific institution. That particular wing.

And that exact man.

Session Six:

[N alone in a prison cell]

She thinks I don't know. The doc.

Of course she does, she wouldn't be coming here if she knew I knew. Funny thing is it only started happening hardcore once I got here – not inside – but in solitary. There's inside and there's *inside* you see. I *have* learned a *bit* over the years, and I don't just mean from learning to read and all them books. That all helped but it was only when I started putting it all together with my actual life that it really began. It was my old cell mate. I'm not a good sleeper at the best of times, the chat that comes out my mouth was nothing compared to what was going on in my head, and nights were always the worst. Anyway, this particular night I was at least trying, had my eyes closed and was lying down and still. And I was literally just about to drift off when Kareem – who I thought was asleep – starts fiddling with his mobile and it's not only the light but the sounds of the digits being pressed. And for some reason it goes straight through me and is all amplified a hundred times, like I'm on acid and the entire cell seems like it's flooded with light and sound until I feel like I am going to explode, my head is literally gonna blow off ... but not – for once – with *anger* ...

And then I open my eyes. And look. And there is Kareem. And he's fast asleep, not just fast asleep, but sleeping and even *looking* like a *baby* ... He just looks so young I can't believe it. I mean it's him, but it isn't him if you know what I mean. And there is no sound now and no mobile phone in sight either, just a regular ugly bastard who suddenly looks like an innocent kid. But it's that light. The cell is completely dark but as I look at this weird throwback version of my cell mate I see that green fluorescent light I had first seen on that girl, years back. And like with her, it's coming from within him, but now, now I see this detail that was never there before, the actual light, it travels through his body see, traces this path through what looks like this network of nerves or capillaries, passing all the way through him. And sometimes it stops, here and there and pulses for a while and when it does this he's flooded with an extra high current or something. And I know, I know I'm being shown something, being taught something that isn't in any of the hundreds of books I have read by then. But there is something else, that wasn't there with the girl, nor when all the water sources in the world temporarily went green on me. There is this fucking stench like you wouldn't believe, like the devil himself had paid us a nocturnal visit and wanked all over us. And that's when I get it. It's Kareem. And his sins. All the violence he has ever done to others is all right there, all the blood spilt and all the tears shed. All residing in him. And I can see it and I can even smell it – but most of all I can *feel* it.

Believe me when I say, I never asked for this. Don't know why the good Lord chose me to see it at that moment, but since then two major things happened.

I kept on seeing it.

And I finally shut the fuck up.

230 The Prayer Rug

Session Seven:

[N and Dr Kahlil sitting facing each other, still in the consulting room.

Dr's notes appearing transcribed on screen: Session 4]

N: How've you been, doc?

Dr: I've been well, thank you, Noel. How are you?

N. I've been good, doc, I've been good

[N gets up and walks around the room in silence, before finally taking his seat.

There are no books anywhere to be seen.]

Do you ever pray, doc?

Dr: It depends on what you call prayer.

N: So what is prayer to you, doc?

Dr: No one's ever asked me that either.

[puts down her pen, moves her notebook and takes off her glasses.]

It's this *[gestures all around the room]*.

N: Being with me? I'm truly flattered, doc—

Dr: Being with you, but not *just* being with you! Being with any client is what I mean. Here in the prison, my practice on the outside, friends, family, strangers – it really doesn't matter. That's what I'm here for, that's what I'm here to do. To give witness to the stories of others. That to me is prayer.

N: And what about you?

Dr: What about me?

N: Who hears your story?

Dr: Who says I have a story?

N: We all have a story. So who hears yours?

Dr: I have my audience out there; you don't need to worry about me.

[Dr now puts her glasses back on and gathers herself, flicking through previous pages of her notebook.]

Seeing as we've already touched on it today, how about you finish your other story? The one I made you hit the pause button on?

N: Anyone ever hit you?

Dr: I'm sorry?

N: With a pause button I mean, doc?

Dr: Of course. No. I mean yes, we're all human and we shut each other down all the time. *[as if seeing the room for the first time]* The room – it's so empty now.

N: No more books to hide behind.

Dr: No more letters …

N: Feels good, doesn't it, to be naked for once?

Dr: There's naked and there's naked.

N: Never a truer phrase spoken. Doc.

Dr: The prayer rug. It was the one about the prayer rug.

N: It would be my pleasure. The absolute least I could do. So our girl here—

Dr: *[interrupting]* She's finally free.

N: You what?

Dr: Her husband is in prison now and even if he is innocent of whatever misdemeanour he was alleged to have committed, at least *she's* free.

N: Whose story is this anyway?

Dr: It's no one's and everyone's. It doesn't belong to any of us.

So now … she can't obtain a divorce, you know, being in a distant land and era – and that is a blessing in itself in her situation, as with no divorce her family can't actually force her to get married again. So with no husband and with no possibility of ever having to endure another marriage – unless she chose to, of course – she's finally free.

N: Right.

Dr: Metalwork, it's all well and good, as long as the only thing you're beating is the metal.

N: Okay.

Dr: Because whatever wifely arts she was raised in, the embroidery – which she did, by the sounds of it, genuinely love – the housekeeping even, I don't think being pummelled with a hammer should have been one of them, do you? A hammer or anything else?

N: And what about you?

Dr: Me? *[pause]*

N: You know the hardest thing? It's not what people think it is. I'm not even talking about sex. It's that there's no one there to listen. It's that any time anyone ever touches you is either to do you harm or to search you in some way, with rubber gloves like they'll catch something. Like a fucking animal, so why not just fucking be one you know? Why not?

Dr: So why not?

N: I never actually hit a woman you know, doc. You'll have seen my files.

Dr: And whose story is this anyway?

Together: No one's and everyone's.

Dr: And files – they always tell the truth, do they?

N: I'm sorry.

Dr: And letters?

[Silence]

N: I'm sorry.

Dr: So, exactly, as you told it, while *his* hands may have beaten out their own tune of destruction, hers – well – they just sung forth the song of her life, in her own way. And that's all we can really ask for, isn't it? Not much else *to* ask for is there?

N: I guess not ... So ... our girl here – she has her freedom now, doesn't want another fella around, so tell me ... what does she do then?

Dr: She takes that one thing, that core part of her, you know that one thing that really makes you feel you're alive when you do it, and she uses that. That is her steppingstone to her new life. And it's hard you know. Having to weave the fabric of our stories and make a thing of beauty with the ugliest and rawest of materials. But it's the only way to do it. But as you said, it's a different time and place and so she has to find her own way. And she knows intuitively that they have to be gifts. So first she starts with the people she knows, the people in her village. While they may have shunned her for a while, there's just something about these prayer rugs and the demeanour of this woman. So every gift is accepted. Sometimes with warmth and other times bemusement, but not once are they ever refused.

N: As what dickhead would turn down the gift of prayer?

Session Eight:

[Dr in her consulting room]

You know what I really love about coming to the prison? It's the journey up on the train. The number of open fields and then woodland I see when I look out the window, just within hiking distance of the HMP itself. Like the people in one of the most deprived boroughs in Europe looking out their windows and seeing the towering phallic offices of Docklands. Right in front of your face but completely out of your reach.

Well that's what it was like for me.

You'd think in my line of work that trauma would be my bread and butter, or my jam and scones, and you'd be right. It's just that the good souls you'd most likely be laying all this trauma on – like me, or maybe not specifically me, but someone like me – would all be carrying their own. And that's fine, that's broadly in the known category, that many of us go into this work to try and heal our own issues, hopefully consciously and safely and with good supervision, haha … I certainly knew that myself. Who do I see when I look at a male client across the table in my consulting room, a prison space, a coffee shop, a theatre audience?

Who's the man I'm really seeing and wishing I could heal, though at the time it was all just beyond me? Even keeping myself safe was. He's still there though. A phantom who haunts every encounter with every soul. Not as obvious as N and his visual representations, that girl is real alright, she's no hallucination, trauma or not. I'm just not visual, you see. Sometimes I wish I was, and say I had my own therapist or one of you had the insight to ask me that question, this is what I'd say:

I don't see it. I don't see coloured pre-emptive lights or a physical form, it's much more abstract than that. It's a feeling, but a feeling that's somehow embodied by these conversational signs. Like the subtlest of reminders, the hints of former encounters, all the clues are there, gradually blending into coherence. You feel like you're not just looking at one man. You're looking right through him into all the other souls that preceded him, all reflections from the mirror of your own soul, all that you're still trying to polish away at, to repair and make whole, so you could actually hang it somewhere, like a waiting room or a hallway without it terrifying all your tasteful John Lewis furnishings, who now turn to you and ask who exactly is this interloper on the wall? We could just about cope with the edgy but not too edgy Marc Chagall prints. You don't want it too tasteful either; some hints of an interior world and sexual territories are fine, but just not verging on porn ... But a cracked and dirty mirror giving you full on fragments of distortion that makes cubism seem naturalistic is not going to put any client at ease.

Mirror mirror on the wall, who's the most fucked up of them all?

Session Nine:

[N in a dark completely bare cell]

It had been months and months.

So I kept on asking, where was the doctor, when could I see her, this was my well-being didn't they know. And you know what, I really meant it. That I was gonna shut the fuck up and stop talking, try and give something back as I could see it you know. Could see all the fists and kicks and slaps, all the put-downs, all the accusations ... and more. It was like looking in a mirror. All them books and all them letters. What do they really do for yer?

And just as I was about to give up was when it happened. I got to see the doc again, and I swear to ya, as God is my witness, I didn't mean none of it. I didn't mean to kick off. After all these years, you would have thought ... you would have thought ... *[becoming emotional].*

But anyway, it is what it is now. I ain't never gonna see her again and that is what I gotta accept. And that's what half killed me; I was just so looking forward to it you see. I always did, right from the first session. Tried not to let it show too much but I'd be counting down the days until I'd see her again.

So when the idiot powers that be finally sorted it out, I was properly made up I was. Went along to the session, sat down at the table and looked across at her. And she has this massive file in front of her today, when normally she would have just her notebook. And I thought that was a bit odd, I did. But I let that go. I could barely see her face over the top of it.

My file.

[A bare room in a prison. A man and a woman sit facing each other across a table, several huge files of paperwork are placed between them.]

N: Sorry, lady, I was expecting to see Dr Kahlil. Who are you?

Dr Rogers: I'm Dr Rogers, the new psychotherapist who's been allocated to this prison. Who's Dr Kahlil? I haven't seen any mention of that name in your files.

N: Dr Kahlil? She's who I was working with here, before your good self.

Dr Rogers: Right, and when was this? You have been in this institution ... quite a while I see.

N: You see? Never mind. I've been with her for ever, every four to six weeks or so, but there'd been a gap for a while and no one seemed to know what was going on. In fairness it was probably only a few months, it just seemed like years, ya know?

Dr Rogers: Well, I'm afraid I don't know. There hasn't been a psychotherapist allocated to this HMP for a long time now. Are you sure you're not perhaps confusing this with someone else you've been seeing? Your art teacher perhaps? You seem to be quite talented—

N: *[becoming slightly agitated]* No, lady. There ain't no one else I've been seeing. There's never been anyone else. Do you understand what I'm saying? There's only ever been her.

Dr Rogers: Noel, I'm going to have to ask you to sit down now; we can talk about this, but there's absolutely nothing here in your file.

N: *[increasingly angry]* And files always tell the truth, do they?

Dr Rogers: What? Of course they do. Evidence is what—

N: And letters? Letters after people's names? Qualifications? Awards? Words, words, fucking words? *[Picks up the top file.]* All these words for example? Are they all truth?

[Starts grabbing papers and reports and ripping them up and throwing them across the room. Phrases then appear on screen in different typefaces and said aloud by different voices via a recording:]

'Prolonged episodes of psychosis', 'borderline personality disorder', 'anti-social behaviour', 'visual hallucinations', 'disordered thinking in cause and effect'.

Session Ten:

[N in his dark cell unwrapping a package.]

Forget about the doc, there ain't no one now.

For a while I thought even that Dr Rogers would be better than no one. But ... nah ...

I haven't even had a cell mate for years – and that's just how I like it.

[N then lays the object on the floor and stares at it.

The cell then starts to brighten until a woman dressed in white becomes visible. She is illuminated by a green light that starts to slowly fill the whole cell before she disappears and it returns to darkness again.]

Glossary

Abaah – father
Ayah – maidservant
Babaji – a respectful term for father
Baloo – bear
Bayaah – colloquial, friendly form of address for a man, matey
Beasharam – shameless
Benarsi – textiles made with intricate gold and silver brocade and embroidery on fine silks
Bettah – son
Bhadnaam – of poor reputation or ill-repute
Bhai – brother, especially an elder brother or relative
Bhai sahib – polite form of address for a man
Biryani – a highly seasoned rice dish made with vegetables, meat or fish
Dhal – lentils
Dheet – irritatingly stubborn
Dhenda – post, stick
Djinn – a spirit in Muslim mythology able to appear in human and animal form and possess humans
Ghazal – a genre of poetry, containing spiritual themes and often set to music
Gulab Jamun - a very sweet dessert of round fried dumplings
Haram – believed to be sinful
Haramzaadah – obnoxious male, bastard
Kameez – blouse
Khusra – a castrated male, often born into poverty and forced to beg or work in various forms of entertainment to earn a living
Kurta – a loose collarless shirt or tunic
Lehnga – ankle-length skirt (with a matching fitted bodice and shawl) worn on formal occasions such as weddings
Loo – very hot, dry summer wind that blows over plains of northern India and Pakistan

Mahal – palace
Mali – gardener
Mithai – sweets, confectionary
Naashta – breakfast
Noogdai dhanai - a snack of small fried sweets, often sold by street vendors
Pathaan – a member of the Pashto-speaking community from the mountainous regions of north-west Pakistan and eastern Afghanistan
Purdah – the practice in some Muslim societies of screening women from men or strangers, especially by means of curtains or barriers
Qawwali – a form of devotional music that expresses the mystical Sufi practice in Islam
Raja – an Indian prince or king
Rhuko – wait
Sahib – a respectful form of address for a man, sir
Sahiba – a respectful form of address for a woman, madam
Salaam – Islamic greeting
Shafaq – twilight
Shaitaan – the devil
Share – lion
Sheerah – syrup
Tablas – typically a pair of small hand drums
Tamaasha – a performance or spectacle
Ummi – mother
Urdu – language spoken in modern day Pakistan and parts of India
Yaar – colloquial, friendly form of address for a male e.g. mate, bro
Zikr – a form of devotional, meditative practice where worshippers rhythmically and repeatedly chant various names associated with God, silently or aloud

Acknowledgements

Thank you to all who have been involved in bringing *The Prayer Rug* to life.

Ben Pestell for his support and encouragement with an early complete draft.

PM for his positive comments on the prison sections.

Nicola Fuller for hearing me read sections of the novel aloud.

Phyllis Cole-Dai and members of The Raft creative community for the space to share the ongoing creative process.

Special thanks to Thomas Shostak and Geri Ortega for being part of a precious ongoing writing group, which has kept my creativity alive since the completion of *The Prayer Rug*.

Jessica Palmer for the lovely artwork.

All at Brown Dog Books who have supported the publishing process.

Family and friends, who have been wonderfully supportive and curious about this endeavour.

The many strangers I have encountered on walks, in galleries and cafes, who I struck up conversations with, never to meet again, and fellow writers and creatives, whether I can even recall you all, who have all helped to bring this story to fruition.

Finally, the mysterious forces that led me to leave my career and devote myself to writing ... and that have guided my every move since ...